THE BURNT OFFERING

Claudia is caught up in the conflict and turmoil of her parents' unhappy marriage; the impact of their incompability making her vow never to follow in their footsteps, and to distrust love... Claudia's fight, however, is not only against prejudice and fear, but against the scheming of a mother who, to gain her own happiness, would sacrifice that of her daughter. In seeking to avoid the misery she believes to be attendant upon marriage, Claudia is drawn into the web of two loves while slowly and remorselessly history threatens to repeat itself.

THE BURNT OFFERING

The Burnt Offering

by

Sonia Deane

Dales Large Print Books
Long Preston, North Yorkshire,
BD23 4ND, England.

British Library Cataloguing in Publication Data.

Deane, Sonia
    The burnt offering.

    A catalogue record of this book is
    available from the British Library

    ISBN   1-84262-454-7 pbk
    ISBN   978-1-84262-454-8 pbk

First published in Great Britain in 1951 by
Hutchinson & Co. Ltd

Published in Large Print 2006 by arrangement with
The estate of Sonia Deane, care of Rupert Crew Ltd.

Dales Large Print is an imprint of Library Magna Books Ltd.

Printed and bound in Great Britain by
T.J. (International) Ltd., Cornwall, PL28 8RW

CHAPTER ONE

To Claudia Lomond the beginning of a new day was fraught with uncertainty and apprehension, and as she left her bedroom and descended the stairs on this particular morning, she kept her fingers crossed, took a deep breath, and swung blithely into the breakfast room as though her very vitality and cheeriness would will her parents into amiability.

Her father glanced up at her uncompromisingly from his paper.

'We've already finished our porridge; you're late, Claudia.'

Her mother said with some spirit:

'Really, Charles! Since Claudia never takes porridge, I cannot see that it matters.'

Whereupon Charles looked at her somewhat critically and retorted:

'Since you never see anything from my point of view, Helen... But I have a right to enforce a little discipline in my own home, you know.'

Claudia hastened:

'I overslept; sorry, daddy.'

'Too many late nights,' he said overbearingly.

7

Claudia wanted to laugh, even while appreciating that it was no laughing matter. Her father's dictatorial attitude and quick temper could, on occasion, strike almost a humorous note and she had long since accepted the fact that he and her mother were wholly incompatible and that from such incompatibility had sprung intolerance.

Claudia, at twenty-four, was a modern who, nevertheless, had retained much of the fragrance of Yesterday. She had spirit without aggressiveness, warmth without cloying sweetness. She was loved and loving, and ready to make excuses for the frailties of human beings, rather than to condemn them unheard.

The problem of her parents' relationship was one that never failed to concern her. As individuals, she knew they were possessed of sterling qualities, but they neither understood each other's viewpoint, nor shared any community of interests. Her father appeared continually to say the wrong thing, and her mother, far from placating him in moments of ill-temper, added her own quota of grievances until that which began as a harmless discussion, developed into a heated argument. Domestically, her mother was an efficient housekeeper, so that there was no discord on that account. Equally, her father was a good business man, who in no way shirked his responsibilities in the home, and had given a great deal, materially, towards its maintenance. To Claudia, however, none of these virtues atoned for the lack of harmony and what she considered to be the right atmosphere. She said, in an effort to change the subject:

'How do you both feel about going to the theatre on Saturday? Just the three of us?' She added laughingly: 'Just one more late night won't hurt, Daddy.'

Her mother beamed and said swiftly:

'That would be lovely, darling.' As she spoke she turned her gaze towards Charles.

'I can't say that I agree with you,' he commented. 'I'm not fond of these half-baked plays.'

'How can you possibly know that it will be half-baked?' Helen demanded.

'They're all half-baked,' he said with an infuriating calm.

'That is absolute nonsense!'

'Very well, then it's nonsense; have it your own way, Helen. The fact remains that I'm not keen on going. That,' he added, 'need not prevent you and Claudia going.'

'I shall not,' she replied stubbornly, 'go without you.'

'That is entirely up to you,' came the swift reply.

Claudia spoke calmly, but with a certain appeal.

'It does happen to be my birthday, Daddy.'

Charles Lomond stared at her a trifle blankly, then:

'So it is! June 6th... Ah, well! That's different.'

'If I may say so,' Helen cried with faintly aggrieved intonation, 'it is hardly flattering to me, Charles, to know that you have to be persuaded by Claudia before you will go out–'

Claudia watched her father's face, realizing that his temper was rising.

'For heaven's sake don't make something out of that, Helen.'

Charles Lomond was fifty-two and in that second he felt every moment of it. His nerves were frayed and his spirits low and this, he knew, Claudia sensed instinctively. In appearance, he was extremely good-looking, with well cut features, broad forehead and shapely head; in addition, he was both tall and slender and carried himself with an air of distinction that always awakened within Claudia a sensation of pride whenever she saw him coming towards her in a crowd.

Helen Lomond, at forty-eight, looked younger than her years and had, in her youth, been an exceedingly pretty woman of the rather fragile, Dresden type. Now, with faintly greying hair to frame a still pink and white complexion, she managed to retain a charm and freshness that made age, as such,

10

wholly unimportant. Claudia realized, however, that an expression of content and composure was missing from their faces and that the glow of true happiness was required to transform and bring them both to life.

'May I,' she hastened, anxious that there should be no further argument, 'get the seats, Daddy?'

'You may,' he said, and smiled. 'We could have dinner somewhere afterwards, if you like. Settle it with your mother.'

It was later that morning that Claudia said suddenly, urged by an impulse she could not resist:

'You know, Mother, I really ought to have a career of some sort. The little work I do in the house isn't sufficient justification for living – and I hate idleness.'

Helen was combing her hair as Claudia spoke and she swung around from her dressing-table stool, consternation on her face as she gasped:

'But you couldn't do that, darling. What would my life be without your companion-ship? I can hardly bear the thought of it. Besides, if you left, I'd either have to do your work or get another maid, so you more than justify your existence ... whatever made you think of that suddenly?'

'I've been thinking of it for a very long while,' Claudia said quietly. She added, breathlessly: 'And suppose I should marry?'

Helen said smugly:

'Let's not suppose anything so gloomy, darling.'

Claudia felt trapped and emotion swelled within her. She in no way misjudged her mother's attitude and she knew that it was not deliberately, or consciously, selfish, but rather had she grown so accustomed to the present situation that the very possibility of any change horrified her.

'But every woman should have a career,' Claudia persisted. 'No one knows their future and–'

'Your future will be amply provided for, darling,' came the swift reply. 'We're by no means wealthy, but we are certainly not poor, and I have always insisted that you must be our first concern.' She gave her hat the last pat, took a pair of gloves from a drawer on her right, stood up and said: 'Please let's not talk of it any more. You're all I have, Claudia; without you I should be lost.'

Claudia said firmly:

'You have Daddy.'

She saw her mother's expression change, even harden.

'Your father and I have no common interests whatsoever. When you are out of the house it is like a morgue to me.' She added swiftly: 'It would be foolish to pretend otherwise.' She shrugged her slim shoulders. 'Just one of those things and no doubt as bad for him as for me.'

'Why,' asked Claudia solemnly, 'did you marry Daddy?'

Helen Lomond smoothed on a pair of very soft kid gloves; every movement was precise and meticulous.

'You might say that I was inveigled into it by your grandparents,' she said calmly, 'or that we were both jockeyed into it; for your father's family were just as eager for the marriage as mine.'

Claudia was moved by an impulse she hardly understood; there was an urgency in her attitude as though her whole future hung on the slender thread of her mother's reply:

'Why didn't you separate?'

Helen gave a rather metallic little laugh.

'Lack of courage possibly; marriage becomes a habit, Claudia; it is a cage from which there is very little hope of escape... Besides, I've had you to compensate and, in any case, a broken home is not a very pleasant legacy to give a child.'

Claudia heard those words without in any way being moved by them; in that moment she felt that two homes, with a carefree parent in each, might be infinitely better than one with two parents wholly incompatible sharing one roof and four walls. And that the unfortunate child of the marriage

13

might, as a result, acquire the precious gift of freedom. She had no illusions but that her father and mother built their life around her and, in the process, allowed a certain selfish domination to creep into their affection for her.

Helen Lomond was a trifle disturbed by Claudia's attitude. She wanted her to be happy and she would have insisted that she was the most unselfish parent in the world; a parent whose one aim was to see that her daughter had everything possible in life, and that she in no way curtailed her pleasures or imposed restrictions.

Never for a moment, however, did it occur to her that she steered Claudia's life along that pathway which most suited her own particular needs; that she encouraged only those friends within *her* circle and frowned on those who might, conceivably, have drawn Claudia away from 'Stoneways', the Lomond home. All this was the more dangerous because Helen was blind to her own subtle efforts. Blatant domination, parental tyranny, made obvious by its very aggressiveness, is far easier to combat and fight than the kindly affectionate devotion of those whose very love for their unfortunate offspring provides both alibi and excuse.

Claudia said thoughtfully:

'I should have to be very sure before I married.'

'I suppose,' came the swift reply, 'we all think like that when we're young.' A light laugh. 'But your father and I jog along as well as thousands of other people.'

'I'd detest that.' Claudia felt a little stubborn.

Helen had no wish to pursue the subject and changed it abruptly as she stated rather than asked:

'You're coming into the town with me for coffee – aren't you, darling?'

'Not this morning, Mother.'

It struck Helen that there was something very firm and decisive about Claudia, which gave her a strength of character and purposefulness greatly to be admired. Claudia could be relied on, she reflected, and found the fact exceedingly comforting. It was like having a staunch ally and Helen felt that she needed such moral support to enable her to make the most of her own unsatisfactory existence. She said cajolingly:

'Oh, do, Claudia. I hate it without you.'

Claudia smiled.

'No; I'm going over to have lunch at the farm.'

'Cloverdell!' It was a rather breathless sound.

'Yes.'

Helen's expression changed. She always felt on edge when Claudia mentioned 'Cloverdell' as though the Russells, who owned it,

15

antagonized her in some wholly inexplicable fashion.

'I cannot imagine what you can see in that family, darling,' she said with an admonishing indulgence. 'Farmers are so dull–' She stopped almost suspiciously. 'Do you see much of Allan when you go there?'

Claudia knew instinctively that her mother disapproved of Allan, in the same way that she disapproved of most of the men to whom she gave her friendship.

'Since Allan is part of the farm as well as the family – naturally. He's always around. Why?'

'No special reason, darling,' came the hasty reply, 'except that he isn't your type.' A pause, then: 'By the way, they say that Raymond Winters – you know the man who has just bought "Old Place" – is a most charming man and terribly wealthy.'

Claudia said disinterestedly:

'Really!'

'You don't,' said Helen with satisfaction, 'care much for men – do you?'

'I've never thought about it,' came the smooth reply.

'I'm glad ... we get on so well together and men always upset everything... Darling–' She looked at Claudia very directly: 'Don't become too friendly with the Russells, I–'

'I'm already friendly with them, Mother – you know that.' There was no compromise

16

in Claudia's tone.

Helen looked pained.

'I never ask anything of you; I think you should respect my judgment–' She broke off and Claudia hastened:

'I can respect your judgment without believing it to be the right decision for me, Mother.'

As she spoke Claudia was conscious of a strange presentiment. It was as though, in some inexplicable fashion, she was standing on the threshold of drama; as though nothing would ever be quite the same after that day. In those seconds she saw the pattern of her parents' life superimposed on her own, and realized the vital issues that same pattern raised and the repercussions it was likely to have upon the future.

'Claudia!' It was a rebuke.

Claudia said steadily:

'You must allow me some freedom of action, Mother. I know you mean well, but there has always been a certain prejudice in your attitude towards the Russells.'

Helen could not deny the justice of the statement; she knew she was jealous of Claudia's affection for the Russell family and she said hastily:

'I suggest we allow the subject to drop, darling. You evidently have no intention of doing as I ask, so that no purpose can be served by continuing the discussion.' She forced a smile and then added: 'It will be like a morgue without you ... enjoy yourself.'

A few seconds later Helen left the house.

Claudia felt a suffocating sense of oppression as she made her way to her bedroom. She wished she could rid herself of the sensation as of being trapped in a very small cage. Within the rather forbidding Victorian walls of 'Stoneways' there was conflict and uncertainty, which impinged upon her life like a swift moving shadow creeping over the face of the sun. Pity for her mother surged within her as she began to change from her working clothes into a dress of primrose linen. And on the heels of that pity and understanding sympathy, came a slight hardening of attitude. Surely she, herself, had a little right to enjoy herself and be gay. Could she be expected to shoulder entirely the burden of her parents' incompatibility and ease their lives by her continual vigil and presence?

All problems, however, were forgotten the moment she reached 'Cloverdell' and she came to life as she stood on the brow of Pendip Hill – some two miles out of the market town of Horsham in which 'Stoneways' was situated – and gazed out across the farm's broad acres which lay like a giant carpet beneath the vivid blue of the sky. It was as if she saw it as her spiritual home and the love of the soil had its inception in her very soul. She had walked the distance from 'Stoneways' and every nerve in her body tingled as she paused to take in the panoramic view. The soft breeze fanned the folds of her dress and caressed hedgerow and ripening corn in a lullaby; silence, deep and profound, lay upon the earth, absorbing those sounds of nature and making them a curious part of the stillness. To the south, the Sussex downs etched themselves against the heavens, their undulating sweep a razor edge against billowy cloud.

Allan Russell coming upon her standing there, said by way of greeting:

'The world seems very far away at this moment – doesn't it?'

She wasn't in the least surprised to be thus hailed; more often than not Allan appeared from nowhere the moment she stepped over the threshold of his parents' lands.

'Very far away,' she said and sighed luxuriously. She went on dreamily: 'This particular spot ... the views, the limitlessness of it all ... I love it, Allan.' She raised her eyes to meet his and, for a second, emotion flowed sharply between them.

Claudia physically had a magnetism which never failed to enchant; her small, oval face was eager and radiant, her hair shone like burnished gold, and there was about her an inner fire, a passion and fervour that matched her fierce sincerity.

Allan, tall, bronzed, towered above her; he was handsome in a virile, masculine fashion and had a disarming smile which was irresistible. His strong character upheld the Russell tradition and he had taken his place on the farm, not merely because it was his father's wish, but because his heart was in it and no task was too menial for him in the interests of 'Cloverdell'. Pride swelled within him at the sound of Claudia's praise; a sweet excitement enveloped him as he said hoarsely:

'You always seem to belong here.'

Claudia's gaze focused the rambling old farm house with its grey stone walls, against which clematis and jasmine were splashed in a riot of colour. It seemed to beckon to her as though holding the secret of living.

'Probably because I'm happy here,' she said simply. 'You and your family have been so kind to me, Allan.'

'That is not difficult,' he said quietly and held her gaze masterfully. Then: 'Shall we go in? Mother's waiting for you, I know... By the way, you're not rushing away – are you?'

'Not until to-night,' she promised.

'Splendid.' He guided her down the footpath leading to the house. 'Martha's foal arrived last night,' he said eagerly. 'I thought you might like to walk over the stables and see it later on.'

'Oh, I would.'

'We could go into Dunston afterwards and have a meal at the hotel.' He spoke tentatively.

Was it her imagination, she asked herself, or was there really some subtle change in his manner towards her; a seriousness and intensity that was disconcerting? The very possibility sent her rushing, mentally, in the opposite direction. Friendship, without complications, soothed and was gay; emotional contacts shattered all peace and awakened disturbing desires ... she knew that she was afraid of losing the serenity of 'Cloverdell' which had been as a sanctuary for her; and while she accepted the fact that her attitude was ostrich-like, it was beyond her power, at that stage, to alter it.

Claudia hastened:

'Perhaps your mother might prefer–'

Allan interrupted her with a carefree laugh.

'She and Father are going to a local hop,' he said lightly. 'Some charity affair; they'll enjoy every minute of it.'

Claudia found herself saying involuntarily:

'They're very devoted, Allan – aren't they?'

'Very,' he said, adding swiftly and without sentimentality: 'Bless them.'

They came to the house and entered its spacious, walled-in garden which, in turn, led to an old cobbled courtyard, dairy and outbuildings. The smell of cattle, compost heaps smouldering and the fragrance of bean fields and honeysuckle all blended into what represented fragrance to Claudia. She walked unceremoniously into the kitchen.

Marion Russell, Allan's mother, was basting a plump fowl as they entered and, now, there was the aroma of cooking – newly baked cakes, the appetizing smell of frizzling fat in clean tins, and of girdle scones rising on the iron...

It was a large kitchen, with a red-bricked floor scrubbed until it shone, and a massive table so clean as to appear to be bleached. An old-fashioned, double-ovened range took up one wall and threw out a glowing fan of light. The heat came to Claudia in a pleasant wave and she revelled in it; revelled in the sound of the kettle boiling on the hob... This was home-life, in her opinion, at its best; life adorned with all the real and enduring things, and shorn of all that was artificial.

Marion Russell had that amazing knack of making the work of five women appear to be the normal task of one. She was never rushed, or nervy and nothing was too much trouble for her, as she coped with farmers' appetites with a glorious and indulgent efficiency. In appearance she was round, plump without being fat; her face held the light of quiet, yet carefree, happiness; she beamed in greeting and her welcome was like that of a glowing fire on a winter's day. She had a frankness and a sense of humour that won the idolatry of her family; she was the pivot of their lives while yet being wholly unobtrusive and completely undemanding. She turned from the oven and put her arms around Claudia as she kissed her.

'Lovely to have you, darling,' she said simply. She looked at Allan over the top of Claudia's head. 'No, you can't eat those cakes; they're hot.'

'Just how I like them,' he retorted with a chuckle and, picking one from the wire tray, sampled it, nodding: 'Good ... best cook on earth.'

Marion spread her small, well-covered hands and looked at Claudia.

'What would you do with him?'

'Just what you do, I imagine – spoil him!'

Allan made a mock bow then lightly implanted a kiss on his mother's cheek.

'You see? She's on my side,' he said absurdly.

'Heaven help her!'

Marion's eyes danced; she looked no more than twenty-five as she stood there, if expression and youthful spirit were the yardstick of age. Her hair, naturally curly and cut short, framed her face and shone like deep brown satin; her skin, innocent even of powder, in no way looked unfinished or greasy, but healthy and glowing.

At this moment there came a cheery exclamation from the doorway and a wind-blown, golden head appeared around the jamb.

'Any admittance to this select community?'

Susan Russell, Allan's sister, had the impish charm of the thoroughly harmless irresponsible. And she presented a picture of glowing youth as she stepped over the threshold, hailed Claudia, nibbled a cake, grinned affectionately at her mother and sank down in the nearest chair.

'My feet are killing me,' she announced, stretching them full length in front of her and resting on her heels, toes pointing upwards off the floor. 'Why I ever chose this photography game is beyond me... Claudia, you're looking pretty good today; I like your frock.'

There was a free and easy atmosphere between them all; Susan and Claudia were staunch friends and observed none of the conventions in relation to that friendship. To Claudia, it was as though she were part of the family and never did she fail to feel light-hearted and gay the moment she entered 'Cloverdell'.

Duncan Russell, Allan's father, joined them all a little later, wandering in with that air of content which reflected his joy and deep-rooted happiness.

Lunch time was, to Claudia, very nearly a party; conversation sparkled, laughter echoed through the old dining-room and Marion's cooking was of such a quality as to make every meal a feast. Here was no formality, but a homeliness that seemed to light a lamp in Claudia's heart. Sitting at that long laden table, she found herself wondering just what it must feel like to have parents in such perfect harmony as Marion and Duncan; to be the child of such a marriage and enjoy the freedom and companionship that followed naturally in its wake. She tried to avoid comparisons and stubbornly refused to dwell on the contrast between 'Stoneways' and 'Cloverdell'; nevertheless there were occasions when it was impossible wholly to keep to her resolutions, and this was one of them as Duncan Russell – still youthful in appearance, despite his greying hair – with rugged features and a skin almost mahogany from exposure to sun and wind – said to her:

'Marion and I were thinking last night, Claudia, that we'd love to have a little party here to celebrate your birthday ... of course,' he hastened, 'not on the actual day because, naturally, you will wish to spend it with your parents, but during the following week. We'd an idea to decorate the "Long Barn" and go all rustic – if that appeals to

you?' His deep, husky voice, well modu-
lated, was as music in her ears.

Claudia swallowed very hard.

'It's a lovely idea.' She looked from him to
Marion and met her tender, affectionate
smile. 'You are dears to me.'

Susan said:

'Let's dress up – fancy dress, I mean.'

Duncan held up his hand and chuckled:

'Oh, no you don't; I'm game for most
things, but the sight of a farmer prancing
around in frills and furbelows ... your
mother and I haven't the figure any more –
eh, darling,' he added.

Marion upheld him.

'Figure indeed,' said Susan, 'you and
Mother look wonderful; I won't have you
maligning my parents! Allan, how about
some support around here?'

Allan shook his head.

'Support for that remark, young lady, yes;
but for fancy dress – it's out; and seeing that
it is to be Claudia's party anyway–'

They all laughed together.

'Ah, well,' sighed Susan; 'it was an idea,
anyway... Wonder if Raymond Winters
could be inveigled into coming.'

'Good grief,' cried Allan, 'why Winters?'

Susan poised a piece of asparagus in mid
air.

'Because he's very eligible and very
wealthy,' she said impishly. 'And because

26

every girl in town wants to know him.'

'And how do you propose to "inveigle" him,' asked her father with a twinkle in his merry, blue eyes.

Susan looked innocent.

'Oh, you're going to help me, darling; at least you have *met* the man and he's very lonely here; and charity does begin in one's own parish, after all... Don't you agree, Mother?'

'You're the limit,' Allan said indulgently. 'As for his being lonely!' A snort.

Claudia recalled her mother's words about Raymond Winters, aware of a curious reluctance to be drawn into his world. In some indefinable way she sensed danger in connection with him, while admitting it to be wholly illogical.

'He's spending a fortune on restoring "Old Place",' said Marion.

Allan, slightly vehement without knowing why, cried:

'I don't like the fellow; there's a certain arrogance beneath his charm. Only spoken to him once but–' He paused imperceptibly; 'first impressions go a long way with me.'

'No man is ever fair in his judgment of another man,' said Susan loftily.

'Nonsense!' Duncan smiled at her. 'You won't know half so much when you are twice as old as you are now...'

'But you'll invite Mr Winters to the party

– eh, darling?' She put her head on one side and looked irresistible.

'I make no promises.' Duncan's voice lacked conviction. He loved Susan deeply and knew that at heart she was innocent of all materialism, but highly romantic and emotional.

'You're a darling,' she said confidently.

Claudia spent the afternoon sitting out in the garden with Marion, and helping her with the family mending. Tall beech trees offered shade and a luxurious sense of peace as they threw their shadows upon the sun-drenched lawn. It was a sheltered spot, cut off, in effect, from the farm rather after the manner of a retreat, which Marion loved. There, she and Duncan would spend their few leisure hours at the week-end, asking no more than the fulfilment of their own company, and the knowledge that every second was being well spent.

Claudia's gaze travelled to a wing of the old house which, in shape, resembled a small cottage attached to the parent building.

'It's awfully nice for Allan to have that to himself,' she said reflectively, certain that Marion would know to what she referred.

'I believe in a boy having privacy,' Marion said firmly. 'In those few rooms, Allan is completely his own master, shut away from all of us. He can have his friends there, talk half the night, or all night, if he wishes. I always said that whatever else my children might *not* have, freedom was the one thing they should and *could* have!'

Claudia said firmly:

'The most priceless legacy any child can inherit. If only all parents had your views.'

Marion was not deceived by Claudia's home-background; she knew the atmosphere that prevailed at 'Stoneways' and deplored its effect upon Claudia's life generally, admiring the courage and loyalty with which Claudia met the handicap, and praying fervently that one day she might welcome her permanently to 'Cloverdell' as Allan's wife.

'It is sad when they cannot appreciate just what freedom does mean to youth,' she said quietly, adding: 'Duncan and I felt, too, that when the time came for Allan to marry he would find benefit from having a small home in which to start, and since it is quite self-contained there would be no risk of interference!' She smiled broadly as she uttered the last few words, but at the same time scanned Claudia's face in the hope of learning from her expression. Just how fond was she of Allan?

In turn Claudia sat very still as one who dares not think too seriously about a given subject. Her gaze focused again the cottage under discussion; the grey stone glistened in

29

the sun, the wide open windows, diamond paned, held a romantic charm that appealed to her; there was all the enchantment of Yesterday in its solid antiquity. Allan's wife would one day share this beauty with him. Her heart-beats quickened and she said swiftly, fighting against the colour that rose in her cheeks:

'How will you feel when Allan marries – or is that a foolish question?'

'Not at all. I shall ask nothing more for him than that he should find the happiness and fulfilment that Duncan and I have known.' She added gently: 'I'm not afraid he'll marry for other than love. That's the important thing.'

'Yes,' said Claudia thoughtfully, 'that's the important thing... Isn't that Allan coming in, now?' She paused abruptly, experiencing a sudden, sharp thrill of pleasure at the unexpected glimpse of him. 'I thought he wouldn't be back until after five.'

Marion said softly:

'You are not here every day, darling.'

For a second they exchanged glances – almost involuntarily. And in that moment both read the other's heart. Marion did not speak, just got to her feet and said, as Allan approached them:

'I'll see about some tea.'

She left them and Allan sat down in the deck chair she had vacated. Claudia noticed the deep tan of his neck and chest where his cream shirt was open – a smooth, soft tan that was exceedingly attractive. She noticed, too, his strong, firm hands, well kept; there was something in his litheness and virility that attracted her, making her physically aware of his presence and of the emotion surging excitedly within her.

'Playing truant,' he said, and turned his gaze to hers as he rested his head against the back of the deck chair.

'Tired?'

He laughed softly.

'No; are you?'

'In this peaceful spot? Never!' Claudia put down the mending, allowing her hands to fall idly in her lap. 'It's so refreshing to talk to your mother; she seems to see everything in the right perspective.'

'How true.' Then: 'Shall we wander off immediately after tea? I want you to myself, Claudia,' he added tensely. 'I hardly get a look in with the family around.'

She averted her gaze and, once again, fear stabbed insistently; a strange fear that awakened the desire both to remain and, contradictorily, to run away.

They left 'Cloverdell' about an hour later, passing through the heavy oaken door of the walled-in garden and so to the farm itself, beginning their walk over its verdant, fertile fields and, finally, reaching the summit of a

31

hillside from which point they could gaze down upon the Russell heritage and take in the broad sweep of lands they had owned for many generations. The evening brought with it a curious hush and shimmering haze; the blue and gold of day took to itself a deeper hue; the warm earth gave off an aromatic smell as of incense and as far as eye could see, the downs kept their vigil, sentinels of past and future.

They paused and rested on the heather-covered slope leading to 'Long Barn'.

'No hurry,' said Allan and it was as though a certain agitation possessed him.

'I think I'm afraid of these hours ending,' he added tensely. He held her gaze masterfully, taking in as he did so, the beauty of her features, aware of the delicate curves of her red lips, the fine texture of her skin, the passionate and eager light in her dark eyes. And suddenly, as one who could stay the utterance no longer, he said: 'I love you, Claudia; you must have known.'

She didn't speak, but there was a fierce emotion in her silence, in the poised tenseness of her body, the almost startled expression that followed in the wake of solemnity.

'Oh, Allan,' she murmured, and there was a curious regret in her voice.

'What is it?' Fear dominated him. 'Darling—' His voice cracked a little in its hoarseness, 'say you'll marry me.'

Claudia's heart was thumping painfully; every nerve was trembling; her lips felt stiff and incapable of movement.

Allan went on almost desperately:

'I'm not much good at making pretty speeches, but there's never been anyone else from the first moment I saw you, Claudia ... darling, what is it?'

'I'm sorry,' she said breathlessly. 'I think I've always wanted to postpone this moment; to deceive myself into believing that we could go on as we have been doing, without anything more serious spoiling it all–'

'Because,' he interrupted her fearfully, 'you are not in love with me?'

'Because I'm afraid of marriage and all it stands for,' she confessed honestly and, leaning forward, went on earnestly: 'I've seen so *much*, Allan, that I am terrified of repeating my parents' mistake. I cannot promise you tomorrow feeling as I do–'

'But,' he protested sympathetically, 'because your parents are not happy it in no way follows that you–'

'I,' she interrupted him, 'know what that unhappiness means, Allan; I've seen it; seen two people, both worthy in their respective ways, ruin their lives by the wrong marriage and I've been drawn into it. That's the trouble: it just doesn't end with those two, unfortunate people. I must be so sure of myself, so confident that–' She stopped appealingly.

'Love brings that confidence,' he said remorsefully.

She shook her head:

'You've lived in harmony and compatibility all your life, Allan, and it has, of necessity, given you that confidence; it's inevitable and right that it should.' She paused thoughtfully: 'But even being able to see *your* parents' marriage as it is, doesn't, automatically, wipe out the picture on which I have always been forced to gaze.'

He put his hands on her arms just below her shoulders and gripped her firmly.

'Look at me,' he demanded. 'Look at me and tell me you don't love me, Claudia.'

She quivered at his touch and said breathlessly:

'I can't tell you that … but oh, don't you see, it's not just how much I love you, Allan, but just where that love would take me… It would be easy to drift and accept all you are offering – so easy and so terribly unfair–'

'Not if I don't think it unfair,' he cried. 'I am the best judge of that.'

She shook her head.

'I'd rather never see you again than cause you unhappiness, or fail you.'

For a second he gazed deeply into her eyes, then, swiftly, drew her into his arms, his lips meeting hers in a long, passionate kiss that seemed it would draw from her all resistance. Then, abruptly, he released her.

She sat there trembling and uncertain while emotion surged in an uprush within her. That part of her brain, dulled by the reality of her parents' life, retreated from the possibility of happiness and knew only scepticism and fear ... the woman in her stretched out to grasp all that Allan offered, yearning for the fulfilment of those secret desires and romantic hopes.

'Will you,' he said huskily, 'think it over?'

For a second their destinies hung on a dangerous thread; but caution urged retreat and she whispered:

'Yes, Allan; I will.' She added: 'But I realize how little I've seen of life outside "Stoneways"; how few people – men especially – I've met.'

'You've had the gloom of experience without the gold,' he said resentfully. 'I can give you that gold, Claudia; show you a new world ... not just a world on which you gaze for a matter of hours. I *know*; I know what makes marriage a success; I know that I have it within my power to give the woman I love the joy and content and happiness that my father has given my mother... I've watched them ... all the little things that far too many people overlook.'

'You could,' said Claudia wisely, 'only give all that to a woman who equally understood those depths of which you speak; a woman who could meet you half-way. I just don't *know*, Allan, what I have to give; everything is so conflicting that I dare not take anything on trust.'

He lifted her hand and held it in his.

'One must always take life on trust, my darling,' he said gently. 'For each one of us the pattern begins afresh. The important thing is to work that pattern with colours that don't fade and threads that don't break. Believing them both to be right will go most of the way to proving it is so.'

'But so many people begin by believing all that,' Claudia said, wretchedly. 'And look at the divorce courts.'

Allan drew her once again into his arms:

'Love is the only thing that, for you, will wipe out the things you have seen in marriage,' he said softly, tenderly. 'The love that tells you, quite plainly and unmistakably, that you cannot live away from me, and that even though your parents' marriage failed ten times over, you are quite certain that yours will not.' He held her almost triumphantly: 'That day will come, my darling, and I'm prepared to wait until it does.'

And with that he kissed her fiercely, hungrily and let her go, jumping to his feet immediately afterwards and pulling her up so that she stood beside him.

For a second they remained immobile,

then he said, his voice slightly uneven with emotion:

'Do you see – those hundreds of acres? It took more than just work over the generations, to keep all that the rich heritage it is today; it took faith and hope and love, Claudia ... and marriages that endured all things in the light of love ... this is no more than a monument to success – spiritual success,' he finished softly.

There was conflict and tumult within Claudia's heart as she gazed upon that panorama. How wonderful it would have been to reach out and embrace all that it symbolized; to turn and, within the sanctuary of Allan's arms, find that harbour which led to escape from all the troubles that beset her... So many problems, however, crowded in... Her mother's future; the knowledge of how she drew from her, Claudia, practically all her happiness; how she relied upon her... And above all, the fear lest she, herself, might, within the framework of her own disillusionment and uncertainty, fail Allan by any impulsive decision. It would have been so perilously easy to allow his doctrine and the example of the Russells to sway her judgment; to forget the reality of 'Stoneways' and to recall it – too late.

Long afterwards, Claudia looked back on that evening with a nostalgic longing, remembering every mood, every moment of its beauty. Allan's tender joy as he showed her the foal, with its absurdly long, slim legs that would grow no longer with the years and intrigued her more on that account; the quiet romanticism of dinner by candlelight at an ancient hostelry at Dunston; the quivering excitement and passionate tenseness of meeting Allan's eyes and knowing that he cared ... eyes that caressed her in a glance, and held the shadow of regret as they pleaded in vain.

At parting she clung to him, again haunted by a presentiment she could not define... Her lips were warm and soft beneath his own, her body curved gently against his and, then, with an increasing pressure as emotion surged wildly and triumphantly, momentarily to wipe out all save the urgent need that overwhelmed her.

'I shall wait,' he whispered, his mouth within an inch or so of her own and his arm still cradling her head. 'You cannot escape me, my darling – try as you will.'

He had run her back to 'Stoneways' in a car hired from the Inn – a rickety village car kept mostly for station work and driven by a rustic who had been in 'them thair parts for nigh on seventy yars'.

Claudia's heart sank with each half mile that was covered and as they came within range of 'Stoneways' she felt that sickness in the pit of her stomach, dreading its atmosphere and longing to creep, unseen to her room, without discussion or argument.

'Stoneways' was one of those gaunt Victorian houses such as might be found on any old-fashioned sea front, with wide double-bays and central door and one floor above. It had two acres of ground, but no one ever did more than notice if the gardener hadn't done his job properly.

To Claudia's astonishment, a sleek coupé Rolls was parked in the drive.

Allan said:

'You have company!'

'No one I know,' she hastened, craning through the window of the chunking hire car. 'Friend of Daddy's, I expect.'

'If he is your father's age, he is welcome,' said Allan with a smile. 'No, I won't come in, darling; couldn't bear an anti-climax. I'll ring tomorrow morning and ... don't forget you're having your birthday party with us next week.'

Claudia felt bleak and lonely as she watched Allan go and then went into the house. After the homeliness of 'Cloverdell' the cold formality of 'Stoneways' struck a certain chill; the rather large, ornamental hall and imposing staircase held no atmosphere of friendly welcome. Voices came to her from the lounge and she opened the door somewhat in trepidation.

Her mother beamed upon her.

'Ah, darling; I'm so glad you're back... Mr Winters waited to meet you...'

Claudia met the steady gaze of Raymond Winters as her mother spoke; a gaze both bold and challenging and her heart missed a beat as he moved towards her and said in a low, faintly mocking tone:

'And you are Claudia? Your mother's description of you was not, if I may say so, in any way adequate.' He flashed a smile at Helen and then turned his attentions again to Claudia.

Raymond Winters was attractive in a rather extravagant fashion, since his fault-less clothes and air of well-being, stamped upon him all the material assets of wealth. He lived in a world where money could buy everything – even the favours of women – but as he met Claudia's steady, uncom-promising gaze he sensed, instinctively, that she would be the exception and was the more intrigued by her.

'Mr Winters very kindly drove me back from the club this evening,' Helen explained.

'Really?' Claudia felt a strange foreboding as she stood there; it was like being drawn into a net she had endeavoured fiercely to escape. Again that sensation was upon her, prompting the urge to escape from this man, and inspiring the wish that they might never have met; she did not want to be thrust into his world or have him impinging upon hers; neither did she want to be caught up in the social whirl of which he was the centre. 'And how do you like Horsham and the district, Mr Winters?' she asked, realizing that it was up to her to make some kind of conversation.

'I love both,' he said, his gaze upon her. Claudia studied his features which were thin, somewhat aesthetic; his eyes were dark; his mouth inclined towards sensuality; in evening clothes his figure was impeccable; he presented a picture of elegant charm which she instinctively distrusted. 'I'm having a house warming at "Old Place" on Saturday and it occurs to me that if you would consent to come – you,' he hastened, 'and of course, you and your husband, Mrs Lomond – the affair could not fail to be a success. I am, after all,' he added modestly, 'a stranger in your midst.'

'We should be delighted to come,' Helen said, accepting with alacrity.

Claudia spoke up:

'Have you forgotten my birthday and the theatre, Mother?... I'm sorry, Mr Winters, but–'

'Your birthday,' he interrupted with an air of charm and decisiveness, 'then most certainly I won't take "no" for an answer: we'll celebrate the two things together.'

He spoke as one used to being obeyed and

to having his own way; his money gave him the power to command and he never failed to use it. Looking at Claudia he told himself that she interested him and he intended to get to know her better. Obstacles didn't exist.

Claudia protested:

'But my father–'

'I'll make things right with your father,' said Helen firmly; 'he will be very grateful to escape the theatre as you well know. I'd love to see your home, Mr Winters,' she rushed on. 'I hear it is simply beautiful.'

At that moment Charles Lomond joined them, greeting Raymond Winters with politeness as distinct from enthusiasm. He had met him without being impressed and, like Claudia, had no desire to be drawn into a world which made no appeal to him.

'I've gate-crashed your home, old man,' said Raymond Winters easily.

Charles remained silent and there was an awkward pause in the conversation which Helen ended by an enthusiastic outline of the arrangements for Saturday evening.

Charles frowned; he hated above all things having his plans made for him.

'That is very kind of you, Mr Winters,' he said stiffly. 'And since my wife has already accepted for me that leaves me nothing more to say.'

Raymond Winters was not deceived. He

made a mental note that Charles Lomond would be an opposing factor, while his wife would be, equally, as helpful.

'I'll send my car for you at seven,' came the smooth announcement.

'Thanks,' said Charles, 'but that will not be necessary; I'll drive my own.'

Helen seethed; it was always the same with Charles; he could be unutterably difficult and boorish and, so it seemed to her, resented anything that she had arranged or organized. And, if the truth were known, she had worked very hard to get Raymond Winters to 'Stoneways'.

It was after Raymond Winters left that Charles burst forth:

'Why on earth invite that fellow here? Can't stand him. Insufferable; thinks he can buy the earth.' He looked at Claudia: 'Don't tell me you *want* to go to his party–'

Claudia said tactfully, realizing that it was the only way she could hope to avoid the blame falling upon her mother:

'It should be fun, Daddy.'

'You see,' said Helen. 'Really, Charles, you think only of yourself. Claudia has little enough social life without your being thoroughly unpleasant to a man like Raymond Winters.'

'My daughter has no need to rely on favours from men like him,' came the instant retort. 'I don't trust the man and I'm

43

asking you not to encourage him. What's more, I suggest that we cut out this affair on Saturday; quite simply to make some excuse; after all, we had our own plans–'

'And difficult enough you were over them,' snapped Helen. 'I flatly refuse to do as you suggest ... Claudia, don't you agree with me?'

Claudia sighed.

'I think it would be very obvious, Daddy.'

'Then you and your mother can go on your own.'

'That's ridiculous,' Helen cried.

Charles picked up the evening paper, poured himself out a stiff whisky and flopped into an arm chair.

'It may be a warning to you, Helen, not to accept invitations without first consulting me.'

Claudia said:

'Oh, Daddy: I'm sorry...'

Helen burst out:

'What does your daughter's birthday mean to you? ... there's just no co-operation whatsoever in this house. I'm sick to death of it – sick to death of it,' she added furiously.

Claudia trembled.

'Let's not talk of it any more,' she said urgently.

Helen, angry, frustrated, strode to the door:

'I'm going to bed,' she cried fiercely. 'Come along, Claudia. I'm sure your father will enjoy being left alone.'

Claudia turned to him.

'Can I get you anything before I go up?'

'No thanks, my dear; run along.' He added stiffly: 'Good-night, Helen.'

Upstairs and when undressed for bed, Helen went to Claudia's room.

'What did you think of Mr Winters?' she began tentatively.

Claudia answered:

'I'm inclined to agree with Daddy. He's just a little too charming.'

'Sheer prejudice; Charles doesn't think any man good enough for his daughter; men are like that.'

'Daddy has never shown any criticism for my friendship with Allan.' Claudia paused then said breathlessly: 'What would you say if I were to tell you that I was thinking of marrying Allan?'

Helen paled.

'Allan!' It was a gasp. 'But, my dear child, you're not serious. It would be a tragedy.'

'For me?' Claudia found that she was holding her breath.

Helen moved from her bedside and walked slowly to the dressing-table, then, abruptly, almost dramatically, she turned and said:

'For you and, indirectly, for me too.' She

sat down again and Claudia knew that she was under a very great strain as she went on urgently: 'Listen Claudia, I've been thinking so much about the future ... things can't go on as they are now and it struck me tonight as I saw you and Raymond Winters together that–'

'Mother!' It was a painful gasp.

'Listen – please, darling. Don't you see, Claudia, Raymond Winters could give you every security in life; the right background and an income that would make you independent so that you'd never, never be tied as I have been. I'm not a materialist, but if I'd had any money of my own I'd have broken away from your father long ago: it would have been better for both of us... But now, if you were to–' She hesitated.

Claudia said sharply, fearfully:

'Are you suggesting that your future and your freedom are bound up with my making a wealthy marriage, Mother – is that what you have in mind?'

And her mother answered quietly:

'Yes ... yes; oh, darling, it *is.*'

CHAPTER TWO

Claudia felt trapped as she stood there, hearing her mother's voice echoing almost sinisterly through the dim recesses of a mind suddenly turbulent and torn with conflict. Fiercely, she resisted being drawn further into the maelstrom. Could anything be more incongruous, or ironical, than that she should be confronted with this plea, having come straight from Allan to whom she had expressed her fear of marriage and her determination not to repeat her parents' mistake? It was like being caught up in a gigantic web that mocked all chance of escape, and a phrase came hauntingly through the tense, dramatic silence: 'History always repeats itself.' She said urgently, desperately:

'But the very idea is fantastic, Mother. I don't even know Mr Winters. Besides, marriage without love would be unthinkable. You, above all people, should appreciate that.'

A shadow crossed her mother's face. She was as a drowning person clutching at a straw as she cried:

'It isn't only love that is important,

darling. There is so much you don't realize. True, Raymond Winters is a stranger to you, but he need not be. It is so easy to adapt one's ideas and so easy to turn one's back on security. Marriage, in any case, even with love, is a gamble – the divorce courts prove that, surely; but given the right background, the material assets, the chances of happiness are so much greater. Money, to the extent that Raymond Winters possesses it, offers diversion, interests, a new world; it also offers escape in failure–'

'When I marry,' said Claudia firmly, 'it will be for all time; I'm not looking for a way out, before I even get to the altar.'

Helen Lomond shook her head.

'Staying is so much easier when one knows one is free to go, Claudia. You don't understand.' She sighed resignedly. 'I'd never ask anything of you that I believed to be against your interests; any sacrifice, but–'

Impulsively, generously, Claudia cried:

'Oh, Mother, I'd do anything to help – anything, you know that, but–'

Helen's lips were trembling; her body was taut, her nerves frayed to the limit of endurance. She interrupted swiftly:

'Promise me just one thing.'

'What?' It was a fearful sound.

'That you will not lightly discard Raymond Winters's attentions, that you will set out to like him rather than to resist him. Oh, darling, to think of seeing you happy with a man like that and of the chance being given to me to get away from this – this *cage*,' she added vehemently. Her expression changed to almost pathetic anxiety. 'There isn't anyone in your life that you would consider marrying – anyone you're fond of?'

Claudia said quietly:

'There's Allan; but I'm so afraid of making the mess of my life that you've made of yours that I've–'

'Allan!' It was a cry as she interrupted her. 'That would be a tragedy; you'd never be happy in that life – never! A farmer's wife, Claudia.'

Claudia was conscious of a wild rebellion rising within her. She was sick and weary of the discussion; appalled by the problems that seemed suddenly to have come upon her.

'I am the best judge of that, Mother.'

Helen Lomond's face paled.

'Do you mean that you would seriously entertain the idea?'

Claudia drew in her breath and held herself tensed as she replied:

'Allan asked me to marry him: he asked me only tonight, Mother. I have not yet given him my answer.'

'Oh, Claudia.' It was a broken sound.

Claudia felt that a part of her heart was bleeding. She loved her mother and pitied

her, too. She was not deceived by the weak-
nesses of her character, but she knew that
such selfishness as she manifested was not
deliberate, but rather the outcome of years
of frustration.

'I'm afraid of marriage,' Claudia exclaimed.

'You – you love Allan?' It was an incredulous query, implying that the whole suggestion was ridiculous.

'I don't know.' Claudia drew a hand across
her forehead. 'I'm confused, bewildered;
I've nothing to steer by ... don't you see?'

'Meaning that nothing in this house has
helped you,' came the bitter reply.

'If I do, then I'm not criticizing, or
blaming, you,' Claudia hastened. 'It is just
that–'

'I know how you feel,' Helen interposed.
'And I know, too, that the stability of a life
such as Raymond Winters could give you
would answer all your questions, whereas
life with Allan–' She puckered her brows
into a frown of horror– 'How long would
mere affection last in the surroundings he
could offer? You want someone older, more
mature. It isn't that I'm unromantic, but
that I believe that romance can thrive only
in the right setting.'

'Romance,' said Claudia softly, 'has
thrived at "Cloverdell" for generations.'

'Because the Russells are simple people

who ask very little of life.'

'That depends on your interpretation of the word "little".'

Helen felt that she was pushing Claudia farther away from her by continuing the discussion. She said quietly, and with a faintly martyred air:

'You know, darling, that I would, as I've said before, never ask anything of you simply to ease my own burden ... let's not talk of it any more.'

Claudia was grateful for the respite; but suddenly it seemed as if she had been thrust into a state of chaos; as if life became a tangled skein that had been handed to her to unravel. She could see the pattern in her mother's mind with a terrifying clarity, even though she did not enlarge upon it and a vision of Raymond Winters rose up before her with almost Mephistophelian significance. His wealth would be the open sesame leading, ultimately, to her mother's freedom. She said urgently:

'And you know that I'd do anything to help; that I *want* to help, Mother. Your happiness means so much to me.'

Helen stooped and kissed her cheek.

'I'm sure it does, darling ... things will work out. Perhaps I ought not to have mentioned it, but the strain of life lately–' She broke off dejectedly. 'Good night, Claudia ... sleep well. And don't worry about me.'

There was very little sleep for Claudia that night. Thoughts of Allan, her mother and father, Raymond Winters, stabbed at her brain with dagger-like precision. Weird and fantastic patterns took shape within her mind. From the semblance of calm she was hurled into conflict. Memories of her evening with Allan crowded in upon her... Was this love she felt for him and if it were was it of such stern stuff, such steadfastness, as to endure for all time? All time. Could she cling to the happiness that had always existed at 'Cloverdell' and offset it against the unhappiness at 'Stoneways'? Could she turn her back on her mother's problems and plunge into what seemed just then as escape?... Allan's kisses still, in her imagination, warmed her lips, excited her ... but passion was not love. She turned over and a little cry escaped her. It was like swirling in some vortex. Raymond Winters... She had instinctively recoiled from the name and felt that, in some strange fashion, her destiny was linked – even against her will – with his.

At breakfast the following morning Helen went back to the question of Raymond Winters' invitation, her voice edgy in anticipation of resistance.

'I don't want to be made to look foolish at the last minute, Charles, and if it is your intention to be thoroughly rude and boorish on your daughter's birthday, all I ask is that

I may be forewarned, so that I can plan accordingly.' She added sharply: 'Some men are proud to go out with their families–'

Charles had sat in stony silence fuming behind his newspaper as the tirade went on. He emerged from it and said, fighting to keep his temper:

'I was ready to go out with mine; it was all fixed: you're making the trouble – not I.'

Helen gave a little shriek of denial.

'I like *that*. Just because I accepted Mr Winters' offer–' She added swiftly, 'And, after all, it will be much more fun for Claudia–'

'Claudia is the best judge of that,' came the steady reply. 'I suggest we leave it to her.'

Helen darted Claudia a fearful, nervous glance. It was as though her life depended on this visit, and she dare not allow the opportunity to slip by.

'Claudia wants to go,' she insisted. 'She told you herself that it would be fun.'

Charles said icily:

'Suppose you allow your daughter to speak for herself, my dear.'

'Don't "my dear" me in that condescending tone.'

Claudia cut in between them, torn in both directions. She knew that were her mother to be frustrated in her desire to visit 'Old Place' serious repercussions would plunge the entire household into gloom. She said tactfully:

'I, quite frankly, Daddy, do not see how we can possibly avoid going to the party. Mother accepted and, in your presence, all the arrangements were made. Had you refused last night, it would have been different.'

Charles's attitude changed. Anger died as he looked into Claudia's dark, fearless eyes; warmth crept around his heart, softening the harshness that had goaded him to fury a moment before.

'You're right, darling. It's just that I don't like the idea of that fellow hanging around you, or thinking that you'd be impressed by his wretched money.'

Helen said scathingly:

'Seeing that all the women in the county are angling for Mr Winters' favours, and that he has obviously appreciated Claudia—'

Charles cut her short:

'Claudia is not "all the women in the county",' he said stiffly. 'But she's worth ten of every one of them.'

Claudia thought as she sat there: How childish it all is; how pathetic is the level to which human beings reduce themselves when goaded by incompatibility. If only they would alter; if only they were happy, what a different world mine would be!

'Naturally,' said Helen facetiously, 'she's my daughter.'

'And mine.' It was an emphatic sound.

'When you've settled the question of my parentage,' Claudia said, deliberately infusing a cheerful note into her voice which she was far from feeling.

The 'phone rang in that second. Charles picked up the receiver from a table within his reach.

'Allan?... Hello, my boy; how are things ... good! Yes; she's here beside me. One moment.' He glanced at Claudia and smiled knowingly as he handed over the receiver.

Claudia felt her mother's gaze jealously upon her and an awkwardness and embarrassment gripped her. She detested 'phone conversations in the presence of other people who appeared to hang on every word uttered.

'Hello, Allan.' (How stiff and formal she sounded.) 'This morning. What time?'

Helen gasped:

'You're coming shopping with me, don't forget, Claudia.'

Claudia ignored that.

'About twelve-thirty. King's Head? Yes; I'm shopping with Mother beforehand,' she added discreetly. 'I'll be there. 'Bye.' She handed the instrument back to her father who replaced it.

'It will all fit in perfectly,' she said in the tone of one who would brook no interference.

'I'd had it in mind for *us* to have lunch at

the King's Head,' said Helen, slightly aggrieved.

Charles said swiftly:

'Don't tell me you're beginning to tie Claudia to your apron strings, Helen. A girl wants something more exciting than her mother – at her age!'

Helen flushed with annoyance.

'I've never interfered with Claudia's freedom,' she snapped.

Claudia got up from the table. She couldn't bear another minute of it.

Later, elated by the prospect of the party on Saturday, Helen began:

'I want you to have a new frock for your birthday, darling. Something *very* glamorous.'

Claudia's thoughts rushed to the party at 'Cloverdell'. She knew she wanted to look her best and a thrill of pleasure engulfed her. The prospect of meeting Allan later that morning gave zest to the outing generally and, for a brief while, she forgot the problems and conflicts attendant upon Raymond Winters and gave herself up to the luxury of choosing a frock that became her. The final selection was a soft blue moss crepe, draped to her figure, with a bustle in the shape of a bow at the back, and the new boned corsage, strapless, revealing her shoulders and giving her an enchanting grace as it moulded her firm, young breasts, hinting at their beauty without blatantly exposing them.

'Perfect,' said Helen as Claudia stood before the long mirror in the salon. 'Turn round once more ... yes, it was just made for you ... pearls and your diamond clip; no one will outshine you.'

Claudia said without thinking:

'Will it be a little too elaborate for a rustic affair. I don't want–' She stopped.

'Rustic?' Helen's brows became puckered.

Claudia tried to sound careless.

'Oh, I forgot to tell you: the Russells are giving a party for me next week – a belated birthday affair. "Long Barn" is going to be decorated,' she said unable to keep the enthusiasm from her voice.

Helen's heart missed a beat.

'Rather odd *their* giving you a party, darling,' she said amiably.

Claudia knew that to her mother everything was either 'strange' or 'odd' when she was in the mood to resist it. The Russells had, silently but remorselessly, become an issue and it was useless trying to deny the fact. The obsession was Raymond Winters.

'I think it a lovely, friendly idea.'

'I see no reason to take friendship to quite such lengths. If you want a party, darling, I can give you one, surely.'

Claudia found herself tensing.

'Oh, Mother, that doesn't come into it. In any case, I'm celebrating my birthday with you… This *is* a heavenly dress.'

'Most certainly it will be out of place in a barn,' said Helen deprecatingly. 'A crime to wear it *there.*'

Claudia dug her heels in.

'No more so than to wear it at "Old Place".'

'Darling! That is really absurd. You can hardly compare "Cloverdell" with the Winters home.' She added hastily, knowing how Claudia detested even a breath of snobbery: 'And that is not, in any way, detrimental to the Russells.'

Claudia said no more. A mood of rebellion possessed her at the very sound of 'Old Place' and Raymond Winters. Both were associated with an impending doom.

The shopping finished, Helen said regretfully:

'And now you're going to run off with Allan.' A pause. 'When will you be home, darling?'

'I can't really say, Mother.'

Helen appeared to be preoccupied with her compact as she went on:

'Barbara and Winifred are coming for tea and I do like you to be around to superintend… You know you do look really beautiful in that frock, darling. I'm so glad we managed to find it for you.'

Claudia in no way missed the subtle innuendo.

'I'll be back in time to help with tea, Mother,' she said with directness.

Helen beamed. She prided herself that Claudia had absolute freedom, but like too many parents that same freedom was but a string from a very tight rein.

Allan was awaiting Claudia outside the hotel. His gaze held hers for an instant before he spoke. Then:

'Hello, darling,' he said softly, intimately, and it was as though his lips touched hers in greeting.

'Hello.' Claudia felt a sudden excitement surge within her; an excitement that died in the bleakness of remembrance. If only she were in the position of thousands of other girls, free to carve out the pathway of her life without fears, inhibitions, complications. If only her mother's future were secure and happy; if only the suggestion about Raymond Winters had not been mentioned to cut across her freedom and build up an edifice of seemingly inescapable sacrifice. She felt rather like someone clinging to a rainbow over a dark abyss... Instantly, however, she began resisting such weakness: self-pity was nauseating to her and rarely did she indulge it. But there was something about that June day, with its soft, fragrant breeze, its golden heat haze; something about Allan's greeting, the implication of his smile, the tenderness of his gaze, that filled her with an aching yearning for happiness; a deep happiness that would light the future like a glowing lamp in her heart; a lamp never to be turned out. She looked up at Allan. 'You came in to market?'

'Yes ... bought a heifer.' He grinned boyishly. 'Very romantic. Oh, and Mother says she's expecting you for tea.'

Claudia had a vision of 'Cloverdell' – sharp, poignant.

'I'm sorry,' she said; 'I promised I'd get back.'

'Couldn't you 'phone and change that?' There was a note of pleading in his voice.

Claudia made rapid mental calculations. Her mother would be disappointed; the wrong atmosphere would greet her without a word being said. Claudia knew what store was set by her presence at home, and how so much friction was avoided through her continual vigilance.

'I'm afraid I can't. Friends coming,' she added swiftly.

They went into the hotel for lunch and a faint uneasiness gripped Allan as he studied Claudia across the table. She was like quicksilver – elusive, tantalizing and his love for her became a hurt in that moment. There was an expression in her eyes that he couldn't understand, and he found himself saying, almost involuntarily:

'Anything worrying you?'

Claudia twisted the stem of her sherry glass and appeared solemnly to concentrate upon the movement. Then, raising her gaze said:

'Many things, Allan; but worries are invariably overcome.'

'Things at home,' he asked fearfully.

'Yes.'

'I wish,' he said earnestly, 'that I could help.'

'You do – with your friendship.' She added urgently: 'Promise me that whatever happens I shan't lose that.'

'What could happen.' It was a sharp sound of interrogation. 'Friendship,' he echoed. 'Is that all you want, my darling.'

The endearment on his lips weakened her, but she fought the momentary desire to confide wholly in him, fearful lest, having done so, his persuasions might influence her. Above all, she told herself, she must be fair; she must not rush into his arms and delude herself that she was in love with him for all time when, quite conceivably, she might merely be in love with love and the idea of escaping from further responsibility where her mother was concerned. Allan deserved the very best that a woman had to give and she knew that, in her present state of conflict and uncertainty, she was in no way capable of giving it.

'Above all, I don't want to be unfair to

you, Allan,' she said with deep sincerity.

'Not to marry me would be that,' he answered hoarsely.

Claudia begged:

'Let's not be serious today.'

A shadow crossed his face. He had hoped that her attitude might have changed, even though he was willing to accept the fact that time was absurdly short in which to bring about a miracle. There was an impatience surging within him, that mingled with his overwhelming love and need for her.

'Very well,' he said generously. 'Tell me what you've been buying this morning.' There was a sweet intimacy in his attitude, a tenderness indescribable.

'A new frock.'

'Evening?'

'Yes.'

He looked at her earnestly.

'For your party?'

Claudia felt a sudden tremor go over her body; a sudden sensation of sickness. She knew that Allan was referring to the celebration at 'Long Barn.'

It was at that moment she saw Raymond Winters enter the dining-room; saw him take a swift look around and then felt his gaze leap to hers.

'Winters,' said Allan sourly. 'I dislike that man...'

Before there was time for further comment,

Raymond Winters had reached their table.

'This must be my lucky day,' he said deliberately. 'How are you, Claudia, although if one is to judge by your looks the question is superfluous.' He paused and eyed Allan with a friendliness that only partly concealed his condescension.

Claudia hastened, feeling wretched because she had not even had the opportunity of telling Allan about the events of the previous evening:

'You have met Allan Russell.'

'Once,' said Allan stiffly.

Raymond Winters was attired in riding breeches and a hacking coat; he looked handsome and elegant and supremely self-confident. There was, in his attitude to Claudia, a certain possessiveness that made Allan squirm, as the conversation proceeded and Raymond said smoothly:

'How many candles on the cake ... twenty?' He smiled, a smile that was admiring, attractive.

Claudia met Allan's eyes; eyes that had become darkly challenging, almost resentful, even suspicious in that second of blind jealousy. She managed to say half in confusion:

'Twenty-four ... but–'

'Your cake will come down from London.' He looked at their table. 'May I join you,' he asked lightly, 'or must I eat my lunch in solitary state?'

Claudia darted a beseeching glance at Allan who, cursing under his breath, managed to say:

'Of course.'

Raymond Winters made a pleasant, but imperious, signal to the waiter and another chair was placed in position. It irritated him to see Claudia with Allan; at the same time giving point to his intentions and stimulating still further his interest in her. He was perfectly aware of the fact that his presence was unwelcome, but the challenge was more than he could resist. He decided that it would be amusing to snatch her from under Allan's nose and, since they were all free people, it became an open contest.

Claudia said anxiously, her eyes meeting Allan's frustrated gaze:

'Mr Winters is giving a house-warming at "Old Place" on Saturday and has kindly invited us to it.'

'How nice,' said Allan in clipped tone. He despised himself for his jealousy, but it burned through him like a branding iron. His fight was hard enough without a rival of Raymond Winters' magnitude. And wouldn't any girl be flattered by the attentions of such a man, no matter how stable of character? Might not his wealth and position provide just that glamour necessary to sway Claudia's judgment and dissipate her fear of marriage, so that she was carried away beyond the power of studied considerations such as she now employed in her arguments on the subject.

'And since it is Claudia's birthday–' He used her Christian name deliberately as one claiming an accepted friendship. 'Well, what could be better?'

Conversation from then on was mostly initiated by Raymond Winters and when he felt that it was discreet to leave, he got up from the table, thanked them for their company, and said to Claudia:

'Until Saturday…'

Claudia watched him go with a sense of desperation. It wasn't in any way what she wanted; his intrusion in her life – the ramifications from the point of view of the future – conspired to make her dejected and depressed.

'I didn't,' said Allan, fighting to hide the bitterness he felt, 'realize that you knew Winters so well.'

'I don't know him well,' she countered instantly.

Allan lit her cigarette and then his own, and flicked the top down on his lighter as though he had an imaginary head in it.

'Then he behaved in an extremely familiar manner,' he persisted.

'I don't like your tone, Allan.' She spoke quietly.

'Sorry; that fellow makes me see red.' He drew in his breath and added generously: 'I know; I'm damned jealous and I admit it. Weak-kneed though it sounds. There is such a predatory, cock-sure attitude about him. I just want to punch him on the nose,' he finished boyishly.

Claudia relaxed; the tension eased.

'He was at the house last night,' she explained. 'It was his car standing in the drive. Mother met him at the golf club and he drove her home. He invited us to the house-warming, the question of my birth-day arose and he managed to arrange the rest. I don't want to go, Allan – honestly.'

'Bless you for that,' he murmured.

'And the new frock was Mother's idea... *I* saw it as new for my real party next week – truly.'

Allan's eyes were dark, intense as he said hoarsely, his gaze holding hers with master-ful possessiveness:

'Marry me, darling – please.'

His voice throbbed; the atmosphere changed. Claudia felt a tugging at her heart and resisted it as she said:

'I can't, Allan; I can't *promise* anything. Please give me time. It was an agreement, you know.'

'I know.' He looked apologetic, and added, 'Don't worry. Sorry, Claudia. But patience is not really my strong point.'

They left the hotel. The heat of the sun beat down upon them, its glare suddenly blinding after the restful light of the dining-room.

'I'd like to whisk you off into the country for the rest of the day,' he said. '*Right* in the country and lock you up in some tower,' he finished vehemently. 'Must you get back?'

'Yes; afraid so.'

'When shall I see you again?' A fraction's pause, then: 'May I come over on Saturday morning – just to say "hello"?'

'Do. Start the day right.' Her eyes were suddenly very solemn as she looked at him.

They parted and she retraced her steps, rather forlornly, home.

Saturday evening began badly, with Charles grappling with his evening bow and cursing the household generally because he was being dragged to 'that fellow's party', against his will. Helen had provoked him earlier and their angry voices carried to Claudia's bedroom to make her heart sink, and her body tremble. She managed to placate her father, however, and flatter her mother, and order was restored, at least temporarily.

'You haven't,' she said to him, 'admired my new frock, Daddy.' She swirled around. 'Like it?'

'Glamorous! You've turned out to be quite a beauty!'

Claudia laughed.

'Why not, with such good-looking parents.' She caught at her breath. What fun life could have been had only those parents cared for each other, she thought dismally.

Reaching 'Old Place' some brief while later, and coming upon it standing in the hush of evening against a quivering turquoise sky, Claudia felt a pang because of its sheer beauty. Its noble façade and stately pillars dominated the scene; it stood almost like a citadel apart from the world, its white walls gleaming against the vivid green of lawns, shrubbery and tall, centuries-old trees. Inside the vast hall Claudia stood awed by that which met her eyes. A large, wide, and circular staircase, dwarfed all else, its deep ruby carpet throwing into relief the cream woodwork and bringing the scene to life. A domed ceiling exquisitely painted, gave height and magnificence. Faint music came intoxicatingly from a room nearby; the swirl of dresses, the haunting fragrance of perfume – all created an illusion which, for Claudia, resembled the splendour of a film set. Yet she could not fault it for any vulgar display.

Raymond Winters greeted them with warmth that was in no way overdone. His gaze appraised Claudia and she had to admit that in his evening clothes he had an attractiveness which, to some women, would be irresistible.

'You like my home,' he said as a statement.

'I can see it by your expression.'

Helen interposed.

'It's simply beautiful.'

'Californian style,' said Charles, it being the only way in which he could deprecate the fact that it was not wholly English.

'Yes; I set out to create that illusion. The whiteness instead of gloom.'

From that time on he gave his attentions almost solely to Claudia. His guests wandered at will; the atmosphere was free and bohemian and drinks were served continuously as were all the delicacies to go with them.

All eyes were turned in Claudia's direction. 'Someone obviously new, my dear,' was said in chorus. There was a radiance about her which was lacking in so many women, and Raymond was quick to sense it. She sparkled, was alive; she could hold the conversation and had a power all her own.

'Will it be too trite if I say you look very lovely?' he murmured as they danced a little later.

'No,' she said tentatively. 'Sincerity can never be trite.'

'And you value that?'

'Don't you?'

'I might value it more if I had the opportunity of studying it more,' he answered cynically.

She looked up at him and met his eyes.

They were dark, wary, and she found herself recoiling from what she felt to be the cruelty that lurked behind them; a cruelty which further manifested itself in his hard, rather thin lips, that could curve in bitterness. Yet there was about him – a strength, even a magnetism – she could not deny; something overwhelming when taken and set against the background of his home, his wealth and position.

'The best way to find virtues in others is first to possess them ourselves,' she said sagely.

'And you don't think me sincere?' His voice challenged her.

'I never make too rapid judgments, Mr Winters. First impressions can so often be very wrong.'

He chuckled softly.

'You're certainly refreshing. Heaven knows I get bored enough by sycophancy.'

'The price of wealth.'

He drew her slightly closer; aware of the smooth whiteness of her skin, the glowing gold of her hair that was fragrant against his cheek as she turned her head and it touched him, sending a tremor over his body, and awakening swift desire.

Claudia wished desperately that he were utterly disinterested in her. She could see her mother watching anxiously from a far corner of the ballroom, and she felt suddenly trapped; as though the very walls were closing in on her and forcing her into a position which, with every instinct, she was fighting. The thought of Allan and 'Cloverdell' came as a clean, downland breeze, holding all the sweetness of life – as though its fragrance had suddenly been wafted through that now enervating atmosphere of heavy perfume. And when the music stopped, she slid from Raymond Winters' arms and, murmuring an excuse, made her way through the throng into the coolness of the night. To get away; to think ... to leave behind the ghost of a future into which she felt she was being relentlessly drawn...

And as she stood there on the terrace, watching the fairy lights that were festooned between the shadowy trees, Helen was saying to Raymond Winters:

'It was very sweet of you to send Claudia those magnificent flowers this morning, Mr Winters; she loved them so much.'

Raymond swallowed a smile. Claudia had forgotten even to mention them, although he had no doubt she would, eventually, repair the omission. He said, and the line of his jaw hardened in determination:

'It so happens, Mrs Lomond, that I want to marry your daughter. I've no illusions about her feelings for me at the moment, but just what *is* the situation between her and Allan Russell?'

CHAPTER THREE

Excitement, triumph, personal relief, surged swiftly upon Helen Lomond as she heard Raymond Winters' words. In the flash of seconds she saw the tapestry of her own life changing; the drab turning to gold; misery to adventure and happiness. But she knew, instinctively, that only careful handling of the situation could bring about such a perfect realization of her hopes. She made a few rapid mental calculations before she said quietly:

'Claudia is a very headstrong girl, Mr Winters.' It would be the height of folly, she argued, to allow this man to imagine that she, personally, would be so impressed by his intentions as to disregard Claudia's point of view.

'I'm aware of that,' he said firmly. 'It is one of the characteristics I like most about her. Spirit,' he said approvingly. 'I detest tame, cloying females. But,' he looked at her searchingly, 'you haven't answered my question about Allan Russell.'

Helen said steadily:

'There is really very little to say, Mr Winters; certainly there is no tie between them; no engagement, or–' She plunged. 'Any likelihood of their being, although Allan is, of course, very fond of Claudia.'

'Meaning that he wants to marry her.' It was an emphatic sound as from one who detests evasion.

'I rather think so. But,' she gave a little laugh, 'Claudia assuredly does not wish to marry him. She likes him as a friend,' Helen infused just the right note of casualness into her voice as to be completely convincing, 'but it ends there.'

'Splendid. I didn't imagine that being a farmer's wife would make any violent appeal to your daughter, Mrs Lomond, but I like to know the strength of my opposition before I start. On the other hand, I shall not underrate my young rival's tenacity of purpose.'

Helen smiled.

'And you?' He studied her intently. 'Are you on my side?'

Helen didn't leap in with foolish effusiveness, she said quietly:

'Claudia's happiness is my concern, Mr Winters.'

'Don't you think I should make her happy?' he asked abruptly.

'I feel sure you would,' she said slowly. 'She appreciates your world, your tastes; also you have both strength and character. She is not the type of girl to fall into any man's arms – least of all the arms of a wealthy man. She hasn't a material streak in her anywhere,' she finished.

'Oh, I know that my position,' he said loftily, 'doesn't impress her.' A little laugh. 'She's frank, disarming, and I like the idea of the chase.'

Helen's heart was beating rapidly; somehow she *must* make Claudia see reason. It was like having the world thrown at one's feet, and yet being afraid lest one might not be able to grasp its wonders.

'Then you can rely on my being on your side,' she said.

'Good; I like an ally... What do you think of "Old Place"?' He spoke eagerly.

'My ideal,' she said honestly.

'Claudia likes it, too,' he said. 'That is a step in the right direction!'

'I'd love,' said Helen, 'to go all over it... Ah, Claudia,' as Claudia reappeared. 'I was just saying to Mr Winters that I'd like to go over this wonderful house.'

'Then you shall.' He turned to Claudia. 'Does the idea appeal to you, too?'

Claudia said naturally:

'Yes; I can never resist houses.'

'Then they should be flattered. How about the owners?' He smiled down at her.

'I never commit myself, Mr Winters, when it comes to human beings.'

'Neatly put... Come along, then.'

He took them through large, lofty rooms, exquisitely decorated and in perfect taste. Magnificent hangings of rich velvets, tapestries, heavy satins, adorned windows first misted with shimmering net. Bedrooms in varying pastel shades, with deeply-piled carpets and divans with padded headboards to tone with quilted satin covers and curtains. Concealed lighting and delicate sconces adorning dressing-tables. Luxury spoke in its most enchanting form. Every landing was wide and spacious and practically all the rooms had their own bath, equipped with all modern devices possible and done in marble of pearly tints.

'This,' said Claudia, 'is a dream house, Mr Winters.' And she meant it. 'A little white palace in the sun,' she added.

He looked down at her.

'It needs only a woman's presence to grace it,' he said pointedly, 'and bring it to life. At the moment it is cold, impersonal. One can never pay for the vital things.'

She glanced up at him with sudden interest. And, instantly, he countered what he knew to be the thought flashing through her mind.

'You imagined that I should think just the reverse: that money could buy anything – eh?'

She didn't lower her gaze or seek any evasion.

'Frankly, that *was* passing through my mind.'

'Claudia!' It was a horrified sound from her mother.

Raymond chuckled.

'How refreshing is the truth,' he said and meant it. 'Perhaps, as time goes by, I may redeem myself in your eyes and overcome the handicap of my money!'

'Is it a handicap?' Claudia arched her brows.

'I rather thought it was – where your opinion of me was concerned.'

'You are entirely wrong,' she said coolly. 'I appreciate all this as much as anyone; what I do resent is the suggestion that women can be bought, or influenced, by it above their own affections.'

'Now you are bringing it down to the particular,' he suggested.

'Supposedly a woman's failing.'

He led them to the end of a wide corridor and said, unlocking a door with its Yale lock:

'This is a complete flat, shut off from the rest. I had it made for my mother. She had absolute privacy and her own front entrance, as you will see in a moment. Unfortunately, she was never able to live in it: she died just as it was completed.'

They moved into a square hall from which five rooms, bathroom, kitchen, etc., radiated. 'Rather unique,' he said. 'It solved the

76

problem for her, or would have done. And they are rather fine rooms – aren't they?'

These, too, were furnished on the same lavish scale, and with every conceivable appointment to add to their comfort and minimise the work.

'They're perfect,' said Helen in a breath.

'One maid and–' He shrugged his shoulders.

'What – what,' asked Helen and a little shiver of excitement went down her spine, 'what are you going to do with it now, Mr Winters?'

'Leave it,' he said, adding very steadily, 'Who knows, my future wife's mother, or a relative of some kind, might one day be glad to have it. And in the meantime, friends like the idea of its privacy. I could never, in any circumstances, have relatives to share my home. My mother was a charming woman, but we should have made each other's life a misery had not our domains been entirely separate.'

Claudia found her gaze drawn to her mother. She could read her mind with the clarity of an X-ray; see the flat as *she* was, then, viewing it – as the perfect sanctuary and escape from the misery of her marriage. Claudia's heart sank; her limbs trembled.

'Someone is going to be exceedingly fortunate,' Helen said.

Raymond Winters prided himself that he

had summed up Helen Lomond very well. He knew that, in showing her the flat and allowing her to realize that it was there for the asking – once her daughter became his wife – he had, by no means, made a false move. He was fully aware of the situation between her and her husband – as were most other people in the town – and knew that she longed for escape.

Claudia's depression increased as they returned to the main portion of the house. It was as though all life, all vitality, had drained from her. She might have glimpsed a prison cell to which she felt she was in the process of being condemned to occupy.

Raymond claimed the dance that was in progress and, looking down at Claudia said:

'I shall be at "Cloverdell" next week – you're having a party there, I understand?'

'Yes.' She hardly heard what he was saying. It was as though her mother's thoughts had taken tangible shape and were haunting her like some pitiful ghost pleading for recognition. She felt suddenly on the defensive, rebellious. 'I cannot quite imagine your enjoying a rustic affair, Mr Winters,' she said coolly.

'That is because you harbour many false notions about me,' he said, holding her gaze. 'I have a great admiration for the Russell family. And Susan is quite delightful. I met her last night, with her father, in the town. Such zest for life.'

'There's something about the whole family,' Claudia said swiftly – and paused, aware of Raymond Winters' gaze searchingly upon her.

'And particularly about Allan?' It was a clipped sound.

'If you choose to put it like that,' she retorted.

He laughed at her with kindly indulgence.

'You're determined not to meet me half-way, aren't you?' he said softly.

Claudia smiled, faintly disarmed.

'I wasn't aware that there was any issue which necessitated anything of the kind,' she said calmly.

His arms tightened their hold upon her as though he would will her to a consciousness of his physical presence. There was something ruthless and determined about him as he said, half roughly:

'I'll give you that hundred yards start and … still win.'

She glanced up at him and fear betrayed itself behind her smile.

'Do you,' she asked with cool confidence, 'live here all the year round?'

'That depends,' he said tentatively. 'I have a flat in town and use it at odd times.' The music stopped and he said:

'This is where you come into the limelight.'

Claudia would not have denied that, in different circumstances, the evening would have been in the nature of an adventure. Her cake, with its twenty-four candles, was the loveliest she had ever seen, and flamed in the darkness as the people gathered around her in congratulation, and she warmed and thrilled to their good wishes, as well as to the gaiety of the atmosphere.

Her mother said in a whisper:

'This is really most kind of Mr Winters; such a charming gesture.'

Claudia could not fail to admit that it was. If only she had not known of the ulterior motive actuating her mother's approval of him; if only the subject of marriage had never been broached, how different it would all have been. It was like watching a stage scene; a scene all set for the appearance of the heroine... It was not vanity on her part that forced home the fact that Raymond Winters was attracted to her, and that his intentions were honourable. His every glance proclaimed that fact and yet, fear accompanied her realization; fear not only of herself, through her mother's need and persuasion, but a certain fear of him, as a man.

She found herself longing, with an acute and nostalgic longing, for the simple and homely atmosphere of 'Cloverdell'. For Marion's loving arms; for Allan's unaffected charm, for his love and all it represented. There was the sanctuary she craved; the peace; the devotion. She caught sight of her father's bored, disapproving countenance and felt a tug at her heart because she was so fond of him, so concerned for his happiness. His future could not fail to depend upon her decisions; the effect of them was of such far-reaching import that she hardly dared to think lest she was dragged into that abyss where sacrifice became a stern and inevitable duty. She tried to imagine her father freed from the inexorable and wretched ties of his empty marriage; to see him happy, carefree, knowing that, in turn, Helen was the happier, too. She knew that never, in any circumstances, would her mother have the courage to make the break unless she had some anchorage, some roots to take the place of those she was relinquishing... She dragged her thoughts away as one tortured by the visions that pursued her. Responsibility weighed down upon her with a suffocating ferocity.

It was long after midnight when the party broke up. Raymond Winters saw Claudia and her parents to their car, walking close beside Claudia with a dogged step and talking amiably as he did so.

'May I call for you and take you up to "Cloverdell" next Tuesday?' he asked as they were on the point of saying good night.

81

'Foolish for two cars to be going in the same direction… About seven? And thank you for helping me out tonight. Without you, all this would have been decidedly boring.'

Claudia said with genuine feeling:

'You have been very kind, Mr Winters.'

'Yes,' interposed Helen. 'So very kind and thank you for showing me over your wonderful house; I've loved every moment of it.'

'Then you must come again – often,' he said gallantly. 'Good night, Mr Lomond; I hope you have not found it too dull.'

They got into the car and Raymond remained standing at the open door, still talking to Claudia.

'Until Tuesday,' he said, as he heard Charles Lomond somewhat impatiently revving up the engine in an obvious hurry to be gone.

Claudia wanted to protest; to be driven to 'Cloverdell' by Raymond Winters was the very last thing she desired; but she could not, without unpardonable rudeness and ungraciousness, avoid it.

'Until Tuesday,' she echoed, faintly.

He stood back and raised his hand in farewell; a tall, imposing figure in the moonlight whose features, nevertheless, etched in shadow, appeared almost satanic. She shivered as one about to plunge to her doom. Long afterwards she looked back on that night as on a remorseless Fate.

Charles began:

'I just can't stand that fellow! He's polite, amiable, the perfect host! But there's something about him that makes me squirm. Insincere – that's it. Reeks of it! And patronizing for all his amiability. Pity the woman who marries him. He'll crack the whip, all right.'

Helen protested vehemently:

'Sheer prejudice! You men make me tired. If you could be half as wealthy, or have half Raymond Winters' position! Jealousy – oh, don't tell me that men are not tarred with that brush; they are – just as much as women. He's charming, wealthy and the owner of a house that could not be equalled, I imagine, anywhere in this county.'

'I'd still prefer to see a daughter of mine marry the village blacksmith,' came the implacable reply. 'I'd trust him further. Winters is a supreme egotist; he'd never make any woman happy – far too selfish.'

'And, of course *you* are an authority on making a woman happy,' came the acid reply. 'Don't make me laugh, Charles.'

Claudia said desperately:

'Suppose we all agree that it was very well done, and that Mr Winters was certainly very kind.'

'By all means,' said Helen gloatingly. 'You see, Charles, your daughter doesn't share your jaundiced views.' A subtle pause: 'And I doubt very much if you ever get your blacksmith.'

Charles rapped out:

'Meaning just – what?'

'Whatever you care to make of the remark,' Helen said jauntily. She leaned over her tub seat and twisted so that she could peer at Claudia huddled up in the back. 'You looked simply wonderful, darling. I was very proud of you.'

'For once,' said Charles, 'we agree.'

A flat, bleak sensation of depression came upon Claudia as they went into 'Stoneways' some minutes later. Its forbidding atmosphere was redolent of the life lived within its walls; there was no semblance of welcome in the silence and the lounge seemed to her fanciful mind to stare at them gloomily and resentfully as they entered as though it, too, had grown tired of listening to the eternal conflict and harsh words that was all to which it was ever privy.

Helen heaved a heavy, discontented sigh.

'What a difference,' she said, 'between that house and this dump.'

Claudia could stand no more; she was in no mood to be drawn into argument and dissension. She said lightly:

'Good night, Daddy – thank you for taking us... Good night, Mother.'

Helen said swiftly:

'I'm coming up, darling ... 'night, Charles.'

She preceded Claudia up the stairs.

'What a wonderful flat that was... To live there in peace and happiness! I'd give my soul for that,' she said as one trying to convey the impression that she was talking without ulterior motive. 'There's one thing: whoever marries Raymond Winters will be a singularly fortunate woman; he improves on knowing and I must say that I appreciated his thought for his mother and his efforts for her comfort. Those are the things that tell in the character of a man... Claudia! Don't look so glum, darling.'

'Sorry.'

Helen wanted to shriek with irritation. To think that any girl in her right senses would be foolish enough to ignore the advantages of marrying a man like Raymond Winters almost drove her mad. A sense of frustration, greater than she had ever before known, overwhelmed her; she could think of no more vigorous approach than that in which she had already indulged, and dared not press home her own claim further lest she jeopardize, rather than improve, her position.

'Perhaps I'd better say good night,' she suggested.

Claudia was in no mood for a further conference in her room; she was weary and longed for sleep and the peace that came with it.

'It is pretty late,' she murmured. 'Good night.' And with that passed swiftly along the corridor and out of sight.

The thought of Allan came insistently, hauntingly. Would she ever be able wholly to forget him; to wipe out the memory of his kiss and find fulfilment in other arms? She distrusted marriage in any case... The mocking thought came back insidiously that in order to open the door of her mother's cage she had to plunge into a mistake as grave as that which her parents had originally made. Yet, could she say that; could she define that word 'mistake' in the connection in which it was then being used; and might she not make as great a failure of marriage as they – irrespective of whom she chose. Almost as one demented she fought to thrust the subject from her mind. Perhaps Raymond Winters would never ask her to marry him. That would solve the problem for her. It might be perfectly true that he was attracted to her at the moment, but he was, obviously, the fickle, philandering type! Thus, wholly illogically, she consoled herself and brightened accordingly.

She saw Allan the following afternoon, having promised to go to 'Cloverdell' to tea and announcing her intention at the lunch table.

'Aren't you,' said her mother sweetly, 'spending rather too much time at the farm, darling. I don't want to interfere but–'

'Then why do so?' interrupted Charles. 'It seems to me that you always have some comment to make, some criticism, whatever Claudia does. I wonder she puts up with it.'

Helen's face went almost deathly white. That Charles should dare to place her in the wrong in Claudia's eyes, try to drive a wedge between them, horrified as well as maddened her. Tears of mortification stung her eyes as she rapped out:

'I suppose you think that will ingratiate you with Claudia. Well, if any girl in this town has more freedom than she–' She choked with anger. 'It wouldn't matter what I said, you'd take the opposite view.'

'Then we'll agree to differ,' came the implacable reply. 'But, personally, I cannot think of a happier, more healthy atmosphere for Claudia than "Cloverdell". I like everything it stands for and every member of its family.'

Claudia warmed to his praise.

'I'm glad,' she said softly. 'You will come to the party there next week – both of you, won't you?' she asked eagerly.

Charles said instantly:

'Rather! Looking forward to it. Duncan's a man after my own heart. To begin with, his people are Scots and that gives him priority over the rest of mankind. I'll take a Scot any day; trust 'em; they are men of action and of their word.' He added pointedly: 'When you marry, Claudia, see to it that your husband has some Scottish blood in his veins, and you won't go far wrong.'

Helen snapped:

'Well, I don't wish to go to the party.' She stopped, realizing the folly of alienating Claudia and, also, that since Raymond Winters would be there, her absence could not fail to be noticed by him. She corrected herself. 'Of course I shall go. Your father knows perfectly well that I like the Russells, and that my feelings in the matter were concerned entirely with the desire that you should meet as many people as possible – as many men as possible–' There was defiance in her voice.

'Ah, now we agree,' said Charles. 'But I was of the impression that, to you, Raymond Winters rather represented all men where Claudia was concerned.'

Claudia introduced a note of lightness:

'When you two have finished arguing over your offspring,' she said, 'I'll take the stand and tell you that, at the moment, I feel very much drawn towards spinsterhood – which is probably how I shall end up! Marriage doesn't seem to me to be a very enviable state ... 'bye both of you.'

'And if anyone 'phones,' Helen asked.

'What am I to say?'

'Tell them where I am,' came the cool reply. 'And that you haven't the faintest idea when I'll be back.'

'Good for you,' chuckled her father. 'Enjoy yourself, darling.'

Helen felt that Charles had placed her at a disadvantage and said sweetly:

'Yes, have a good time and remember me to Mrs Russell.'

Claudia swallowed a smile. She was not deceived.

'Well,' said Allan, as she reached the farm some little while later: 'How did the party go off?'

'Just as you would imagine.' She looked up at him, the joy of being there surging upon her like sun pouring through from dense, black cloud.

'And, of course, Winters was most attentive,' he said trying to curb his jealousy.

'Not,' said Claudia, 'because I encouraged him, Allan.'

He stared at her gloomily.

'I wish I could rid myself of the feeling that he's out to come between us,' he said gruffly. 'You know he's invited himself – it was more or less that, with a little prompting from Susan – here on Tuesday. Blast him.'

'Yes.' She hastened: 'He offered to drive me here – or, us here.' She made a helpless gesture. 'What excuse was there?'

'Nothing short of telling him to his face that he's jolly well not wanted.' A pause. 'Oh, darling, if only you'd give me the right to—'

'Let's not be serious,' she cried desperately. 'Oh, Allan, let's pretend that life is as glorious as this heavenly scene and that only you and I exist in the world...'

'That is simple,' he whispered, as he drew her into his arms.

The night of the celebrations arrived, bringing with it, for Claudia, the glow of excitement. She was determined, on that occasion, to leave every problem, worry, and responsibility behind her and go forward on a billowy cloud of happiness.

Not even Raymond Winters' presence irritated her and as he drove them through the quiet lanes to the farm, she talked gaily and inconsequently until he said:

'You are in good spirits tonight, Claudia.'

Helen was swift to appreciate the significance underlying the remark and put in:

'You seem to have a magic effect upon her, Mr Winters and, indeed, upon us all.'

'Cloverdell' came into view at that second; its golden acres lying beneath the blue heavens like a rippling carpet; its peace and serenity giving to the countryside an enchantment that seemed to draw music from Claudia's very soul so that tears misted her eyes as of one moved spiritually by its splendour, its simplicity.

'Wonderful scene,' said Charles.

'I love farms,' said Helen, 'from a distance! The smells do not attract me, otherwise.'

'Long Barn' as they came upon it, seemed to quiver with pulsating life; to be splashed against its background of green and brown, in a mass of rich colour, with its fairy lights and Chinese lanterns. There was a reality and richness about the atmosphere that manifested itself instantly one glimpsed it and crossed the threshold. A wood-block floor had been polished like a golden mirror; the cabin-like log structure lent a certain rustic and romantic charm to the decorations, streamers and masses of flowers. People for miles around – rich and poor alike – converged upon it in the same hearty spirit; there was no formality and no sophistication. Clothes varied from prints to brocades; from satins to cotton. Men wore all manner of garments that had been shaken out of their moth balls; some suits too large; others too small; others impeccable; but no one cared or, for that matter, noticed; they intermingled with all the good-naturedness and friendliness that the true country knows and lives by. Here was sincerity born of the very soil on which existence depended; lord and labourer smiling across the dividing space, bridging social gaps and enjoying themselves spontaneously.

Cheering started as Claudia entered. For she was known and loved by them all. Allan, instantly, took his place by her side; Marion kissed her, so did Duncan and Susan. They greeted Helen and Charles with all the warmth of which they were capable.

Allan whispered:

'Darling, you look simply wonderful.' Surreptitiously he squeezed her hand.

There was a crowd around her almost instantly and she had a charming word for each one in it. Allan remained beside her, *en garde*. Raymond Winters, who had been forced a little way further down the Barn, retraced his steps and said almost possessively:

'I claim the first dance, Claudia.'

Instantly Allan countered:

'I am afraid, Mr Winters, that you are too late. The privilege is mine.'

Raymond Winters took that, inclined his head and exclaimed:

'Then, the second and – the last. That can be far more important, on occasion, perhaps!'

Susan joined the little group and Raymond gave her his arm as the music began. She smiled up at him in delight. This was exciting and she knew she would get him there she told herself confidently!

Allan's arm went around Claudia's slender

waist; they moved away to the strains of a lilting waltz and she murmured:

'This is a real party, Allan: every minute is precious. I'm floating in space tonight – gay, happy–'

'Shall I ever bring you to earth,' he asked tensely. 'Oh, my darling I want to so desperately … love you so *much*–' As he spoke his lips touched the top of her head and, almost convulsively she pressed against him, emotion surging upwards, all the passion of youth demanding expression. Her sigh was touched with ecstasy and it thrilled him. She could hear his heart, feel it thudding against her breast, as he could hers. For a second they were held together by an enchantment that made it seem as though they were of one body and spirit.

Claudia shut her mind against any analysis; she would not spoil that exquisite moment by argument.

'Darling,' he breathed hoarsely.

'Oh, *Allan!*'

'You love me,' he said triumphantly… 'I know you love me. My sweet, let's tell them we're engaged – say that–'

'No!' Fear came back instantly. 'I can't – not yet, Allan. I must be sure; there is so much for me to study; problems and–'

'Very well,' he said gently. 'I'm an impatient devil – aren't I? But your eyes say one thing, my dearest, and your lips another.

What is a poor man to do!'

She found herself crying involuntarily:

'Keep loving me a little longer until–'

'I shall love you for always, my darling – always,' he said huskily. 'Tonight, you look bewitched; all moonbeams and silver; I want to run off with you–'

'If only you could.' It was a little, passionate sigh. 'If only nothing counted beyond that which we feel – emotion, desire–'

He looked down at her and drew her gaze to his, passionately:

'Emotion is the beauty, the poetry of life, my darling. You cannot live without it and you cannot fight against it for long!'

Again his lips touched her cheek – swiftly, unnoticed in its very swiftness and she thrilled to his touch. Just then the music stopped and Marion, who had stood watching them with hope in her heart, said:

'Allan dear, just give your father a hand with the drinks and then come back and keep a tight hold of Claudia: she's far too lovely to be let loose!'

Raymond Winters appeared seemingly from nowhere.

'I couldn't agree more, Mrs Russell.' He glanced at Claudia. 'May I offer my protection, meanwhile?'

Allan scowled, but Claudia could do no other than smile and move away with him as Allan disappeared.

'Let's wander outside for a few moments,' Raymond said easily.

'Long Barn' stood slightly raised from the rest of the farm, looking down on it so that, as they gazed, the whole countryside seemed to spread like a mosaic pricked out in silver. The light from the moon diffused upon it, like limes upon a gently darkening stage; there was a hush, a stillness, that made Claudia catch her breath.

'Poetry,' he said slowly. 'I wish I had the right quotation, Claudia – for all this and for you.' He looked down at her and his gaze became more intense as he said suddenly, as though the words were forced from him: 'I'm madly in love with you, my darling. Claudia ... marry me – marry me.'

For a second she stared up at him aghast and almost before she could speak, his arms went around her, his lips found hers.

And it was in that moment Allan joined them.

CHAPTER FOUR

Claudia managed to free herself from Raymond Winters' possessive embrace; she was breathless, incapable of uttering the right words, or of grappling with the situation forced upon her as she met Allan's stormy, accusing and faintly contemptuous, gaze. She heard his voice, clipped, unnatural, as from a great distance as he said:

'Forgive me ... I'm afraid I arrived at a most inopportune moment.'

And with that, he swung around and strode swiftly away.

Raymond felt a sense of elation. He had not intended to betray his love for Claudia at that early stage, but realized instantly the advantages that could not fail to materialize in the present circumstances. Allan was jealous and headstrong; and the little scene he had just witnessed might well prove fatal. Allan, he appreciated, was in a somewhat delicate position, and at a distinct disadvantage when it came to fighting wealth and position, and just the sensitive type to withdraw quixotically, imagining that, by comparison, he had nothing to offer. Obviously, he was in love with Claudia... And she? He looked down at her and said hoarsely:

'I'm waiting for my answer... Will you marry me?'

Claudia was restraining the impulse to rush from his side and seek Allan out; but a tiny flame of anger burned fiercely within her. How obvious it was that Allan had imagined the wrong thing; possibly believing that she had encouraged Raymond Winters' attentions. Strange how so much that was vital in life happened in a few split seconds, for she had a premonition that nothing would ever be quite the same from that moment and that the shadow of Raymond had already been cast. She managed to say weakly:

'You must know that is quite impossible.'

He stood there firm, implacable, looking down at her in the moonlight.

'Nothing is impossible,' he said smoothly.

'I'm not in love with you,' she said firmly.

'Of that I am fully aware.'

She spread her hands in a little helpless gesture.

'Then, why—'

'Dear, foolish child,' he said softly. 'I'm not afraid that such a state will remain between us for very long. I'll make you care, Claudia... I've never,' he added almost sternly, 'asked any other woman to be my wife, and I'm used to getting what I want – and fighting for it, too.'

It was a challenge and she rose to it. 'Human beings are not always malleable clay, Mr Winters.'

'Agreed.' He added: 'But you are free, and I love you; my attentions, therefore, have at least the advantage of sincerity in your eyes. I may have been impulsive just now, but that was all. I'll wait, not patiently, but...' He smiled.

'Please,' she said almost desperately.

'What you ask is quite impossible and–'

'Do I detect a certain fear in your voice,' he said with faint cynicism, 'fear of yourself?'

'No.' Claudia was wrestling with a dozen conflicting issues. The thought of her mother obtruded with shattering significance. And in that second, Raymond Winters assumed almost sinister shape – as though he were inescapable, not because she would ever love him, but because he had so much to offer that would revolutionize the lives of those whom she loved. And because her conception of marriage, in any case, had been distorted to a point where she was incapable of constructive thought regarding it. Bewilderment, uncertainty pursued her. If only he had not asked her to be his wife: if only the tormenting problem had been taken out of her hands by his silence.

He laughed at her.

'You deceive yourself so beautifully, my dear.'

She flashed him a warning glance.

'I think it is you who are guilty of that.' Her gaze darted from one point of the scene to another. She added urgently: 'We must get back–'

He interrupted her.

'The word "must" isn't in my vocabulary, Claudia. What is it ... Allan?' He spoke commandingly.

She countered.

'Yes' – defiantly. 'The music has already started again and–'

'The second dance was mine – remember?'

She did remember and tried to overcome the hateful depression that had settled upon her, as a result. The evening that had begun so joyously was now clouded by the spectre of the future.

He put his hand against her elbow and guided her to 'Long Barn'.

'We shall look back on this night, you and I,' he said as one who makes a prophecy. 'But don't forget that I have in no way accepted your refusal. We will just leave the matter for a little while… You are beautifully tantalizing, Claudia,' he added tensely. 'But you'll have to give in; there is far too much in my favour for you to escape me.'

She looked up at him in startled gaze, but his smile was inscrutable. Then:

'Since you have asked me to marry you,' she said with dignity, 'I rather think that only the fact of my loving you could cover that issue.'

'Women have been known to marry first and love afterwards,' he said persistently.

Claudia longed to dismiss him now and for all time. In normal circumstances this she would have done in strong, unrelenting terms. As it was, she dared not be too decisive lest she know the remorse of having failed her mother and shirked her duty. The position was wholly invidious to her, but she was caught mercilessly in its trap.

Allan was not in sight when she and Raymond began to dance.

Her mother appeared as from nowhere when the waltz finally ended, beaming upon Raymond with affectionate gaze and saying:

'You seem to be enjoying yourself, Mr Winters.'

'I could do so very much more,' he replied swiftly, 'if your daughter would promise to marry me.' He flashed Claudia a smile.

Helen felt that all the air had been squeezed from her lungs as she gasped:

'You mean that–'

'She has refused me,' came the steady reply. 'I suppose there is nothing you can do to help my cause?'

The words were in no way uttered idly. Raymond wanted the situation brought into the daylight where Helen Lomond was concerned, and he was exceedingly doubtful as to whether Claudia would have confided his proposal.

Claudia's heart missed a beat. That her mother should know the truth at this stage was the very last thing she wanted. In fact she had already decided to keep the matter to herself. Now, however, she realized just what lay ahead.

Sudden bitterness showed in Helen's face. She saw her world crumble, her hopes fade and she said, almost harshly:

'I'm afraid, Mr Winters, that I have absolutely no influence over Claudia. My wishes are the very last she would consider.'

Claudia felt that every muscle in her body had become taut. Rebellion seethed; frustration gripped her in a vice. There was no mistaking her mother's attitude, and it was almost as though war had been declared.

Helen, realizing she had betrayed her hand with reckless disregard for discretion, added with a honeyed smile:

'But women do change their minds, Mr Winters...' A little sigh. 'I only want Claudia's happiness and have never persuaded her over anything.'

Claudia, hot, uncomfortable, feeling almost like an exhibit in a murder trial said politely:

'If you will excuse me...'

And with that she made her way to the furthest corner of the Barn, her gaze darting about in search of Allan and then suddenly focusing him, as he stood talking to a girl whom she had never seen before. Susan's voice at her elbow came lightly, blithely:

'A new one on you, eh, Claudia?' She glanced at the girl as she spoke. 'That's an umpteenth removed cousin of ours – Meg Ainsley – quite a dear and crazy about Allan.

Always has been and, as far as I can see, always will. Attractive, too, isn't she?'

Susan, shrewd, knowledgeable, studied Claudia intently as she spoke, watching every shade of expression that crossed her face. She was well aware of the situation between Claudia and Allan and of the intrusion of Raymond Winters. What she could not settle to her own satisfaction, however, was precisely what Claudia's true feelings were.

'Is she staying long?'

'Oh, a few weeks – just depends. She only 'phoned this afternoon to say she was coming.' A light laugh. 'Allan's very devoted to her. So are we all. Come and meet her.'

'Don't let's butt in,' she said swiftly.

'Nonsense! Ah, the elegant Raymond Winters is watching you, my dear. I'm going to dance with him again if it kills me. Attractive animal.'

Claudia said:

'You think so?'

'Definitely. Quite ruthless, and very hard but–' Susan chuckled. 'One could bear a great deal against the background of "Old Place"!'

Claudia, a few seconds later, found herself greeting Meg Ainsley and liking her gentle brown eyes and sweet smile. There was an untouched charm about her, a sympathy that was appealing.

102

Allan stood rather stiffly, talking in mono-syllables. He despised himself for the fury that had gripped him as he saw Claudia in Raymond's arms and even the memory of it whipped him to anger and violent jealousy.

'I hope,' said Claudia, addressing Meg, 'that you'll come over to see us while you are here.'

'I'd love to.'

While Claudia was sincere in the suggestion, her thoughts were completely absorbed with Allan whom she felt had withdrawn from her and was talking to her from a distance. At last, as the music started and a partner claimed Meg and Susan, he said:

'Shall we – dance?'

She answered quietly:

'I'd rather go outside, Allan.'

'As you wish,' he said coldly.

Once alone, with the moonlit darkness to offer sanctuary, Claudia began:

'Listen Allan–'

'I'm sorry,' he interrupted, 'that I butted in on that touching little scene just now.' A pause. 'Just where does Raymond Winters fit into the picture of your life?' A harsh sound. 'Or don't you know that, either?'

Claudia felt angry and miserable. There was so much she couldn't explain; so much that she felt involved the whole story of her parents' life, that she said swiftly:

'It so happens that Mr Winters has asked me to marry him.'

Allan's face paled.

'*Marry* him!' It was a gasp.

'Is that so hard for you to believe?'

'No – no, but–' He stopped, then: 'Oh, darling, I'm so damned jealous that I can't see straight when he's anywhere near you. Sounds feeble and I'm ashamed of it but–' Relief surged over him like balm upon a throbbing wound. 'And you refused him?'

'Yes.' Claudia shivered. The word sounded empty and oddly mocking.

Instantly, as though by telepathy, Allan burst forth:

'But you didn't slam the door against him – any more than you slammed it against me! Is that it?'

'No,' she cried fiercely, 'it isn't. And your attitude is unpardonable. I've been absolutely honest with you, Allan. At this moment I wish I could run away to the utmost ends of the earth,' she said desperately. 'I'm so weary of conflict and uncertainty and indecision–'

'I'm sorry.' His voice was calmer. 'The argument that you applied to me applies to him, I take it?'

'The fear of repeating my parents' failure?'

'Yes.' He looked at her earnestly. 'Don't you see that you are shutting your heart out of all this, Claudia…'

She sighed. If only she could stand there,

now, with nothing more than an inbred fear to overcome; stand there, free and un-hampered. But whichever way she turned she was torn in the opposite direction, as though some mocking Fate had predetermined that she should, finally, be the burnt offering on the altar of her parents' folly. And it lay within her power to set them free. Could she ignore that obligation, shut her ears to her mother's pleading? How far the tentacles of unhappiness spread, like some foul disease condemning the children almost before they were born. Could she be blamed, in any case, for hesitating, for caution as she stood on the brink of that precipice which might well force her to follow in their footsteps... She could not divorce her problem from their own: she was a part of it, and to escape with remorse for ghostly company... Yet there was no one – not even Allan – in whom she could confide that phase of the grim truth. Allan could only accuse her of shutting her heart out of all this. She said with a certain urgency:

'It isn't that.'

'Are you in love, or infatuated, with Winters?'

'Neither; shouldn't I have agreed to marry him, otherwise?'

'I suppose so.' He looked at her in bewildered silence for a second then: 'And you are not in love with me,' he added tensely: 'Are you?'

The stillness of the night seemed to beat around them as with imaginary wings; the air appeared to be drained suddenly of all oxygen; emotion throbbed on a note of passion as she cried:

'I told you exactly my feelings, Allan; I've nothing more to add. I distrust love; I can't surrender to the first rapture I feel; I only know that I'd give all I possessed in the world to understand the things that are a part of your mother's life. Don't you see? It is so easy for you – you are following in a tradition when you talk of love and marriage … the tradition of happiness and success… It becomes vastly different when that tradition has been failure and *un*happiness. I don't want to harp; I just want to be sure about everything – everything,' she added brokenly. Her eyes met his like glistening stars. 'I can't cheat you, Allan; and if you cannot stand my honesty then please, please leave me alone,' she said fiercely.

'Darling!' His arms went around her with a passionate tenderness and she clung to him, feeling every nerve tingling at his touch, aware of him and of her need for him to the exclusion of all else as their lips met in a long, suffocating kiss that seemed to be a part of the warm tide of ecstasy engulfing them both. Claudia ached for the forgetfulness of surrender, while knowing that

106

rapture – the stirring of the senses – could be no more than a transitory glory masquerading as love. And as she drew away from him she said with a great intensity:

'If life could stop in these moments – how heavenly it would be.'

'These moments could be forever,' he insisted. 'Emotion, passion, deepening and merging into a greater love and devotion. Don't you *see*–'

She rested weakly against him.

'I want to, Allan – more than anything in the world; I want to *believe*–'

'You will, my darling,' he said softly as he kissed the top of her head. 'You will.'

It was an hour or two later that Helen said to Marion:

'Do I sense a romance between Allan and Meg – a lovely girl. I talked to her just now... Of course she's in love with Allan–'

'I'm afraid she is,' Marion said with directness.

'Why "afraid"?' Helen waited, tensed, for her answer.

'Because he is not in love with her. There is only one girl in Allan's world – Claudia. And,' she said firmly, 'I believe that Claudia is just as much in love with him, although she isn't so sure of herself as he.'

Helen said very quietly and convincingly:

'I'm afraid that is where you are very wrong, Mrs Russell. Claudia is most certainly not in love with Allan… Raymond Winters will prove to be the man in her life.'

'Mr *Winters!*' Marion's heart seemed to drop a few inches. 'But–'

'He has already asked her to marry him, and while she didn't accept him, she will do so – I know it.' She added with telling inflection: 'I'm afraid that Claudia would not make a very successful farmer's wife and that would be *your* tragedy, as well as his, even had she really cared for him.'

'But Claudia loves the farm.' It was an emphatic sound.

'True – but for a matter of hours, or a day. Not for a lifetime. It is my belief that farmer's wives are born and not made. I have a profound admiration for all of you, but I'm afraid that *my* daughter would in no way measure up to your standards.'

Marion was out of her depth with Helen Lomond. Naturally a shrewd and discerning woman, an excellent judge of character, in this case it was impossible for her to see the tortuous workings of Helen's mind, or in any way appreciate the ulterior motive behind her every remark. She could only accept as truth the opinion Helen expressed. She said breathlessly:

'It is not for me to contradict you, but–'

'Shall we say that we both know our children best.' Helen smiled. 'Susan, for instance, probably strikes me as being quite different from the girl you know her to be; so it is with Claudia. Claudia is the most loyal person in the world and will make a man like Raymond a wonderful wife.'

'You speak as though their marriage were a foregone conclusion.'

Helen smiled knowingly.

'It is, really. It doesn't do, in my humble opinion, for a girl to accept a man the very first time he proposes – at least not when money and position are involved, as in this case.' She hurried on: 'You know it was awfully sweet of you to have gone to all this trouble for Claudia.'

Marion felt suddenly very unhappy; she realized, in that moment, just how greatly she had set her heart upon Allan and Claudia marrying; it had been so much a foregone conclusion as almost to be ignored by her, and she had been quite content to await the day when their engagement would be announced. It had occurred to her that this particular night might have marked that celebration, but now her hopes dwindled, for it was not possible for her to discount the news that Helen Lomond had imparted.

In turn Helen considered that she had acted very wisely. She was incapable of seeing the matter in its true perspective because her own interests were so closely allied to Claudia's future as to be indivisible, and she had it fixed firmly in her mind that anything she might do to further the marriage between Raymond and Claudia was fully justified since, in any case, it was the very finest thing for Claudia herself. The fact that such a marriage would revolutionize her own life just didn't come into it – thus she argued, and arguing, convinced herself that she had every moral right to interfere.

Raymond Winters approached them in that moment, making himself thoroughly agreeable, while in no way appealing to Marion who sensed that beneath a charming exterior, there was an inbred snobbery and insincerity and that, in truth, he held the entire gathering in contempt – which he did. For he had already decided that when Claudia was his wife he would forbid any further association between her and these people.

'Your daughter has eluded me,' he said lightly.

Marion enjoyed saying:

'She went out with Allan again some minutes ago.'

Helen frowned. It was quite obvious that Marion Russell wished to secure Claudia as her daughter-in-law.

'They are,' said Helen swiftly, 'just coming in.' She added: 'And I think we really must be going, Mrs Russell.' It struck her that the sooner she removed Claudia from the romantic atmosphere now surrounding her, and from Allan's attentions, the better.

'But,' Marion protested, 'the party isn't half over.'

'I'm afraid my head is splitting,' said Helen, firmly. 'Mr Winters, would you rally my family? Charles must be somewhere around and if you would send Claudia to me – immediately.'

'Certainly.' Raymond flashed her a meaning smile. He was not deceived and he knew that, in her, he had a very scheming ally.

Claudia and Allan appeared within a matter of seconds. Allan said:

'Perhaps if you were to lie down for a little while–'

'I'm sorry, but I must get home... Claudia will help me, won't you, darling? I feel so – so faint.'

Charles and Raymond joined them in that second. Charles demanded brusquely:

'What is all this?'

Claudia told him, at the same time assisting her mother, who appeared suddenly to be a dead weight, from her chair.

Slight confusion followed; many alternatives to breaking up the little circle were suggested but, adroitly, Helen managed to kill them all. Claudia felt instinctively that some ulterior motive prompted this sudden indisposition – or rather, the degree of it, for a headache and faintness could conveniently be magnified out of all proportion.

'I could,' Allan insisted, when they were ready, 'run you back, Mrs Lomond – you and your husband.'

Raymond Winters said cuttingly:

'I have my car here, Russell. I will attend to all that.' A pause, then: 'And I certainly feel that Mrs Lomond needs Claudia with her.'

A numb kind of unhappiness settled upon Claudia as they drove away from that gay scene.

Helen played the part of the wilting invalid throughout the short journey back to 'Stoneways' and then, as they turned into the drive, she said suddenly:

'The air has done me so much good... Thank heaven that terrible faintness has gone. Of course that Barn was stifling; those places just seem to lack all oxygen and it was so *crowded* ... you'll come in, Mr Winters?'

'I'd like to,' Raymond said with enthusiasm.

'No reason,' interposed Charles, 'why Claudia shouldn't go back to "Cloverdell", seeing that you have recovered so rapidly,' he finished not without sarcasm.

Claudia hastened:

'I'd rather not – now.' Her voice was strangely lifeless.

They went into the house and Helen languished on a deep settee, her legs up and her head resting against the cushions. She congratulated herself upon a rather clever move. Claudia was so wildly impulsive that there was no telling what she might have decided upon, should Allan unduly persuade her.

'I feel very guilty,' Helen said, in a small, rather whining tone. 'But I really am much better, Claudia darling, and if you and Mr Winters would like to go for a little run or – or anything–'

Raymond seized upon that.

'Just ten minutes... We'll pop over to "Old Place". I've just the very stuff to put you right, Mrs Lomond. Brought it back from the Continent with me. My mother swore by it for headaches.'

'That would be kind of you. The usual drugs just don't touch me these days.'

Claudia hated the idea, but to protest would have created a scene and invoked her mother's wrath for no constructive purpose.

'Very well,' she said acquiescently.

Charles, seething, infuriated beyond words, said the moment he and Helen were alone:

'It worked – didn't it? Transparent though it was, the scene worked. Your head no more aches than mine aches... You just wanted to get Claudia away from there, from Allan, and throw her at that damned fellow's head.

Well, I won't stand for it, Helen – do you understand? And I'm not going to bandy words with you.'

Helen kept her temper as she said coolly:

'I don't expect sympathy from you, Charles. And since Claudia is over twenty-one and has her future in her own hands–'

'That's my point,' he said with a deadly inflection. 'I mean to see that it is left in her own hands.'

'You want her to marry Allan Russell.' It was a challenge.

'Yes,' he rapped back. 'Because I believe that to be where her happiness lies; because I believe that she is in love with him, although I don't wonder she shrinks from committing herself to marriage after all she has seen in this house.' He added: 'Allan is fine, sincere–' He caught the faintly ridiculing light in Helen's eye and almost thundered: 'And you want to see her married to that – that spineless boob, Winters.'

'I shall,' said Helen composedly, 'see her married to him, what's more, Charles. This is war between us ... only I shall win.'

She reached out and picked up the telephone receiver from a nearby table as she spoke, answering its sudden ring before Charles had the opportunity.

'Yes... Oh, Allan, how nice of you to call. Yes, much better, thank you. I shall be perfectly all right in the morning. I feel very guilt about upsetting the party.' She caught at her breath, then: 'No, of course I shouldn't mind your coming over to fetch Claudia back, but I'm afraid she isn't here... No;' a subtle pause, then: 'She and Mr Winters have just gone out – over to "Old Place" as a matter of fact. I'm so sorry ... of course... Good-bye.'

At the other end of the telephone Allan said as he jammed the receiver down:

'That's the last straw!' He spoke as one talking to himself, oblivious of the inquiring faces of his mother and Meg who had just come into the sitting room.

'What is the last straw?' said Marion anxiously.

Allan felt the last remnant of his control snap as he burst out:

'Claudia! She's gone over to "Old Place" with Winters. If you ask me the whole thing was a put up job to get away from here.'

'Allan – no!' Marion spoke with swift reproval.

'I don't think that Mrs Lomond was really ill,' said Meg quietly. 'But that doesn't follow in any way that Claudia was a party to the deception.'

Marion made a few rapid mental calculations, then:

'I don't, as a rule, repeat anything told to me, Allan, but this affects you... Mrs Lomond left me in no doubt whatsoever

115

tonight of her belief that Claudia would marry Raymond Winters and that he was, in truth, the real man in her life.'

'I see.' It was a grim sound.

'You know how deeply I care for Claudia,' Marion hastened, 'but I don't want you to be – hurt. Probably you know far more than I and I'm with you whatever the fight.' She drew in her breath sharply. 'Just sometimes one has to face up to the possibility of defeat – that's all. I know that Claudia has given you no promises – she isn't the type to make them unless she can keep them.'

'True.' It was a harsh sound. 'And thanks, Mother, for telling me. I'd like to–' He stopped. 'Oh, never mind.' He turned to Meg. 'Not very entertaining for you,' he said with rueful apology. 'Let's dance; let's go gay, Meg, and forget the world. What do you say?'

She smiled at him.

'Haven't I said "yes" to you since I was about two?'

'I know … bad for me.'

'Certainly it is.'

Marion looked on with a worried frown. Meg's appearance at this juncture was not perhaps the best thing for Allan. Had she been foolish to tell him what Helen Lomond had said … yet how could she encourage a relationship that was foredoomed to failure? She wished that her own, instinctive feelings

116

had refuted the very suggestion of such a marriage between Claudia and Raymond Winters; but there was the hateful fear lest every word might be proved true. Raymond Winters was the type of man who possessed every advantage and few women would be able to resist his attentions.

Meg said jerkily, as she and Allan danced together a few seconds later:

'You care for her very much – don't you?'

'Yes.' He looked down into Meg's frank, honest eyes. 'But I shall get over it, no doubt – people do.' It was said cynically.

'Don't be too sure of that,' she murmured. 'I've never got over you. I say it unashamedly, cursing you very often for the fact when some thoroughly nice male presents himself... We're too close in our friendship for me to feel any loss of pride in the confession.'

'You're terribly sweet, Meg.'

'You won't fall in love with me for that reason.'

'Damned senseless emotion, love,' he said angrily. 'Don't usually talk to anyone like this, but to you–'

'I just don't count,' she said disarmingly. 'Shall I stay for a while?'

'Will you?'

'If I shan't be in the way.'

'You know the answer to that.'

'Do you want a little advice?'

'No; but I'll take it – go ahead.'

'A woman admires the constancy of a man who is always there waiting patiently for her, but far more often she loves the man who keeps her in suspense.'

'Such wisdom!'

'Or the man who delivers an ultimatum.'

Allan's expression changed.

'I'll remember that,' he said sharply. 'Thanks, Meg.'

Claudia was thankful when, on their return to 'Stoneways' Raymond Winters declined her polite suggestion that he should 'come in for a drink'. And she saw his long, sleek car drive away with a sense of relief. The ordeal of the evening had been almost more than she could bear and her nerves were strung to breaking point. She let herself into the house and moved in the direction of the lounge from whence the angry voices of her parents greeted her. She heard her father say:

'This situation cannot go on, Helen. The whole thing is impossible.'

And her mother's reply:

'Do you think that I would stay here for a moment if I were financially independent, or had anywhere – anywhere to go?'

Claudia shivered, took a deep breath, and ventured into the lion's den, handing her mother the capsules which Raymond had sent.

'Nice to have one thoughtful person around,' said Helen. 'Mr Winters has sympathy.'

Claudia said wearily:

'Is there anything else I can get you, Mother?'

'No, thank you.' Helen spoke acidly. In the morning she would go into the question of Raymond's proposal. 'Are you going straight to bed.'

'Yes; I'm rather tired.'

Charles said with vehemence:

'I'm afraid that the evening has been completely ruined for you, darling.' He looked at Helen with a certain challenge: 'By the way, Allan 'phoned while you were out. He wanted to know – since Helen told him she was feeling better – if he could fetch you back–'

Claudia felt her heart miss a beat. Her whole body became tense.

'What – what did you say?'

'Your mother' – he stressed the word 'mother' – 'explained that you had just gone out with Mr Winters.'

Claudia was trembling; the implication of that statement from Allan's point of view struck her with all the force of a blow ... it was unbearable that he should think the wrong thing... And suddenly, almost like a mist clearing from the face of the sun, she knew that she loved him; that only in his arms could she ever find happiness... And that never had the barriers that separated them seemed so formidable as at that moment.

CHAPTER FIVE

Claudia had always been a decisive, consistent person who loathed any form of vacillation, so that the position in which she now found herself was doubly painful, and the more she struggled to reconcile duty with desire, the greater became the conflict and the more obscure the future.

When, the following morning, her mother sent for her, she knew precisely the nature of the argument ahead, and as she opened the door of that familiar bedroom and crossed the threshold, she sensed that this was the climax, not a mere discussion trailing into ineffectuality. Calmly and dispassionately, she studied Helen who was propped up rather attractively against massive pillows on a luxurious divan bed; her face was pale, her eyes dark and hunted of expression. Pity tugged at Claudia's heart; the misery of the whole situation washed over her like a grim, relentless tide.

Helen said quietly:

'Come and sit here beside me, darling. I want to talk to you.'

Claudia sat down, seeming to sink inches into the soft mattress. On the one hand she wanted to fight, rebel, assert herself; her love for Allan swamped all other thoughts and impulses. She ached for the freedom and peace of mind that would have enabled her to rush over to 'Cloverdell' and promise to marry him; to tell him that she would risk the hazards of marriage and fight to preserve the ideals that her love for him, and his for her, had inspired.

Her voice was strangled, uneven as she said:

'You want to talk about Raymond.'

Helen felt a tightening of the muscles at her throat. She was, she told herself, a victim of circumstances whom life had forced into this unenviable position. She wanted Claudia's happiness and she craved happiness for herself. It wasn't, she argued, selfishness that was driving her to fight for that same happiness; surely she was entitled to know a little peace before she died. But she knew that Claudia was in no mood to be dictated to; no mood to tolerate aggressive, or demanding, tactics and that to win the battle she must show tolerance, sympathy, and awaken understanding in Claudia's heart.

'Yes,' she said quietly; 'it is. Do you think

you are being wise over all this?'

Claudia had not expected that approach.

'A woman is always wise to refuse to marry a man whom she does not love,' she said steadily.

'That is a popular belief – often erroneous.' Helen sighed. 'I am in a very awkward position,' she went on. 'You know my life; you know how I long to escape from it all and that, if it so happened that you had cared for Raymond, your marrying him would not only have secured your future, but given me – and your father for that matter – another chance of happiness.' She waved a hand. 'That, however, is of no consequence; I suppose I can go on being unhappy without it killing me. But there is your side of all this. At the moment you are infatuated with Allan; but that doesn't make you any the more fitted to be a farmer's wife and, after the glamour has worn off, you will begin to realize the hideousness of marriage that offers no escape because, financially, the upkeep of two homes is out of the question.'

Claudia said wearily:

'This is just going over old ground, Mother. That marriage is a gamble, no one will deny; but, equally, it is absurd to suggest that because yours was a failure mine will be, or that marriage to a man I don't love is a better proposition than marriage to

122

one whom I do.' She stopped; the last sentence had slipped out unawares.

Helen cried:

'So you admit your love for Allan?'

'Yes.'

Helen shivered in the bleak wind of defeat and the gentle tolerance faded slightly.

'Love is so transient; it means nothing – nothing, my dear.'

'But position and money do?' It was a rebellious cry.

'Yes.' Helen spoke forcefully. 'I'm not a materialist in the ordinary way, Claudia; I don't think, either, that you would call me mercenary, or mean; but I have learned, through bitter experience, just what free-dom of action money can give a woman; and I couldn't deplore the idea of your marrying Allan more than I do – more than I should do even if I, myself, were absolutely happy with your father.'

'I believe you are sincere in that,' Claudia admitted. 'But I equally believe that you just cannot realize how far your self-deception goes.'

A dull flush spread over Helen's cheeks; she could neither deny, nor confirm, the statement. Nevertheless, she saw an open-ing and took it:

'I will not insult your intelligence, darling, by suggesting that I cannot eliminate myself from this problem – I can't. I'm only human, after all,' she said somewhat pathetically. 'Had it so happened that you'd been willing to marry Raymond, I should have been given a new lease of life. Nothing can alter that.'

Claudia said desperately:

'But you could still have that new lease, Mother.'

'And how?' There was still a pathetic expression in her eyes, far more impressive that any anger could have been.

'If you left Daddy; agreed amicably to separate; you'd both begin again. Even divorce and perhaps a fresh start in an entirely new world. I'm no stumbling block and I'm devoted to you both–'

Helen was trembling.

'And just what do you suppose we should do for money? I've gone into this with you before. Your father most certainly wouldn't delve into what little capital he has and his income wouldn't keep two homes. Do you realize, too, that if I were to leave him I could hardly claim more than a few measly pounds a week? Do you seriously suggest that, at my age, I should live in two rooms, deny myself every comfort and luxury and find pleasure in doing so – or happiness?'

'You are,' insisted Claudia, 'taking a very extreme view.'

'I'm looking facts in the face,' came the somewhat irritable reply.

'You once told me,' Claudia went on still

in that urgent, faintly breathless, tone, 'that Father was by no means a poor man and that I had no need to bother with a career because my future was taken care of – financially.'

For a second Helen was taken unawares, then:

'Which was true,' she rapped out. 'Your father's life is very heavily insured, but those insurances, while benefiting you one day are merely a liability to him – to *us* – now.' She sighed wearily, dejectedly. 'It's all right, Claudia. I knew that you wouldn't be affected by anything I might say ... or be prepared to compromise in any way. Let's leave it at that. I hope you will be very happy with Allan – evidently you have made up your mind to marry him. I'm afraid I just feel that you are showing very poor taste.'

Claudia bristled.

'Daddy wouldn't share that view.'

'Your father never shares any views with me – on principle,' came the bitter retort.

'That isn't true, Mother.' It was said quietly.

'Of course, if you are on your father's side then–'

'There is no question of "sides",' Claudia interrupted fiercely. 'I'm forever torn between you both; seeing your point of view *and* his. Do you think it is a happy kind of life for me, either? What happiness have I ever seen in this house,' she finished vehemently.

Helen began to cry.

'To throw that up at me,' she wailed, 'just because I hoped that you'd marry Raymond ... it's cruel, cruel,' she sobbed. 'You just don't care what happens to me.'

Claudia quietened her.

'My nerves,' Helen said brokenly. 'They won't stand much more.'

Claudia said suddenly, almost sharply:

'And suppose I were to marry Raymond ... what then?'

'You know, darling, the answer to that question.' Helen's expression changed and, watching her, a knife turned in Claudia's heart, as she realized that even in the joy of contemplation her mother seemed to shed many years and come to vivacious life as she went on: 'I should begin really to live, Claudia... Raymond would let me have his gorgeous flat at "Old Place" and that would be such an asset in itself that any allowance Charles could make me ... well, it would be quite perfect. I should have a background and security and still not be away from you, or left with a feeling of isolation – even though, obviously,' she hastened, 'our lives would be entirely separate. The very idea makes me feel young again.'

'And you wouldn't miss Daddy – when it came to it?'

Helen puckered her brows.

'Are you serious? No, my dear; I'm afraid we should neither of us miss the other. And both feel like prisoners released from a life sentence.' A faint pause. 'But why waste time; you have no intention of allowing any of that to happen since you–'

'That's unfair,' Claudia said miserably. 'It isn't a question of "allowing". I can't make myself care for Raymond and–'

'Oh, *darling!* If only I could put some sense into your head; make you understand that life isn't a romantic novel.'

'Don't you think,' said Claudia gravely, 'that you and Daddy might have made a greater success of your individual lives had you regarded it as such? I cannot feel that you are good examples of marriage without romance, Mother. And can't you see how I dread – yes, dread – following in your footsteps and making your ghastly mistake?'

Helen knew that she had blundered, but she manœuvred her way out by saying:

'All that is true, darling; but the divorce courts are not wholly filled with marriages that began as ours … love is hardly a serviceable quality. But money and position last forever, and prevent the boredom of a middle-class monotony when romance fails. You'll learn to appreciate my words after a few years as a farmer's wife.'

Discretion prompted Helen to speak as though Claudia's marriage to Allan were a foregone conclusion, but she had no intention of regarding it as such or of declaring the battle lost – yet. She was sufficiently wise to know that this was the last time the matter would ever be discussed between them and that any further move she might make must, of necessity, be by stealth.

Claudia got up slowly from her position on the bed. She stood looking down at her mother and there was great compassion in her eyes, and a searing, tearing pain of divided loyalties, uncertainty and a desperate desire to see her parents happy.

Helen said softly, holding out her hand:

'Darling, don't think me selfish … it just isn't that. I'll go on bearing things … be happy; I've endured so much that your happiness is my most vital concern.' She stopped effectively. 'You know I'd never have you make any sacrifice for *me.*'

Claudia choked down the sobs that rose in her throat. She was tender-hearted to a degree and the very thought of her mother's misery weakened her.

'It will all work out,' she said, scarcely above a whisper.

'Of course … what are you doing today?'

'Going to the farm – first of all.' She looked at her mother very steadily. 'Allan must have thought it very odd my going out with Raymond – why didn't you explain the facts?'

'*Darling!* It just didn't occur to me; I wasn't exactly feeling well, you know.'

'I shall soon put matters right, anyway,' said Claudia. 'I'm afraid the Russells must have been very disappointed at our leaving as we did.'

'One cannot help being ill, Claudia.'

'I know that, Mother...' Claudia moved away from the bed to the door.

'You'll be back for lunch?'

'I'm not sure. Expect me when you see me.'

Helen felt sick at the thought of Claudia going to the farm. If only there was something she could do to alienate her from Allan ... but what – *what?* She said dolefully:

'Come back as early as you can, darling. I still feel rather ill and don't like being alone.'

Claudia promised that she would.

'Daddy hasn't taken the car with him today, so I shall borrow it,' she said swiftly. 'Save time and that wretched wait for buses.'

Claudia raced over to 'Cloverdell' some few minutes later. A certain nervousness possessed her as she went towards the familiar door at the back of the house. She was in love with Allan ... in love ... and it appeared to her that the very fact must be written on her face for everyone to see. She tried frantically to shut out the memory of her conversation with her mother; she tried to tell herself firmly and defiantly that she owed a duty only to herself and that her parents' unhappiness was no concern of hers and that for her to be sacrificed to it was fantastically unfair.

Marion greeted her father solemnly and Claudia was instantly aware of the subtle difference; it wasn't less friendly, but, rather, more distant, as though some shadow had thrust itself between them.

'I came,' she said breathlessly, 'to apologize for last night; it was so awful to have to go like that.'

Meg sauntered into the kitchen at that second and, somehow, at the sight of Claudia, jealousy flamed violently and surprisingly. But for this girl Allan would think of her in terms of marriage... A sudden bitterness flooded through her. She wished there was something she could do to influence him against Claudia without revealing the ulterior motive of which he would, in any case, be well aware. She told herself that she had no desire to be vicious, nothing was more foreign to her character, but it maddened her to think that Claudia, who wasn't even in love with him, could cause such havoc and wreck all her hopes.

She said with an attempt at a smile:

'I hope the charming Mr Winters helped to atone for the disappointment.'

Claudia met Meg's eyes very levelly and

recognized, suddenly, an enemy, without blaming her for the fact. It was obvious that Meg was in love with Allan, even as Susan had said and, now, Claudia could gauge her hurt. She answered quietly:

'I think you know my answer to that.' She looked at Marion. 'My mother sends you her apologies once more–'

'My dear–' The words came gently for Marion sensed a certain confusion and unhappiness in Claudia's manner– 'I'm so sorry she wasn't well. I hope she is better today.'

'Much,' said Claudia loyally, 'although not really well. Mother lives on her nerves, I'm afraid and excitement mostly upsets her.' She glanced about her. 'Is Allan around?'

'He was here a few moments ago – most probably you'll find him if you go towards "Long Barn"...'

'Thank you.' Claudia felt a sense of loss as she stood there; it was almost as though Meg had usurped the place she had once held and although she realized the absurdity of the idea, nevertheless she could not rid herself of the belief that the events of the previous evening had, in some abstruse manner, already cast their shadow.

She found Allan standing at the brow of the hill overlooking 'Long Barn' and, at the sight of her, he turned sharply and said with faint cynicism:

'So early in the morning?'

'Too early.' Her eyes met his and in the light of her love for him, she felt the exquisite thrill which she recognized as a blending of physical and mental, that quickens the pulse and brings a heady intoxication because of its fierce and ecstatic impact. And, as she stood there, she longed, ached to be free; free to go to him and ignore all family issues and to forget that Raymond Winters existed, or that marriage to him would transform her mother's life.

'No.' He spoke guardedly. His gaze was critical. 'I hope you found "Old Place" more to your liking than – this.' He inclined his head in the direction of 'Long Barn'.

'You know my feelings about "Old Place",' Claudia countered.

'Do I?' – sardonically. 'Could any man be expected to know anything about you.' He broke off. 'Oh, why discuss it.'

Allan wrestled with imaginary devils as he stood there. The memory of all that Helen Lomond had said to his mother the previous night came back to sting anew. In the light of that conversation Claudia appeared to lose much; to be the type to encourage the attentions of one man while knowing, in her heart, that she intended to marry another.

'Because I wish to do so,' she managed to say calmly. A hateful sickness struck at the pit of her stomach. 'My mother omitted to tell you last night that Mr Winters and I had merely gone over to "Old Place" to get some special tablets for her head and–'

'Couldn't he have made the journey alone?' Allan spoke rather sarcastically. He looked at her searchingly: 'Last night, Claudia, I was jealous and admitted it; this morning I'm beginning to feel that my jealousy is not without foundation. If you, even as you say, have no time for Raymond Winters you have only to dismiss him from the picture. He could not pester you with his attentions against your will. One word and he'd be out,' he added fiercely.

Claudia felt that invisible bands were tightening around her wrists, tieing her hands, strangling all movement.

'Your suspicions are so wrong, Allan. If only I could explain–' She stopped.

'And why can't you? Your attitude is quite beyond me.'

She looked up at him, longing to feel his arms around her, knowing that one word from him, in that second, would have meant her surrender. But he stood there, cold, withdrawn and aloof, and her pride rose fiercely.

'I have no "attitude",' she insisted.

Allan heard again the tormenting echo of his mother's words: 'Mrs Lomond left me in no doubt whatsoever of her belief that

133

Claudia would marry Raymond Winters and that he was, in truth, the real man in her life'.

'Not even that of clever deception,' he said, his love for her whipping him to anger. Claudia's face paled; she was trembling as she cried:

'I don't understand you in this mood.'

'No,' he said tersely, 'perhaps not.' Meg's advice hammered at his brain: 'The man who delivers an ultimatum'. And he plunged: 'Then perhaps it would be better if I made myself quite clear. I've asked you to marry me; I've told you that I was prepared to wait indefinitely for your answer ... well–' His mouth became set in a tight, uncompromising line as he fought against the overwhelming impulse to take her in his arms and crush the breath from her body until she agreed, there and then, to be his wife. He went on: 'I can see the folly of that. I would like my answer within a week, Claudia. We cannot go on as we are and if you cannot choose between me and Raymond Winters then–' He shrugged his shoulders. 'Perhaps this may make the decision for you.' His expression hardened: 'One is either in love or not – there can be no possible argument about that.'

Claudia was shaking so violently that she was afraid her legs would refuse to support her. A week! But for her mother it wouldn't have taken her a second to decide... And as she stood there she found herself resenting bitterly the whirlpool of her parents' unhappy marriage; resenting the manner in which its tentacles had spread out to strangle her freedom and endanger her future. She wished she could be ruthless and ignore the problem as set by her mother ... turn her back on it all. Now, she was ready to risk marriage; to dare all in her love for Allan... But it was as though her mother wielded some uncanny domination, inspired some strange, and even terrible fear, that was as a conscience within her forbidding her to take her own happiness... The very misery she had seen and shared at 'Stoneways' was as a judgment exhorting her to sacrifice herself. Could she ignore her mother's pleas and find peace of mind? Her whole soul seemed to be bruised by the conflict; the love now consuming her was as an unquenchable fire.

The moment Allan had uttered those words he wanted to retract them. Suppose Meg had been wrong? The thought of losing Claudia struck as sharply as an arrow piercing his heart. With an effort and, in an agony of suspense, he waited for her answer.

She said, very quietly, and he saw her wince as in pain.

'No, Allan, there can be no possible argument as to whether one is in love, or not... And you shall have my answer within a week. Although–' She stopped and her gaze lifted to his while passion surged wildly between them and she felt that he must see the love that blazed in her eyes for him.

But at that moment, Meg's voice hailed them, and as she reached the spot where they were standing and took up a position at Allan's side with what seemed to Claudia to be a little possessive gesture, she said:

'Claudia, your mother and Mr Winters are waiting for you at the house.'

Claudia stared at her.

'For *me?*'

'Who else?' Meg said lightly, 'I'm not Mr Winters' type.' She laughed. 'Nor he mine.'

Allan inclined his head and said to Claudia:

'Don't let us detain you.'

Claudia said involuntarily:

'You – you are not coming back to the house?'

'No; I can well do without the privilege of meeting Mr Winters.'

Meg said subtly:

'Which will not grieve him, my dear man. So long as he is so popular in other directions he'll survive your prejudice.'

Claudia wanted to comment on the remark, but a bleak, isolated sensation gripped her. It was as though she and Allan had suddenly become strangers, while Meg ... belonged. The thought stung and her love did nothing to alleviate the pain, rather did it inflame her imagination so that she built up Meg's relationship with Allan until it became a vital and dangerous menace. Had Allan given her that ultimatum in the hope that she would refuse to marry him; was it his way out of the situation?... Yet what could have caused so violent and sudden a change, were that so. She dismissed the idea as fantastic and ridiculous... But Meg loomed, nevertheless, as a rival to whom Allan might well turn and with whom he might find solace.

She left them and returned to the house. She was puzzled by her mother's visit and not a little suspicious. But Helen was to her amazement, sitting in the kitchen watching Marion making pastry while Raymond looked on, seemingly at home. The explanation was that she 'simply had to come and apologize for spoiling the party' and, also, that 'Mr Winters had 'phoned and then offered to drive her over.'

Raymond moved swiftly to Claudia's side, aware that Marion was mindful of his every movement.

'I've come to whisk you off to town,' he said possessively. 'I promised Lord Moreton I'd bring you with me for lunch. You'll love his house in Grosvenor Square–'

Claudia stared at him, completely taken by surprise and when she started to protest, he charmingly interrupted her by saying:

'Your mother has been kind enough to say that she would drive your car back ... simple? You can return with me.' He looked at Marion. 'If this is most unconventional behaviour – forgive me, Mrs Russell, but I'm sure you know how things are.'

'Yes,' said Marion quietly.

It was then that Claudia turned and saw Allan's tall figure framed in the doorway and heard his voice smooth, deliberate:

'We all understand–'

She took a step forward; it was as though she were suddenly caught in a trap which was no less terrible because it was invisible. She glanced at her mother who appeared completely disinterested and was engaged in ardent conversation with Marion. She hated the thought that stabbed at her brain: was this little scene engineered by her; was there some conspiracy between her and Raymond? And, instantly she despised herself for what appeared a treacherous and wholly unfounded suggestion.

In that second she met Allan's steady gaze and the tumult and conflict awakened by their love for each other seemed to leap between them in a fierce and violent emotion. There was a dark intensity in his eyes that met hers half-mockingly, challengingly; while in hers was a bewildered, almost angry rebellion because, somehow, the situation had got out of hand. Defiantly, then, she turned to Raymond Winters in assent.

Helen sat there tensed to the point almost of exhaustion. She had engineered this entire scene; 'phoned Raymond in the first place and she heard, again, his voice, smooth, reassuring, as he said to her: 'The day that Claudia becomes my wife, I will hand you over the keys of my flat at "Old Place" and it shall be yours for life... There is nothing that you cannot rely on my doing for your comfort ... just persuade your daughter to marry me – that's all. I know your life and I'd like to see you happy.' He had added: 'I see no reason why we should be squeamish about all this. Let's face the facts and have done with it. You have Claudia's interests at heart, and you know that the very idea of her marrying that fellow Russell is fantastic.'

Claudia turned to her.

'You will be all right, Mother?'

'Perfectly,' Helen said without any over-done effusiveness. 'I'm going to stay for lunch.' She glanced casually at Raymond. 'Goodbye, Mr Winters; thank you for running me over here.'

Claudia looked at Allan as she passed him on the way out. An anguish of longing swept over her; longing to feel his arms around her, his lips on hers. Never had she loved him more or more despairingly. His gaze met hers, softening in the light of passion which seemed to leap like some living force between them and to draw her to him with a compelling desire that took all her strength, and his, to resist. Then, as one not daring to trust himself further, Allan said tersely:

'Good-bye, Claudia.'

The words echoed like a requiem. She shuddered and, long afterwards, remembered them ... and their tragic prophetic quality.

Helen sighed as they left. It was an effective sigh that dispelled all question of suspicion.

'All I hope is that she will really be happy,' she said quietly. 'I have a feeling that their engagement will be announced after tonight.'

Marion said swiftly:

'I understood that you were entirely happy with the idea of Claudia marrying Mr Winters,' she said deliberately, anxious that Allan should hear the conversation first hand.

'I am,' Helen said reflectively. 'But one never knows and one always wants the very best for one's children... Still, love is the controlling force – particularly with Claudia. Her heart has always ruled her head. I suppose I must be grateful that it so happens that, while she will not marry for money, nevertheless, she has fallen in love where money is...'

She turned as she spoke to glance at the effect of her words upon Allan. Without a word he had swung on his heels and walked out of the room.

Alone with Meg a few minutes later, Helen began tentatively:

'Are you saying here long?'

'That rather depends.' Meg spoke slowly, taking Helen's measure as she did so.

'On Allan?'

'Yes.' There was a piercing, questioning look in her eyes.

Helen traced an imaginary pattern on the kitchen table as she said:

'I think you will find that Allan will be quite – free, shall we say – before long, my dear.'

Meg sat down opposite her; her voice was hoarse and a little breathless as she asked:

'Is Claudia really going to marry Raymond Winters?'

'I firmly believe so,' came the instant retort. There was a subtle pause, then: 'That is what you are praying for – isn't it?'

Meg said:

'I hardly think that–'

'Come, child,' Helen said gently, persuasively, 'I understand and I might even be able to help. I know, as well as you, how disastrous it would be, both to Claudia and Allan, were *they* to marry. In fact, for that very reason I would do all I could to dissuade Claudia. Not that I believe in interference,' she added swiftly, watching every shade of expression on Meg's face.

Meg said tensely:

'If she *loved* him, it would be different–'

'Exactly,' said Helen. Her smile was warm, tender. 'Don't worry, my dear – you'll get your Allan. And my advice is to fight for him. All's fair, after all and, as Claudia's mother I cannot be hypocrite enough to wish to see her married to him knowing that it could but end in disaster. Claudia is not cut out to be a farmer's wife.'

Meg looked at her earnestly:

'Then you are – are on my side?'

'Definitely.' She put out a hand impulsively. 'We'll be allies, you and I, Meg... If you need me – well, I'm always there,' she said with telling emphasis.

'And I,' exclaimed Meg, almost chokingly. 'Oh, Mrs Lomond, you don't know how you've heartened me.'

'Bless you,' said Helen. 'These things work out. We'll pull together and just see that they do – eh?'

'Oh – yes!' It was a thankful, impulsive sound.

Helen said resolutely:

'Claudia will never marry Allan – never.'

It was just after midnight that Claudia returned to 'Stoneways'. Her father was already in bed; Helen had waited up. A strange premonition gripped her as she greeted Claudia and asked:

'Where is Raymond?'

Claudia appeared to square her shoulders.

'He went on.' A faint pause, then: 'Mother, I've something to tell you; something you won't like, I'm afraid.'

Helen caught at her breath.

'Well?' It was a fearful sound.

'I've decided to marry Allan,' Claudia said resolutely. 'I love him and I cannot give him up. Please understand.'

CHAPTER SIX

Throughout the entire day with Raymond, Claudia had wrestled with the problem of the future, torn, uncertain and desperate in her need of Allan until, finally, she knew that she could fight against him no longer, and that the natural desire for love, and all that it embraced, outweighed all other consideration. Now, as she faced her mother she was determined not to be weakened by persuasion or moved by a pity that could well prove of no avail.

Helen said very slowly:

'I see.'

'Do you?' It was an urgent sound. 'I want you to, Mother; it would be dreadful if you–'

'Suppose we don't become sentimental,' Helen said and her voice was crisp, almost business-like. 'You cannot expect me to show an enthusiasm I shall never feel. On the other hand, I am fully aware that I have absolutely no influence, or power, over you: you must do as you wish and take the consequences.' She sighed. 'All I hope is that Allan will be worth the sacrifice you are making for him.'

'Sacrifice!' It was an incredulous sound.

'Yes – sacrifice. To give up, or rather to throw away the chances of marrying Raymond in order to spend the rest of your life with a man who will never give you more than drudgery! If that isn't a sacrifice then I do not know what is.'

'But, you don't seem to realize,' Claudia protested, 'I am in love with Allan, therefore the sacrifice would be *not* to marry him.'

Helen was fighting to control her emotions; to beat down the anger that was fast degenerating into violent temper. Thus to have her hopes irrevocably smashed was almost more than she could bear. She said deliberately:

'And just where does Meg come into all this?'

144

Claudia stared at her.

'*Meg?* Whatever has she to do with it?'

Helen said swiftly:

'I was of the impression that Allan was becoming more than interested in her – that's all. But if you haven't noticed a difference in him ... perhaps I am unduly sensitive on your behalf, darling, but I must say that he seemed to pay her a very great deal of attention today while I was there and, in fact, they were discussing the idea of going away for a holiday together – to stay with relatives in Scotland. Allan seemed most anxious to get out of the district.'

Claudia's heart missed a beat. The ultimatum Allan had given her only that very day ... could she deny that she had allowed the thought to register lest it might be his way of backing out of any further association... But that was fantastic, ridiculous ... and yet–

'If Allan were interested in Meg he would hardly be anxious to marry me, Mother.'

'Very well ... you know best; but don't say I didn't warn you.' She paused. 'When was all this settled between you and Allan?'

Claudia said truthfully:

'It isn't settled, inasmuch as I have not yet given him my answer – told him that I will marry him.'

'Oh!' Light pierced the gloom of Helen's thoughts. She was making rapid mental calculations as she talked, realizing that she must not alienate Claudia and thus forfeit her confidence. She went on carefully:

'Strange, isn't it, how a few words can change the whole pattern of a person's life?'

Claudia raised her gaze and stared almost fearfully into her mother's faintly pained and faintly reproachful eyes.

'Meaning – what?' She spoke breathlessly.

Helen forced a note of lightness which was in no way intended to deceive Claudia.

'I was really thinking of my life and how all this affects me, darling. Ah, well, my dream of freedom was short-lived.'

Claudia's heart sank.

'I'm sorry, Mother, but–'

'That's all right,' Helen said swiftly. 'In fact if that happened to be the only issue it would all be very simple. However, let's say no more. I only pray that you are not going to be – hurt.'

'By Allan?' It was an incredulous sound.

'Yes, by Allan.' She added hurriedly: 'And Meg.'

'That is absolutely absurd, Mother.'

'Well, we are all entitled to our opinion. But Meg is rather like the wife to whom the man always returns – the reality. You are merely a dream that will fade.'

Claudia said firmly:

'That is quite absurd, Mother, seeing Allan and Meg are related. Of course they are good friends and he pays her attention. Why not?'

'Why not, indeed,' said Helen meaningly, feeling that to create suspicion would be a step in the right direction, 'provided that is where it ends.'

'I don't think,' said Claudia stiffly, 'that you understand... Good night, Mother.'

'Good night, darling... My fear is that I understand too well,' she added as an after-thought.

Claudia tried to bask in the luxurious happiness of contemplation as she lay awake in the darkness, watching the moonlight paint grotesque, yet friendly, shadows upon walls and ceiling. To marry Allan; to walk forward into the future with him; to know that the misery and conflict were over... Surely she had a right to build her own life – a life divorced from that of her parents.

And as she lay there, Helen, in a frenzy of fear, uncertainty, 'phoned Raymond Winters.

'I had to talk to you,' she said earnestly. 'Forgive me for troubling you at this hour.'

Raymond Winters sat upright in bed, moved this way and that until he was comfortable, took a cigarette from a box on the table beside him, lit it with a deft movement of his lighter and, puffing a tiny cloud of smoke into the air, said reassuringly:

'I am quite sure it is something urgent.

Take your time and don't worry about disturbing me... Well?'

Helen told him all that had transpired.

Raymond's gaze travelled around the massive bedroom as he listened and although it might have appeared that he was wholly indifferent, his whole body became taut as he said:

'Now don't panic. Claudia will not marry Allan – I can promise you that. I've always been prepared for this, but it was useless making any move until I knew, for certain, her intentions. Do you think that I am the type of man to let anything I really want slip through my fingers?'

At the other end of the telephone Helen was trembling violently; in a state of acute nervous tension.

'But what can be done,' she asked despairingly.

'So long as you have your daughter's welfare at heart and are ready to co-operate with me,' he came back at her smoothly, 'all will be well. The thing that concerns me is: have you her welfare so much at heart that you'd be prepared to go to any lengths to save her from this disastrous marriage?'

Helen thrust aside the issue as it affected her, telling herself that, in truth, her chief concern *was* only Claudia's happiness and that her own was entirely secondary.

'Of course I have,' she insisted. 'I'd do anything – anything to prevent this marriage. It will ruin her life and–'

Raymond played up to her. He knew that he was dealing with a weak and frustrated woman, rather than a cunning or vicious one; a woman easily led; a woman capable of deceiving herself at every turn and one who was sincere in the erroneous belief that, by acquiring those things she most ardently desired for herself, she would indirectly be benefiting the daughter whom she professed to love! Her outlook was, he knew, entirely distorted by her own unsatisfactory marriage, so much so that it was wholly beyond her power to see the situation in its true perspective – for which he had just cause to be thankful. He said persuasively:

'Then, in the morning – early – 'phone the Russells. Speak, obviously, to whichever member happens to answer the 'phone. Invite them to a meal – anything – but manage to have a word with Meg. If she answers the 'phone so much the better. Tell her of Claudia's decision and advise her for everyone's sake, to get Allan away ... you said something about a visit to Scotland? And if that isn't possible, then suggest that she gets him well out of Claudia's range today. Quite simple. And don't forget that she is just as anxious to keep Allan away from Claudia as you are!'

Helen's voice came back faintly:

149

'But that is a purely temporary measure and–'

'I know what I'm doing,' he said curtly, and authoritatively. 'Trust me.'

'Of course.' Helen, in the rather deathly silence of her room, glanced around almost as one expecting a ghost to appear. It was not her nature to conspire and scheme, but some force within her, stronger than all else, goaded her on. She could not give up this heaven-sent opportunity of freedom and comfort; and she could not sit back while Claudia wasted her life on a farm. And suddenly, guiltily, she started as she saw Charles's tall, commanding figure come into the room.

Instantly, the receiver went down. She said:

'How dare you come here at this hour?'

Charles tightened the cord around his dressing-gown almost as though he had it around an imaginary throat.

'I'm here,' he said, 'to know precisely why you are telephoning Winters at this hour. And because, most likely, I know the answer.'

'Then why,' she flung at him, 'want any explanation from me?'

'Because I don't like the look of things,' he said grimly. 'You know my opinion of the man; you know how I feel about the idea of any marriage between him and Claudia.' He paused and drew in his breath sharply: 'Yet you persist in encouraging him, and,' he almost thundered, 'what is more I believe that you'd go even further than that, and scheme with him.'

Helen snapped:

'My actions are no concern of yours. And now will you please go: I'm tired.'

'What were you saying to Winters?'

'That is my business.'

'Claudia shall never marry him.'

She laughed.

'Don't put on that early Victorian father act – it makes you look quite idiotic,' she said maddeningly. 'Claudia will do exactly as she pleases.'

Charles felt an overwhelming sadness as he stood there looking at the woman who was his wife. If only their lives had been different; if only, now, they could both pull together and rebuild for the future on the wreckage of the past. He said quietly, yet with a certain urgency:

'Listen, Helen; we've not made a success of things, you and I, but can't we now, for Claudia's sake, see this matter through together in some semblance of harmony? Won't you respect my viewpoint over Raymond Winters and give me credit for–'

Helen interrupted him:

'I give you credit for trying to be smarmy because you want your own way, Charles;

want me on your side for once. Well, it just won't work. I'm not interested in your ideas, or wishes, and I detest your absurd prejudice over Raymond Winters.' She added and her voice rose menacingly: 'As for accusing me of scheming with him against Claudia's interests. That is something I will not tolerate.'

Helen loathed the thought that, quite probably, in the morning, Claudia would discuss her decision to marry Allan; tell Charles of her intention and, thus, form a solid block calculated to defeat every plan which she, herself, had made. Yet Raymond had assured her that he would never give in and always had his own way ... that, at least, gave her fresh hope and confidence.

'But you don't deny the accusation? – yes, it is an accusation, Helen,' he said fiercely.

'I wouldn't lower myself,' she rapped out. In that moment her emotions became wholly uncontrollable. She hardly knew what she was saying as she rushed on: 'I'm sick to death of your arrogance and condescension. If our marriage was a failure to begin with then it is a farce today. Do you imagine that I want to see Claudia tied to a farmer all her life; tied so that she has to remain with him simply because she hasn't the money to leave him and is as financially dependent upon him as I am upon you? Anything – anything,' she said vehemently, 'would be better for her than that.'

Charles gave her a steady, searching look.

'And if you had the money you would leave me?'

'I most certainly would.'

His face became darkly suspicious:

'Then am I not near the mark when I say that you see in the possible marriage of Claudia to Raymond Winters, your own ultimate freedom ... at Claudia's expense.'

A dull flush mounted Helen's cheeks, but she burst out:

'I refuse to stand here and listen to your insults.'

Charles stared at her as a man accepting an ultimatum; a man hesitating on the brink of a momentous decision. Then:

'We will settle all this, once and for all, Helen – in the morning,' he said stiffly and, with that, turned and went swiftly from the room.

Helen remained awake the entire night and, before eight o'clock, feverish with anxiety and terrified lest Claudia might burst upon her, or overhear her conversation, got through to 'Cloverdell'. Duncan Russell answered the 'phone and Helen immediately asked to speak to Meg, reasoning, rightly, that Duncan was far too preoccupied with his own affairs to consider the strangeness of the request. Meg's voice came a trifle fearfully, some seconds later.

Helen explained the situation, finishing with:

'You know how I feel about such a marriage which could only bring misery to them both. And if you are prepared to save Allan from ultimate disaster ... then get him away from the farm – on that trip you were discussing and, above all, away from it, somehow, today... I know you cannot talk freely and should you be questioned about my 'phoning, say that I wanted to arrange a little party for you – which I do, my dear and we'll go into the details, later. Why shouldn't it be your engagement party – to Allan.' A pause, then: 'I must go now; keep me informed.'

Meg stood at the 'phone as one transfixed, after having replaced the receiver. Her heart was thudding violently; all this was foreign to her, even distasteful, but so intense and overwhelming had her love for Allan become that she was prepared to go to any lengths to win him.

Susan, flying around as she prepared to go to business, cried:

'What's all that in aid of and what on earth did Mrs Lomond want with you?'

Faint colour stole into Meg's cheeks; she hastened:

'Something about a party.'

'Queer woman,' said Susan. 'I thought it most odd her coming over here as she did.

154

Some motive behind it. Just can't make out what... Of course she's simply dying for Claudia to marry Raymond.'

'Which, I imagine,' said Meg and her voice was rather clipped, 'is precisely what Claudia will do. She's obviously attracted and impressed by his flattery.'

Susan stared at Meg as one seeing a new facet of her character for the first time.

'You don't like Claudia – do you?' she said quietly.

Meg bristled. The soft grey eyes flashed, the docility vanished as she countered:

'How perfectly ridiculous. What reason have I either to like or dislike her?' She added with some violence. 'I cannot say that I appreciate the manner in which she has kept Allan dangling on a string.'

Susan, wise beyond her years, said firmly:

'That's not fair; if you ask me, Claudia is in a most difficult position. I've an idea that so much goes on at "Stoneways" that no one knows anything about – so much that makes Claudia's life pretty miserable.'

'That,' said Meg, 'has nothing to do with Claudia's relationship with Allan.'

'That's where you are so wrong,' said Susan. 'Ah well, I must get going! We've got "the nose" coming in this morning.'

'Who on earth, or what on earth may that be,' asked Meg forcing a laugh.

'A woman, my dear child, to whom nature

has given a very large nose, but who deludes herself that it is a mere dot and … that is how she wants it to look in a photograph! 'Bye. See you tonight.'

'Always late,' said Allan, coming in from the farm and surveying Susan with affectionate indulgence.

'Always,' came the blithe reply. And with that she was gone.

Meg moved to the doorway and looked out on the gold and blue of the summer day, across a patchwork quilt of fields, and so to the uplands beyond. She said suddenly, impulsively:

'Allan, take me out today. Let's wander … find an old inn for lunch; put the clock back and be kids again.' A light laugh. 'I heard you say that Tom could keep watch for you. It would be such fun and we haven't been out like that since I came…' She looked up at him. 'Or am I being a nuisance?'

Allan's thoughts of Claudia were visual in that moment, as though she were, in reality, standing there beside him; he could feel the passionate, vibrant strength of her personality; feel his heart beats quickening as the fragrance stole from her… And he said almost curtly:

'Why not! Let's get away – now.'

'Allan – how lovely. Yes; I'm ready – just get my bag… You bring the car round and tell the others… No, I won't be long.'

She watched him go, almost exhausted by the suspense. The 'phone went and she lifted the receiver before it could even be heard by the rest of the household.

'Claudia... Allan? I'm afraid he isn't here. Any message... Ask him to 'phone you when he comes in. Of course. Good-bye.'

Meg felt a certain desperation as she stood there. Somehow she must follow Helen Lomond's advice and get Allan away. There wasn't any time to lose because, obviously, Claudia would ring again ... even if Allan didn't 'phone her. Meg's expression became hard. Certainly she was not going to pass on *that* message.

At the other end of the wires, Claudia experienced a sick sensation of disappointment, but she overcame it and decided that, later on, she would go out to the farm. Allan was always there around twelve when they had their lunch. She thrust aside the fears that had haunted her previously. Nothing could endanger the happiness that lay ahead. Allan loved her and she loved him and, when she explained the situation in which she had been placed – as she fully intended to do in fairness to them both – he would understand, and the ghost of Raymond Winters would be laid forever. Her heart stopped its painful thudding, and seemed to sing instead. She and Allan ... the whole glorious future theirs to mould to their will. 'Cloverdell' and that little, snug cottage all ready and waiting for them... Peace and content and – Paradise. She turned away from the 'phone, humming to herself. Nothing could damp her spirits on this magic day – nothing. She strode into the breakfast room, but it was empty. And, suddenly, in an agony of suspense, she listened to the angry voices coming from her mother's room above. And it was as though the very blood in her veins became chilled in apprehension.

Upstairs, in the cold, merciless light of day, Charles and Helen faced each other in sullen, smouldering anger.

'There appears,' said Charles, 'to be no possible basis for compromise, Helen. Heaven knows I've tried.'

'So have I,' she snapped. 'I shall never be able to understand your attitude over things – particularly over the subject of Claudia's marriage. As her father, I should have thought–'

He cut in:

'Let's not go over all that again,' he said wearily.

'You refuse to study my wishes in anything,' she snapped.

'Then,' he said, and his voice was deadly in its calm and implacable decisiveness, 'I think the time has come when it will be for our mutual benefit if I make my home elsewhere.'

She stared at him.

'Leave me?'

'Yes,' he replied gravely.

Helen stood there in stunned silence as she tried to grapple with the problem and anticipate the repercussions likely to result. The thought of her freedom was exhilarating ... but just what would the effect be upon Claudia?

'I see.'

'Don't tell me that you – mind.' It was said cynically. It struck him as he stood there, that such a move might well be to Claudia's advantage. Helen would then be able to build a new life; he overlooked the fact that, equally, she might assume the role of the lonely, disillusioned woman who needed companionship more than ever.

'Mind!' Her tone was sarcastic. 'I couldn't care less.' She looked at him and there was a hard glint in her eyes: 'I'd like you to leave at once – since you've decided to go.'

'Don't worry, I will.'

'Today.'

He gave her a cynical glance.

'This morning. I hope that will suit you.'

'Perfectly.' She stared at him. 'You will be fully responsible for my maintenance – you realize that.'

'Naturally; you shall have the limit I can afford.'

'Which,' she taunted him, 'will hardly be a

fortune. Certainly not enough to keep this house going.'

'You will hardly require anything so large. Claudia will be married, and that will leave you free to live where you choose.'

It was at this juncture that Claudia knocked on the door and was told to go in. Once over the threshold she glanced anxiously from face to face, her attitude eloquent of inquiry, even fear.

Helen said rather shrilly:

'Your father is walking out on me, Claudia. What do you think of that? Leaving me.'

'I think,' said Claudia instantly, 'that it may enable you both to find a little happiness. I see no reason why there should be any enmity or bad feeling between any of us.'

Charles said, greatly relieved:

'Thank you for that, darling.'

Instantly, Helen was on the defensive, jealous of the affection that existed between Charles and Claudia.

'Spare me any touching, sentimental scene,' she said. 'Walking out on one's wife is not, after all, such a laudable procedure.'

'Neither,' Claudia retorted, 'is hypocrisy and it would be rank hypocrisy for me to assume that you desire Daddy's presence here.'

'I will not be spoken to like that.'

160

'I'm sorry, Mother; but do,' she pleaded, 'let's not get all this out of perspective.' She turned to Charles. 'There's something I want you to know – something that will please you,' she added swiftly.

Helen cried out; for a reason she couldn't define she didn't want Charles to know about Claudia's decision to marry Allan.

But he guessed instantly.

'Allan?'

'Yes.'

'Good for you,' he cried, and there was a note of relief, even triumph, in his voice. 'I knew you'd never think twice about that mountebank, Winters.'

Helen kept her temper by the expedient of biting her lower lip and clenching her hands. It was torture for her to be forced to listen to all that; it undermined her confidence in the machinery which she and Raymond had set up for the perfection of their plans. Slowly, insinuatingly, however, she said:

'I only hope that your trust in Allan is warranted.' Her pause was significant. 'It is my belief that Allan's affections have undergone a very marked change since the arrival of Meg. I pray you won't have to suffer the humiliation of finding yourself unwanted now that you have, at last, made up your mind, darling,' she finished.

Claudia retorted:

'I am quite prepared to risk that, and not one scrap afraid lest you may be right.'

'Splendid,' said Charles stoutly.

Claudia felt a tug at her heart as she asked suddenly, abruptly:

'Where will you – live, Daddy?'

'I'm not sure,' he answered. 'As a matter of fact I have to go to Canada on business and plan, now, to start almost immediately. That will take care of two or three months. When I return – well,' he said. 'A hotel, most likely.'

'Your solicitude for your father is most touching,' said Helen.

'Please, Mother.' Claudia spoke quietly, but admonishingly. Her mind was in turmoil; she knew that she would miss her father, while equally realizing that he was taking the very wisest course and she could not help seeing that, from her own point of view, it would help enormously: now, her mother would be free; the burden of her unhappiness no longer the ghost standing grimly in the shadows. 'Can I help you pack,' she finished unsteadily, addressing her father.

'If you would... I'll collect the bulk of my things, later.'

Claudia felt a pang of regret; to see her parents thus estranged was a bitter blow, even though she fully realized that their separation was inevitable; but she craved the joy and happiness of a real home and the hurt went deep because of all she had missed and, now, could never experience.

Breakfast was a farce eaten more or less in silence. And when it was over Helen got up, looked across at Charles and said:

'It would be more comfortable for us both, Charles, if I go to a solicitor. This whole thing must be done legally.'

'As you wish.'

'Then I'll make the necessary arrangements and get him to communicate with your lawyers. And I suppose I must begin to look around for some pokey little flat somewhere – it will be all I can possibly afford, now ... good-bye,' she added all in a breath.

Claudia was conscious of a hateful suspicion as she heard her mother's remarks ... 'all I can possibly afford' – was that the weapon now to be used in advising a marriage with Raymond ... was that the angle on which she would turn the fierce light of her own reflected wishes. She thrust the idea aside and concentrated on the moments ahead when she would see Allan. Nothing – not even her parents' problems – must marr the ecstasy of this day and its glorious promise.

'You'll be happy with Allan, Claudia,' her father said gently. 'I'm so thankful you've been guided by your own heart.'

'Bless you for supporting me, Daddy.'

'Don't allow anyone, or anything, to interfere with your plans – promise me.'

'I promise as far as I am able … when will you be leaving for Canada?' she asked suddenly.

'In a matter of days; I've decided to take the cancelled passage I was offered, and that means sailing at the end of this week.'

'I shall miss you.'

'I shall soon be back.' He put a hand on hers. 'Then we'll get together, Claudia; really get to know each other. And when you're married, I shall inflict myself on you sometimes for week-ends! How's that?'

'Wonderful.'

Charles's expression changed.

'Look after your mother,' he said gently. 'She needs you.'

'Don't worry.'

Charles got to his feet. He had hated almost every moment of his life in that house, but, now, when he was on the point of leaving it, he felt a curious pang – a pang of regret for what might have been and a reluctance to gaze upon it for the last time. But he squared his shoulders, kissed Claudia and, picking up his case from the hall, went swiftly out to his car.

'Say good-bye to your mother for me,' he said unevenly. 'I'll 'phone you, darling…'

The next second he was gone.

164

Claudia went back into the silent, empty house. Her heart was beating heavily, her eyes misted... A chapter had ended ... what of the new one about to begin?

Allan hadn't 'phoned...

Her mother's words came back tormentingly and even though she told herself they were fantastic and untrue, nevertheless fear struck sharply ... suppose Meg... No, she would not begin to harbour such treacherous suspicions.

Helen called to her and she went up to her room.

'Well, now we're alone together,' Helen began, somewhat tearfully.

'Now you are free,' Claudia reminded her forcefully. 'Daddy has done for you what you felt my marriage to Raymond would achieve.'

Helen gasped:

'Don't be so ridiculous, Claudia... What is my position now? Financially, I shall be hampered – condemned to some small hole called a flat, no doubt, for which an exorbitant rent will be charged. And I shall be quite alone. A slightly different picture from the flat at "Old Place" with you near me and my income intact... Oh, it doesn't matter but don't, please *don't,* suggest that your father has freed me... I shall merely be spared his irritating presence, that's all. It seems that you are both to desert me ...

you, when I need you most. Ah, well!' She sighed. 'How wonderful it would have been now had it so happened that you were to marry Raymond. I shouldn't have a care in the world and my future would be absolutely secure.'

Claudia tried to ignore that as she said decisively:

'I'm going to see Allan; we'll talk when I get back, Mother.'

Helen said pathetically:

'I doubt if he will be there and please don't leave me alone today, darling; I feel so strange and lonely.'

'I shall not be gone long,' Claudia persisted. The suspense of listening for the 'phone to ring; the waiting and torment of conjecturing was more than she could bear.

Half an hour later she made her way to 'Cloverdell' and as she walked along the short pathway to the house, she saw Allan – with Meg beside him – driving towards her. And as he pulled up sharply to greet her, Meg said swiftly:

'We're just off to Scotland to stay with my cousin.' A light laugh. 'I love a holiday arranged on the spur of the moment – don't you?'

CHAPTER SEVEN

Never for a moment had Claudia taken her mother's remark seriously about Allan and Meg going to Scotland and now, faced with the truth, she felt that, even as she stood there, her world was disintegrating around her. She stared at Allan and her eyes momentarily betrayed the shock she was experiencing; then with an iron control, she managed to say casually, brightly:

'I agree; the unexpected always has possibilities. I hope you both have a marvellous time ... when will you be back?'

Allan hastened:

'Early next week.' A hateful confusion, a bleak depressing sense of insecurity engulfed him. He had no wish to go on this trip, and had been persuaded simply because he found the tension of waiting for Claudia's answer almost more than he could bear and because he imagined that a change of scene might help the days to pass more swiftly. But it was one of those arrangements that was outside all reality for him and he had packed as one in a dream. His gaze held Claudia's; suppose she had come there that morning to give him his answer...

His lips twisted almost cynically, a reflection of the thoughts that possessed him... A most unlikely idea. She would keep him waiting the full week and then, in all probability, tell him that she was going to marry Raymond. It seemed, from all he heard, that she was continually in his company. 'Was there,' he asked tensely, 'anything you wanted to see me about?'

'No – nothing.' Claudia's thoughts were racing. Would a man go on a trip of this kind with a girl, unless he was more than normally interested in her. Suspicion piled up on suspicion, assisted by a sullen, painful jealousy. Suppose her mother had been right in her fears about the instability of Allan's regard. He might even be fearing lest she, Claudia, would finally accept his proposal and behaving in a manner calculated to antagonize her. All the joyous anticipation, the mood of happiness in which she set out, vanished as, suddenly, it seemed she stood in shadow where, but a few moments before, all had been sunlight. Allan seemed remote, withdrawn, no longer a vibrant part of her life as he sat there with Meg; she knew the anguish of feeling unwanted and pride came fiercely to her rescue. She hastened: 'I rather wondered if we might all arrange a show before Meg leaves.'

'But how sweet of you,' Meg almost

purred, knowing she had the advantage. 'We must go out sometime – but I'm not returning for ages yet – am I Allan?'

Allan, oblivious of Meg's scheming, aware only of her devotion and apparent sincerity, said:

'No, certainly not.'

'What – what part of Scotland are you making for?' Claudia managed to say.

'St Andrews.'

'Give it my love,' said Claudia wistfully.

Allan met her gaze and the impact was as a magnet drawing him to her; a sense of frustration overwhelmed him.

Looking at him, Claudia longed to ask why he had not 'phoned her, but pride forbade it.

Meg, fearful lest that telephone call might be brought up said swiftly:

'We really ought to be getting along, Allan.' Her voice changed to a smooth delight. 'And look who is here! Mr Winters. I doubt if we'll ever manage to get Claudia to herself again.' Inwardly she smiled. Helen had telephoned her to warn her of Claudia's visit and to say that she was hoping to contact Raymond Winters and get him to fetch Claudia back from the farm. As usual, she had been successful.

Allan jammed the car into gear, flashed Claudia a stormy and somewhat cynical gaze, as he said:

'I don't think we will interrupt the party, Claudia... I was going to suggest that you drove into the town with us but... Goodbye.' And with that he raced the engine and shot forward, skimming Raymond's sleek, shining car, by a matter of inches.

Claudia stood there helpless, baffled and wretched to the point of tears.

Raymond Winters stopped beside her.

'We seem fated to meet here,' he said carelessly and convincingly.

She wanted to accuse him of following her, but that seemed almost presumption on her part. Defiantly, she exclaimed:

'Perhaps you would run me back home?'

'By all means... I was going to ask Russell. To send over some stuff for the horses, but it can wait, and my man can attend to it, anyway.' He opened the door for her and she slid down into the beautifully upholstered seat beside him, and relaxed.

'Our friend was in a hurry,' he commented dryly.

'To get to Scotland,' Claudia announced.

Raymond said subtly:

'She's a very charming girl and they should be very happy together.'

Claudia puckered her brows.

'I cannot quite see the connection.'

'Can't you ... or perhaps I'm speaking out of turn. Forget it. I understood from Susan that their engagement would be announced on their return.'

Claudia stared at him.

'You mean that – that you knew they were going to Scotland together?'

He looked slightly bewildered – a simulated bewilderment wholly convincing.

'Shouldn't I have known?' he asked.

'Yes, but–'

'You didn't believe that there was any truth in the idea that Allan and Meg were … I'm sorry, Claudia. I knew this would happen that night at the dance at "Long Barn". And I'll say this: Meg was determined that it should. I'm certain that Allan didn't intend deliberately to hurt you.'

Claudia said stormily:

'Isn't your defence of him a little out of character?'

'And isn't your annoyance with me a trifle ungracious?' he retorted boldly.

Claudia had reached a point where she was seething with indignation. That Allan should deliberately have ignored her 'phone message and, while professing to love her and awaiting her answer calmly go off to Scotland with Meg was surely quite unpardonable. Yet … was that quite fair since he might well maintain that he was continually forced to watch her with Raymond in attendance while Meg, after all, was a relation; also that his desire to get away from the district during these days of suspense was merely human…

171

Raymond studied Claudia in a few swift glances, aware that she was upset and, above all, that her confidence in Allan was beginning to be shaken. He played up the advantage with subtlety.

'You know my feelings in the matter, Claudia; for me to pretend that I am sorry because of this turn of events would be sheer hypocrisy. I'm well aware that the fact of Allan's possible marriage to Meg does not, automatically, make you love me, but at least it does remove my most dangerous rival. And even if you should never change towards me, I still feel confident that you would never have been really happy with Allan.'

'Suppose,' said Claudia, sick at heart, 'we discontinue the subject.'

'If you wish … but, tell me, why had you come out to the farm?'

'For a purely personal reason,' she replied steadily.

'Yet you left without so much as going to the house?'

'And just how could you possibly know that?' she flashed at him.

He smiled significantly.

'For the simple reason that had you already been to the house it was almost certain you would have left with the others in the car: they, also, were to drive through the town … but, you asked *me* to take you back–'

'Sherlock Holmes?'

'Elementary deductions, Claudia.' The car purred along the quiet countryside. 'Where would you like to go?'

'Home,' came the prompt reply.

Raymond Winters frowned. He was annoyed beyond words to think that he was thus obsessed by this girl, when he was well aware of the fact that there were dozens of others ready to fall at his feet. But something about Claudia attracted him in a way he had never before known and he faced the fact that he was, literally, prepared to go to extreme lengths to make her his wife.

'Why not to my home?'

'Thank you, no.' She added, realizing that he would have to be told about her father's decision: 'Mother is alone today... I promised her I'd get back quickly.' She looked at Raymond very levelly: 'It will not surprise you if I tell you that she and my father are separating.'

He stared at her. The car slowed down and stopped.

Claudia protested.

'I want to talk to you,' he said firmly. 'Is your mother making the break?'

'No – Daddy. It will be far better, really.'

'Your mother will be on her own – when you marry.'

'Yes.' Claudia's voice was a trifle defiant.

Raymond's arm went along the back of

her seat, he drew nearer as he said softly:

'There's so much I could do, Claudia, if you'd only realize the true position.'

She cried desperately:

'Please let's not go over the old ground, Raymond. My mother will be perfectly all right; she has always wanted freedom, well, now it is hers.'

'Aren't you being a little hard,' he suggested subtly, playing upon her emotions.

'Hard.' It was a breathless sound. 'You are certainly the first person ever to accuse me of that.' But she was shaken by his words, flung back into that state of tumult and conflict where duty rose as a grim spectre before her.

Raymond went on, with clever innuendo. 'I couldn't disagree more with people who expect children to sacrifice themselves for their parents, but there are times when to give them happiness and security without any real hardship to themselves–'

'In short,' said Claudia bluntly, 'you are suggesting that I marry you in order that my mother's life can be more comfortable – is that it?'

'No,' he said sharply, 'it isn't. I was merely pointing out the many ways in which I could help if only you'd realize the truth: that you care for me... The truth, above all, that Allan Russell will marry his cousin and that, if you have set your heart on becoming his wife, you are wasting your precious life.'

Claudia's face paled; she felt suddenly ill for there was so much conviction behind those words. She said stubbornly:

'Aren't you rather presuming and–'

'I am claiming the right to point out obvious facts to you; facts to which you persistently blind yourself,' he added fiercely.

'That is quite absurd.'

He looked down at her with a dark intensity, a compelling determination.

'I told you the night you refused to marry me that I in no way accepted that refusal, Claudia. I repeat the sentiment. I am impatient because of the time that is being wasted; sad to see you going around in circles rather than admit you were wrong.'

'*Wrong!*' It was a gasp. 'About – what?'

'Allan,' he said imperturbably. 'If watching him go off with another woman won't convince you, then nothing will.'

Instantly, Claudia said:

'There is nothing whatsoever in Allan and his cousin going to stay with relatives.'

'You are now being naïve,' he said infuriatingly. Then, changing his tone he said softly: 'However, I'll bear with you, my sweet; the deeper you get into this situation the more you will need me in the end. So simple.'

'If only you'd realize how I feel,' she said desperately.

'That's just it: I do realize,' he said impressively. 'And I am very surprised at your attitude; I gave you credit for a certain wisdom, shrewdness.' He sighed.

Claudia sat there beset with doubts, puzzled as she thought of Allan and Meg, unable to cling to any solid beliefs, her confidence shattered. She could not get away from the fact that Allan had not 'phoned her and, honest herself, never for a second would it occur to her that Meg had deliberately withheld her request.

'Suppose,' she said lightly, 'we stop this inquisition! I asked for a lift home, not a sermon.'

He looked deeply into her eyes and, again, she was struck by the light of cruelty, that gleamed just behind the smile. Yet his manner belied any such characteristic and she could not deny his solicitude.

'Is that your way of dismissing me?'

'No ... Raymond, I'm sorry,' she said impulsively. 'But–'

'You're confused, bewildered, and hurt,' he said softly, congratulating himself on an unbeatable approach.

She glanced up at him swiftly:

'You are very sympathetic,' she murmured while yet not making the remark seem a compliment. It was as though it were quite beyond her power to keep the cynicism from her voice.

Slowly and deliberately, Raymond leaned down and pressed his lips against hers in a kiss, stifling, passionate. Then, without a word, drove on again.

Claudia's cheeks were flushed. She wanted to protest but, as always, some power almost beyond her control held her back; a power having nothing to do with personal, or physical attraction, but with that which was bound up with the domination of her mother who, on these occasions, appeared to stand like a ghostly sentry on guard.

They returned to 'Stoneways' and Helen simulated surprise at Raymond's presence, welcoming him nevertheless and in her own subtle fashion conveying a certain rather forlorn and pathetic attitude as she said:

'I suppose Claudia has told you that – that Charles–'

'Yes,' Raymond hastened. 'I am sure that things will work out and if I can ever do anything–' He paused impressively.

'You are so awfully kind,' Helen murmured. Then: 'You'll stay to lunch, won't you?'

'I think,' Raymond said easily, 'that it would be far better if you both came to lunch with me.'

Instantly Claudia wanted to avoid prolonging the meeting, but Helen said swiftly:

'I must confess that the very thought of going to that lovely home for a few hours cheers me beyond words...'

'Splendid. We could run up to town tonight for dinner and the theatre.'

There was no question of any refusal being possible. The commanding note in Raymond's voice conveyed his determination not to be overruled. He avoided Claudia's eyes as he spoke, relying on Helen to give him the support he needed and then, discreetly, to back out at the last minute so that he and Claudia could go alone.

And it worked according to plan. In different circumstances it would have been a perfect day. The luxury and peace of 'Old Place'; the glory of the setting amid shady cedar trees, the tranquillity of sitting in their cool shade while tea was served effortlessly and with efficiency, held a certain glamour even for Claudia, but her thoughts were obsessed with Allan whom she pictured with Meg as she tortured herself by imagining him making love to her... Hurts that stabbed with the sharpness of a dagger thrust.

Later, as she and Raymond were driven to London by his chauffeur, first to the theatre, then to the Hungaria, with its gypsy orchestra and atmosphere of gaiety and dignity, that same obsession for Allan increased, becoming a nostalgic anguish as she longed for his arms and for the touch of his lips.

Raymond was at his best that night; courteous, subtly flattering, attentive in his most intriguing manner.

'Would you,' he began as they glided through a slow waltz, 'like to travel, Claudia?'

'Very much.'

'A world tour for a honeymoon?' His eyes seemed to burn with a passionate, desirous flame as they met hers.

Claudia said breathlessly:

'That sounds like Elysium.'

'It could be with you, my darling.' His voice was low, tender.

She said honestly:

'One cannot control one's heart. Life would be very simple, otherwise.'

'And very dull.' He looked down at her. 'You make the chase very tantalizing and the tension almost unbearable.'

She shook her head and said remorsefully:

'I don't mean to, Raymond.'

'And your attitude always leaves me that margin for hope,' he said deliberately.

Claudia hated the truth of that statement. No one, she knew, could accuse her of encouraging Raymond's attentions, on the other hand, the domestic situation at 'Stoneways' prevented her from slamming the door in his face. Life took to itself a new complexity as she dwelt upon the position in which she now found herself with Allan. The true significance of his visit to Scotland might elude her, but she could not ignore all that Raymond had said – and obviously innocently so she believed – about an engagement. Her mother, also, would not have adopted the attitude she had. For Claudia, in her loyalty, refused to believe but that her mother, at heart, desired that which was most calculated to bring her happiness.

Nevertheless, black though it all looked, Claudia resolved that she would not jump to conclusions that might well mean the wrecking of her future. Allan's attitude on his return from this holiday would be the deciding factor ... the week would be up and if he were contemplating marriage with Meg, the truth would, of necessity, have to be told. Flatly she refused to plunge into folly; both Raymond and her mother might be doing no more than quote conversation which, taken out of its context, might well be entirely fictitious. The thought calmed her and her love for Allan rose on the wings of an exultation inspired by trust.

They danced until just before midnight and then returned, through deserted streets and quiet lanes to 'Stoneways'.

Helen was still up as Claudia had imagined her being.

'I knew I should not sleep,' she explained, 'and I thought you might be glad of some coffee or sandwiches.' She smiled. 'Or both.'

Claudia said swiftly:

'I don't know about Raymond, but for me – only bed!'

Raymond forced a smile.

'Don't let me detain you from the luxury.' He wanted to speak to Helen without making it too obvious, knowing full well that she had remained up for the same purpose. He edged to the door and Claudia, grateful to be excused further conversation with him, said swiftly:

'Thank you for a very enjoyable day... Good night... Good night, Mother.' And with that she went up the stairs.

Helen said:

'I hoped I might have a word with you, alone.'

He inclined his head and followed her into the lounge where, at her invitation, he poured himself out a whisky and soda. Then:

'Well! You see how little need there was for your panic.'

Helen said solemnly:

'We must not overlook the fact that the whole position will change when Allan returns. We've managed to build up a very good story, but–'

'Suppose you let me do the worrying?' He looked at her and decided that she was a very weak woman incapable of grasping the deeper significance of the issues around her. 'Meanwhile, you have the strongest weapon, now. Your own position; your loneliness; a depleted income ... even debts,' he added carelessly. 'Claudia is already torn between you and Allan; already struggling within herself to find out just where her duty lies–'

Helen said with foolish haste:

'Claudia isn't in love with Allan.' The thought flashed through her mind that, after all, Raymond might weary of the fight, particularly since, now, Claudia's affections were admittedly elsewhere. 'She is merely infatuated.'

Raymond said pointedly:

'You do not need to have any fears on that score ... I know precisely how things are between Claudia and Allan. You can put your mind at rest, however, that I shall not be deterred because of Claudia's regard for Allan. I've imagined myself in love many times, but I've lived to love again. So will Claudia. At the moment, however, her world centres around Allan and I'm not so crassly stupid as to deceive myself on that score. It is up to me to alter that. And,' he paused, his expression becoming almost satanic as he went on with a cold, merciless inflection: 'the simplest way to achieve that miracle is to make quite sure that he is given every reason to feel that she has treated him badly.'

Helen said in a breath:

'I hardly think that–'

'My dear Helen,' he cut in with cynical tolerance. 'Can't you realize that his attitude towards her will then change accordingly and she will imagine all the wrong things – particularly that the idol had feet of clay?' He gulped the remains of his drink. 'I've it all worked out; don't worry. And you will soon have the key to that very coveted flat in your possession,' he added bluntly. Then: 'Fortunate that you've got rid of your husband. I must say I considered him a decided bore... Now, I must be going.' He looked at her very levelly: 'Go on as you are; play up your own position, your concern for Claudia and your distrust of Allan, and leave the rest to me.'

'I will.'

'And keep me informed.'

Helen nodded, and walked to the front door with him. She was in a state of acute nervous anxiety. At heart she hated the deception, but told herself that it was, after all, for Claudia's ultimate happiness.

'I shall 'phone in the morning,' Raymond said authoritatively. 'Now go to bed and – sleep,' he admonished. 'You haven't a thing to worry about. Believe me.'

'I do believe you,' she said unsteadily.

Raymond went out to his car and decided that Fate had been extremely generous in enabling him to solicit the help of a woman like Helen Lomond. A cynical smile twisted his lips dissolving into contempt. She was definitely not the type he admired.

It was the following morning that Charles 'phoned and asked Claudia to have dinner with him in London that evening. She accepted with alacrity and, gaily, imparted the news to Helen.

'I see.' Helen's lips were pursed into a thin line. 'So I am to be left here alone while you dine with your father. Do you think that quite fair – after all that has happened, darling.'

Claudia said very firmly:

'And just what has happened that in any way detracts from my good opinion of Daddy?'

Helen grew flushed under Claudia's searching gaze.

'I think,' she insisted, 'that your loyalty is to me.'

'And I,' came the implacable reply, 'think that my loyalty is to you both.'

'You cannot run with the hare and hunt with the hounds.'

'But I can think for myself and see this whole situation in true perspective,' Claudia countered. 'What is more, Mother, I flatly refuse to be placed in the invidious position of taking sides, or in any way endangering my position with Daddy. I can assure you of one thing: he will in no way expect me to be other than loyal and affectionate towards you. So let that be understood.'

'I don't like your tone,' Helen said angrily.

'I'm sorry; I don't like yours. Had Daddy wronged you in any way, behaved badly, it would be different, but when I remember how anxious you have been to secure your freedom, it would be quite impossible for me now to assume that the loss of Daddy's presence here involves you either in hardship or heartache.'

Helen began to sniff into her handkerchief.

'And what else does it involve me in – if not hardship,' she demanded. 'Having to give up this house, move into some dump ... it isn't fair; my position is horrible. If your father had a spark of decency he would never have left me.'

'Oh, *Mother!*' It was an impatient, exasperated sound. 'That is sheer hypocrisy and you know it.'

'I know,' said Helen, 'that my life is nothing more than a burden, now. Here I am buffeted about, not knowing what my future may be, while your father can gad off to Canada and enjoy himself. What hope have I of enjoyment? Oh, I might have had...' A sigh. 'To be at "Old Place" yesterday was sheer exquisite torture; realizing that I might have ended my days amid that peace and beauty and security... But no; you're too selfish to consider me... Only your father merits your consideration and sympathy.' Frustration overruled discretion in that moment and although Helen knew how foolish she was being, she had not the will-power to stop.

Conversation was stopped at that juncture by the ringing of the telephone. Helen grabbed at the receiver, her voice changing to a honeyed sweetness as she said:

'Raymond... Can we go to Torquay with you? But that sounds simply wonderful. When? Eleven *today*... Stay at the Palace; but we'd love it. Of course.'

Claudia's voice came sharply, authoritatively:

'*I* cannot go, Mother; I am seeing Daddy tonight – I've told you that.'

Helen thrust a hand over the mouthpiece of the instrument.

'Be quiet,' she snapped. 'The very idea of... No, Raymond... Oh yes, she's here. One moment...' Reluctantly, she relinquished her hold of the receiver and as Claudia put it to her ear cried in a whisper: 'I'll never forgive you if you spoil this arrangement.'

Claudia ignored that as she began:

'Raymond, I'm awfully sorry, but I cannot possibly go to Torquay today. No; I'm having dinner with Daddy tonight: he is sailing on Friday... Yes, it would have been nice, but I know you understand.'

Raymond swore beneath his breath at the other end of the 'phone. But he knew that Claudia would not take kindly to opposition and said:

'Of course ... we'll fix something of the kind later. How about having lunch with me today – to atone.'

'And – Torquay?'

'It can wait,' he said coolly.

'Very well.' She laughed. 'Yes, eleven ... you'll call for me? 'Bye.'

She replaced the receiver and turned to face Helen's wrath.

'How dare you,' Helen cried, white with rage. 'A lovely trip like that, which would have done me a world of good – all thrown away because of your father. It – it is almost more than I can bear. You haven't one spark of consideration for me – not one.'

Claudia felt utterly sick at heart. Her mother's tears both weakened and angered her; every day, it seemed, the situation grew more impossible... Would even marriage to Allan give her respite? Was there no ending to the grim repercussions of an unhappy marriage? Now, more than ever, the burden appeared to rest upon her shoulders, since it was obvious her mother had no intention of rising to the occasion and building a new life. Rather did she apparently intend to wilt and rely solely upon others for her happiness and security. Claudia, however, stood her ground.

'That is grossly unfair,' she said quietly. 'I have a perfect right to see Daddy; I promised him and I want to keep that promise. Torquay with Raymond means absolutely nothing to me–'

'And,' Helen said shrilly, 'I mean nothing to you; my pleasure ... you are not prepared to sacrifice even a day for me... No, your father comes first. Ah, well; it was ever thus.' She sighed dramatically. 'One must not expect gratitude from one's children. I least of all from you. Very well, go with your father. Go to Canada with him. I shall manage somehow. You've ruined all my chances of happiness, anyway, in your refusal to marry Raymond.' A malicious light came into her eyes, anger and disappointment whipping her to a point where she in no way realized or meant the bitter things she was saying as she cried: 'But you'll live to regret it; no good will come from your selfishness... *Allan!*' She uttered the name scornfully. 'Do you imagine that he is coming back from Scotland to marry you? I gave you credit for more intelligence... Everyone else but you realizes how things are between him and Meg... I can't think where your pride is–' She broke off, silenced by the stricken expression in Claudia's eyes.

Claudia felt that a blow had been struck at the pit of her stomach. Was that what people were saying?... And did it matter what they said? Of what use her love for Allan if she was not prepared to trust him? Love without faith... She said quietly:

'I never believe anything that "people" say, Mother. When Allan tells me himself that he is in love with Meg, or is going to marry her, then I shall *know*... When he comes back from Scotland I shall have the opportunity of talking to him and letting him know how I feel... Until then, suppose we do not discuss the matter further. It can only make the gulf wider between us.' And with that she walked swiftly from the room. Her heart was thudding wildly, she felt physically sick, but above the tumult and uncertainty her love remained inviolate. When Allan came back all this would seem as a nightmare that was past...

And in Scotland, some few days later, Allan said to Meg:

'Would you mind very much if we started back tomorrow, Meg?'

Meg caught at her breath.

'No,' she said unsteadily. 'But why?'

He said honestly:

'Claudia! I've got to see her; this whole thing is driving me mad. Suppose that morning we left she had come to—'

'To tell you that she would marry you,' Meg prompted gently.

'Yes ... our going off might so easily have

seemed odd and there was no time really to say anything. Oh, I know Winters would have butted in but even that–' He broke off. 'Sorry to inflict this on you, my dear, but–' He stopped, then: 'What is it Meg; why do you look at me like that.'

'Because I hate the thought,' she said convincingly, 'of telling you what I must tell you.' As she spoke she handed him a letter. 'It's from Susan,' she went on quietly, sympathetically. 'The announcement of Claudia's engagement to Raymond Winters was in the local paper this week.'

CHAPTER EIGHT

Allan stared at Meg in startled, pained disbelief. He took Susan's letter and read it swiftly. The silence of the room became electric and to Meg it seemed her hopes and dreams were crystallizing in what for her was a moment of dramatic suspense. Allan said harshly:

'Well, that seems to be that.'

Strange, he thought, how one could fight against a truth, resist it, refuse to believe in any innuendo, mesmerizing oneself into that mood of complacency, which refused to admit any possibility of defeat and then, suddenly, inexorably, the grim fear dissolved into inescapable fact and further self-deception was rendered impossible.

'I did try to warn you,' Meg said quietly.

'I know; I just didn't want to believe any of it,' he said ruefully. His lips twisted into a feeble travesty of a smile. 'And I was just deluding myself that she had come to "Cloverdell" that morning to tell me she would marry me and worrying myself to death lest there was a misunderstanding.'

Meg said sympathetically:

'Do you still want to return?'

His expression hardened.

'No; we'll keep to our original plan, my dear.' He looked at her with sudden gentleness: 'You're a splendid companion, Meg. Forgive me for vapouring as I have but–'

'It helps sometimes to be able to think aloud, knowing that the other person understands.' She put out a hand and clasped his. A surging happiness enveloped her; her heart was throbbing wildly; where, but a matter of minutes before, her world was darkened by ominous, threatening clouds, now it was illuminated by a dazzling light. Just how had the miracle of that engagement come about. Certainly, she reflected, she had found an ally in Claudia's mother and now there was nothing to prevent her coming into her own and winning Allan for herself. She dismissed entirely the question of his love for Claudia, maintaining that it was no more than infatuation, in any case... Only one thing was important to her: the fact that Claudia was now out of reach.

Allan tried to still the painful thudding of his heart which appeared to beat in the gaping void of his body. It was as though all strength drained from him, leaving him weak, faint to the point of sickness, and no matter how he derided the sensation, he could not overcome it. The thought of Claudia marrying Raymond Winters seared him; the vision of her in his arms was agony, as was his own longing for her.

Anger struck to take a little of the edge from the anguish of contemplation. She had played with his affections, kept him on a string without intention of marrying him, hiding – in the first place – behind the smoke screen of her parents' unhappy marriage to provide an excuse for caution, and no doubt using him to awaken jealousy in Raymond's mind and, thus, render her own position more advantageous as she set out to ensnare the wealthier man. He winced because such thoughts hurt him beyond the pain of his own wrath – wrath in which he had sought refuge as a wounded man craves morphia. He despised any sign of weakness; loathed the idea that he had been reduced to this state of intense and bitter disillusionment. Claudia... *Claudia*...

It was unthinkable that she, of all people, should have behaved thus.

Meg was thinking rapidly, building imaginary castles, planning for the future. What attitude to adopt now, she asked herself. How best to insinuate herself into Allan's life permanently. Her eyes met his and she said deliberately:

'I know how you feel, Allan, and I want to help. One's pride comes into these things, no matter how one disputes the fact. And you, I am certain, are like me: you'd hate sympathy or pity of any kind – even from your own family.'

'How true,' he said bitterly.

She got up from her chair and moved until she stood beside him; her gaze was downcast and, then, suddenly, almost disarmingly, she raised it to the level of his own as she said:

'May I make a suggestion that – that will probably seem outrageous to begin with, but which may help in the end?'

Allan's eyes contemplated her with tender affection.

'You know the answer to that, Meg.'

'Yes,' she said uncertainly, 'but I don't want to presume on our relationship.'

'You could never do that.' It was said with great conviction.

'Then, how would it be if *we* were to announce our engagement? Oh,' she hastened,

'I'm not suggesting that it should be in any way serious, merely that it would tide you over any family curiosity and—' She paused impressively, before adding severely: 'I'm quite prepared to admit that I see red when I think of Claudia cherishing the idea that you are nursing a broken heart because she has ignored you; I've never known any girl treat a man so – so abominably.' She held her breath as she watched for any sign that might betray his reaction and added: 'Obviously, when I leave "Cloverdell" the "engagement" can be broken. For the time being, however, I'm sure it would make things a great deal easier.'

'But,' said Allan, blissfully blind to the dangers attendant upon such an arrangement, 'that would hardly be fair to you, Meg.' Emotion was seething and churning within him; bitterness, regret, frustration – all jumbled into a violent resentment of his position and rebellion against it... Impulsively, like a man swaying dangerously on the edge of a precipice, he said almost sharply: 'Is there any reason why there should be any pretence about it at all?'

'Allan!'

'I don't,' he hastened, 'mean to insult you – anything but that.'

'*Insult* me—' Her voice cracked with a sudden delirious joy. 'But are you sure—' It was the last thing she wanted to say, but was sufficiently astute not to force the pace.

'I am quite sure,' said Allan, 'that feeling as I do, I shall never be more fond of anyone than I am of you – little enough to offer, I know, my dear but, if it *is* enough–'

Meg's eyes were misted as they met his.

'My love for you will increase the measure of yours for me, darling,' she said softly, 'as time passes.' Her voice grew wistful and appealing: 'I think we need each other, you and I, Allan. And I'll never fail you – never.'

'I'm quite sure of that.' He looked down at her. 'But there must be no false pretences on my part, Meg,' he said gravely. 'One cannot turn love off like a tap–'

'You wouldn't be trying to tell *me* that, would you,' she said, and a half-smile hovered around her mouth. 'I know, Allan; and I want to help – as I can. Trust me.'

Allan stared at her. It was quite unreal, yet he argued that the whole fabric of his life had appeared to be woven with foreign threads during the past weeks; that nothing merged into the correct pattern and that his engagement to Meg was no less fantastic than the idea of Claudia's engagement to Raymond.

Meg, on safe ground, said:

'I don't know, darling, but I think it would be rather nice to get back to "Cloverdell", after all – that is if you don't mind.'

'Not in the least,' said Allan. And he

thought cynically: Scotland or Timbuctoo –
it was all the same so far as he was
concerned.

It occurred to Meg that if there should be
any mistake about the announcement of
Claudia's engagement, then the sooner she,
herself, returned to broadcast the news of
her own the better. And, as a precaution, she
sat down immediately and wrote to Susan.
That, she thought, viciously, would settle
Claudia.

To Claudia every hour of those days
seemed like twenty-four. The brightest spot
in that interminable period of waiting for
Allan's return, was the evening spent with
her father. The sullen resentment which
Helen had shown, in no way abated during
that fateful day and when, finally, Claudia
left the house for London, she had said: 'I
shall not forgive you for this. It is grossly
unfair and disloyal.'

Claudia had learned much from that
evening. Charles, away from the stultifying
atmosphere of 'Stoneways', appeared to be
years younger; the rather irritable, over-
bearing attitude was no more and instead,
he was tolerant, cheerful, interested in life as
it surged around him.

'You've changed, Daddy,' she had insisted
gaily.

'Perhaps my mind is at peace, darling.' He
had looked at her very intently: 'Quite apart

from my own affairs, and the composure brought about by my decision, I am so mightily relieved to know that you are to marry Allan. A great load off my mind; I was so afraid lest you might be persuaded–' He smiled. 'But I might have known you weren't that type. By the way, I rather hoped Allan might be meeting you tonight–'

Claudia's voice had faltered as she said:

'He and Meg are in Scotland.'

Looking back, now, Claudia trembled at the recollection of the pained surprise that had come into her father's eyes as she told him that news. How he had tried to make light of it and the sudden tenderness with which he had said: 'You're worried – aren't you, darling?' And had added swiftly: 'Don't be; Allan is as true as steel; he'll never let you down.'

She clutched at that memory now as she went slowly down the stairs to breakfast, telling herself that, in three days, Allan would be back, the 'ultimatum' week over, and this whole, miserable and unsatisfactory situation at an end. Nothing was so wearing as suspense and she was living in its shadow, no matter how she might try to tell herself otherwise.

'And what,' Helen asked, 'are you doing today?'

Claudia said promptly:

'Going over to "Cloverdell".'

197

'Allan won't be there,' Helen exclaimed tartly.

'I'm aware of that … but I happen to love the family, too,' came the steady reply.

Helen sipped her coffee.

'You haven't overlooked the fact that Raymond is returning from Torquay, or rather, that he returned late last night – have you? He is bound to come over and–'

Claudia said firmly:

'Raymond's movements are no more my concern, Mother, than mine are his; if he should call you have only to tell him I'm out.'

Helen mastered her temper.

'Very well,' she said stiffly. Then: 'Good gracious, there is Raymond now – or his car,' she corrected herself as she looked out through the wide open windows on to the drive. Her lips curled as she added: 'At least one man knows how to be attentive to the woman he loves. Pity there are not more like him.' And with that she went out into the hall and personally admitted him.

Raymond came swiftly into the house, bringing with him an air of consternation as he asked breathlessly:

'Is Claudia about?'

'Yes,' Helen answered, instantly alert and anxious.

Raymond gave her a meaning glance and, looking down at the newspaper folded beneath his arm conveyed, silently, the reason for his visit.

He followed Helen into the breakfast room where Claudia sat imperturbably finishing her meal. At the sight of him she looked up casually:

'You certainly get around,' she exclaimed lightly.

He drew a chair into position opposite her.

'So you haven't seen this,' he said unfolding the paper as he spoke.

Claudia was aware of a sudden unbearable tension as she asked fearfully:

'Seen – what?'

Colour flooded Helen's cheeks. How assiduously she had kept the local 'paper from Claudia; how carefully she had guarded the 'phone.

'The announcement of our engagement,' he said briefly. 'It was pointed out to me this morning by my butler.'

Claudia gasped:

'"Our *engagement!*"' Then, once the initial shock was over, suspicion and indignation betrayed itself in her expression, and she exclaimed accusingly:

'How could such an announcement possibly get into the papers?' Her eyes were challenging. 'Unless someone deliberately gave away the information.'

Raymond maintained an attitude of

impressive composure.

'That is precisely what I intend to find out – just what is behind it all.' He added: 'I'm afraid that the London press carry it as well. I'm most terribly sorry, Claudia.'

She retorted:

'It is an infuriating business.'

Helen made some feeble excuse and slipped from the room. It was more than she could bear to think of all Claudia was throwing away by her attitude.

Raymond got up from his chair, and deep in thought, paced the floor for a few seconds. Then:

'I must be honest,' he began, meeting Claudia's uncompromising gaze very levelly, 'seeing that announcement gave me a very great thrill. *My* annoyance is out of deference to your feelings. Certainly, I am proud to be identified with you – even for a brief while.' He lowered his voice appealingly: 'Can't you see it my way too, darling, and let it *be* the truth?'

Claudia moved restlessly from the table. She hated the idea that others had read that newspaper item and accepted it. What of Allan's parents?... And the news might even have reached Allan himself. She said swiftly and emphatically:

'What you ask is impossible, Raymond.' She flung out her hands. 'I've told you so before.'

His expression changed, but he managed to curb his annoyance and impatience sufficiently to say quietly:

'As you will.'

'And you will get it contradicted at once?'

'If you insist.'

'I do.' She puckered her brows. 'I cannot fathom how it ever came to be put in.'

'Oh,' he said carelessly, 'we've been seen about together quite a bit and they were probably hard up for news.'

Claudia was by no means satisfied and she insisted:

'I may know very little about the running of a newspaper, but I should have thought that an announcement of that kind could be made only with the full consent of the parties concerned.'

Raymond laughed.

'I hardly think that policy would take them very far, dear innocent! It is mostly the things that people don't want printed about themselves that inspire the headlines... By the way, Allan home yet?'

'No,' Claudia moved to the door. Plans were taking shape in her mind and she conveyed the impression that she was anxious he should leave as she said: 'I'm just going to "Cloverdell".'

'I'll drive you there–' blandly.

'Thanks, no.'

'So anxious to be rid of me... To atone for

the discourtesy, will you come with me to the Hospital Ball tomorrow night?' He smiled somewhat tantalizingly: 'The story will have been refuted by then and–'

'Thank you all the same but–'

'You will not come?'

'Oh, Raymond,' she cried half impatiently.

'No, my dear: I won't take defeat lying down. Sorry. Your coldness adds zest to the fight – to say nothing of the competition with which I am faced... Yes, I'm going, don't worry: and, incidentally, if you should change your mind about the Ball just 'phone me... Good-bye.' He added slowly: 'But not for very long.'

They walked to the hall together where Helen awaited them. Claudia made her excuses and ran up the stairs and, as she disappeared from view, Helen murmured:

'Not very successful – that announcement.'

He smiled at her almost pityingly.

'On the contrary, my dear, I think you will find it has already served its purpose and,' he added significantly: 'reached Scotland. Susan is bound to have relayed the news–' A confident sigh.

Helen beamed.

'Nothing escapes you – does it?'

'Nothing... By the way, I'd like you and Claudia to be my guests at the Hospital Ball tomorrow evening. Claudia has already

202

refused my invitation but ... I shall expect you both, nevertheless. Use your persuasion.' There was a challenge in his voice. And with that he left her.

Claudia came down the stairs and sighed in relief.

'Did you have to rush away in that rude manner?' Helen demanded.

There was an air of defiant determination in Claudia's attitude as she said:

'I'm in a hurry, Mother.'

'I wanted your help this morning,' Helen insisted.

'I'll do anything you want when I get back,' Claudia said smoothly.

'You're going to the farm?'

'Eventually, yes.'

'What – what do you mean by that?' It was a breathless sound. And as Claudia went to the door and opened it, Helen demanded fearfully: 'Just what is in your mind – this – this dashing out of the house–'

'I'll tell you later,' Claudia cried and the front door shut behind her.

It struck her as she made her way to the road and boarded a bus into the town, that she had allowed matters to drift far too long. Well, now she was in an aggressive mood. If Allan had seen that announcement and, rightly, been incensed by it and its possible implication, she would, at least, have a strong answer, backed by action and not feeble indecision. Someone inserted that 'engagement' in the paper and she intended to get to the bottom of it.

Accordingly, some few minutes later, she strode through the doors of the *Morning Courier,* gave her name and demanded to see the editor. After some ceremonial she was shown into a sparsely furnished office and received by Mr Rufus Wright who beamed benignly upon her and said:

'This is a pleasure, Miss Lomond. And what can I do for you?'

Claudia looked at him with a steady gaze.

'You can tell me,' she said firmly, holding out a copy of the *Courier* and indicating the item of news in question, 'on whose authority the announcement of my engagement to Mr Winters was printed.'

Mr Rufus Wright stared at her aghast, took off his spectacles, wiped them and said breathlessly:

'But, my dear Miss Lomond, on the authority of Mr Raymond Winters himself.'

Claudia curbed the anger that rose within her and said with a deadly calm:

'Then it just so happens that there is not one word of truth in it...' She added challengingly: 'And I suggest – demand – that on *my* authority you have it retracted.'

'But–'

Claudia said firmly:

'There are no "buts" Mr Wright. I am not

engaged to Mr Winters, nor am I likely to be engaged to him and I have the right to *insist* that you do as I say–' Claudia moved to the door as she spoke. 'Good morning,' she finished with an air of finality, and strode from the building.

Never had the longing to smash something been more acute – something that should, in her imagination, take the shape of Raymond Winters' face! How dare he! How dare he imagine that a few words in a newspaper would so appeal to her vanity that she would fall into his arms. She paused, her turbulent thoughts twisting and turning in the dark labyrinth that was her mind... Suppose he had some far deeper reason than that? But what? Allan? She caught at her breath in fear and then laughed at her own folly. She had only to deny the story and far from widening the breach between her and Allan it would, in fact, lay the ghost of Mr Winters once and for all. This time, she told herself resolutely, there should be no loose ends; nothing in abeyance – only a complete confidence. Her heart quickened its beat; the promise of happiness had never seemed quite so perfect as then, as, with an air of one going into battle, she made her way to 'Old Place'.

Raymond received her in his study; he was quiet, even grave, aware of the anger that blazed in her eyes, aware of her poised, tense body and the passionate fervour of her voice as she said:

'This will be the last time we cross swords–'

He interrupted her.

'It may save you a great deal of trouble if I tell you now that Mr Wright has already been on the 'phone to me.'

'I assumed that,' she said cuttingly. 'You flatter yourself that you see all and know all and are never at a disadvantage.'

'Indeed.'

She looked at him very levelly.

'Just what you hoped to accomplish by such an announcement, I cannot imagine,' she said and now she was calmer. 'I just want you to know how much I despise you for it and for the act you put on for my benefit earlier this morning.'

Raymond lit a cigarette and made a few rapid calculations. The situation didn't please him and his concern was to extricate himself from it as gracefully as possible, at the same time reclaiming any sympathy he had lost. What 'line' would most appeal to a girl of Claudia's courage and spirit. And suddenly he knew that which might, all things being equal, serve his purpose best as he began:

'I could offer you my humble apologies; I could say many things in mitigation, but frankly, Claudia, I have no intention of

206

wasting my time or insulting your intelligence.' His dark eyes narrowed slightly, their expression of cunning concealed by a simulated gentleness. 'It is my belief that a man has every right to fight for the woman he loves – fight to win her love in return – I've done no more than that. A newspaper item–' He clicked his fingers scornfully. 'No harm is done and I might have won. Come, Claudia, you are far too good a sportswoman to hold that against me. If I loved you less I'd be content spinelessly to sit back, harbour all manner of grievances, indulge a morbid self-pity... But a man in love–' He shook his head. 'Nothing – nothing deters him,' he insisted, 'and nothing will deter me until the day I am condemned to see you the wife of another man–' He paused dramatically. 'Somehow, I've a feeling that day will never come and it is not altogether wishful thinking on my part.' He drew in his breath sharply: 'I'll be hanged if I'll offer you any apologies – they'd only be damned hypocritical.'

Long afterwards Claudia had reason to recall those words and, then, they turned like a knife in her heart.

Raymond went on coolly:

'And now, suppose you sit down, remove that forbidding expression that doesn't suit you one scrap and ... have a glass of sherry with me.'

Claudia exclaimed:

'Thank you; but I would rather not...' She glanced at the grandfather clock. 'I intended being at "Cloverdell" long before this.'

Raymond asked almost curtly:

'Was your mother aware of your intention of visiting the newspaper office?'

'No.' Claudia caught at her breath. 'Why?'

'No reason.' Raymond thought that if that damned silly woman had panicked and created further suspicion in Claudia's mind she would have him to reckon with.

In that second Claudia felt suddenly sick. It wasn't possible that her mother was in all this and yet... She wrenched her thoughts away, hating herself for the disloyalty. It was true that her mother wanted her to marry Raymond, but that she would scheme with him to gain her own ends... No, never that. All the same, a shadow crept over her heart and the niggling fear remained.

To her surprise and concern on reaching 'Cloverdell' some half an hour later, she saw Allan's old car drawn up outside the front door. Agitation possessed her. Why hadn't he contacted her... She began to tremble and just as she was approaching the front door, Meg came out – almost rushed out – to greet her; a greeting lacking nothing in warmth or effusiveness.

'Claudia! How nice – and we were just talking about you... Only got back an hour or so ago.' She smiled a rather dazzling, provocative smile. 'Things have certainly been happening since last we saw each other – how a few days can change the pattern of one's life!' She eyed Claudia with interest, watching every shade of expression in her eyes as she added: 'Allan and I are engaged ... we wanted you to be the first to know – outside the family of course... Ah, darling,' as Allan approached and joined them. 'I was just telling Claudia about – us.' She slipped her arm through his as she spoke, and her attitude was indicative of complete possession; a woman creating an impression of being in love and, above all, beloved.

Claudia felt that a brutal hand had clutched and squeezed her heart in a vice; that some unseen power had drained every scrap of strength from her body, leaving her shaken, physically ill as the torment of jealousy consumed her. To be condemned to see Allan and Meg standing there together, arm in arm, to watch their apparent oneness, was almost more than she could bear... And she had thought of this reunion as one of bliss and perfect understanding when she should give Allan his answer and know the sanctuary of his love for her... And, now, he was to marry another woman. Almost involuntarily, she cried:

'This – this is quite sudden, isn't it?'

Allan's eyes met hers with no more than

polite interest.

'It might appear so,' he said evasively. His nerves were jangling dangerously. How could she stand there so calmly in the circumstances and simulate surprise at his engagement, when she had not even had the decency honestly to reject his proposal but had, instead, promised to marry another man the moment his back was turned. Yet, looking at her, loving her – it seemed to him that never had that love been so deep or so desperate as in that second.

Claudia, nervous, bewildered, incapable of thinking beyond the agony that gripped her, asked swiftly:

'Are you to be married – soon?'

Meg smiled up into Allan's face and, almost sharply, he replied:

'Yes – next month.' He paused for a second, then: 'And now I think it is time we wished *you* all the happiness–'

'Yes,' Meg hastened, 'we read of your engagement to Mr Winters and were terribly thrilled. Not, of course, that it was any surprise.'

'No,' Allan interposed, with faint cynicism, 'I think it has been a foregone conclusion for quite a while... And when is the great event to take place?'

Claudia took a deep breath and met his gaze very levelly:

'It so happens that it isn't to take place at

all, Allan,' she said with quiet emphasis. 'You see, I am not engaged to Mr Winters. The newspaper announcement was a mistake.'

CHAPTER NINE

There was a moment of deadly silence; a silence in which drama, even tragedy, throbbed as Allan realized all that his precipitate actions now involved. He stared at Claudia as one refusing to believe her as he stammered:

'But – the newspapers!'

Claudia managed to maintain an iron control as she exclaimed:

'Newspapers are not infallible.' She longed to add: 'Is your opinion of me so low that you imagined I could become engaged to Raymond without having given you your answer.'

Allan's tone was harsh as he burst out:

'Then they ought to be.' He stopped awkwardly, aware of Meg's steady gaze, and not daring to make further comment lest he betray himself completely.

Meg stood there tensed, implacable. She had given Allan the opportunity of making their engagement a temporary measure, to be broken when she left 'Cloverdell', and he had not wished it that way. So be it, she argued firmly. Now, she had not the slightest intention of being generous and setting him free; of smoothing his pathway to Claudia... Claudia whom she hated. Obviously, she was in love with Allan and would stop at nothing to achieve her own ends. Not without reason had she refused to marry Raymond Winters.

Claudia moved into the hallway so that the kindly and more mellow light might hide the emotion she was sure must reveal itself in her eyes. She was as one stricken as she nerved herself to face the ordeal of talking to the rest of the family as they came forward to greet her. Susan began blithely:

'Well, well, I seem to be the only one on the shelf, now. And I had it all planned for the eligible Raymond to fall for me! What do you think of these two,' she rambled on, looking at Allan and Meg. 'Dark horses – eh? Although that sudden trip to Scotland was a bit suspicious, I must admit!'

Marion chided:

'Darling, how extravagantly you talk, not allowing us a second in which to wish Claudia happiness.'

Allan spoke and his attitude was grim, his expression inscrutable:

'It so happens,' he said almost bitterly, 'that Claudia is not engaged at all; the announcement was untrue.'

'What!' Marion's voice broke on a note of surprise and fear. Her reactions to what had appeared to be the turn of events were decidedly unfavourable. That Allan had loved Claudia she knew beyond all doubting and she had, at one time, felt confident that Claudia reciprocated his affections... But the advent of Raymond Winters had changed all that... And Helen Lomond's insistence on the marriage had strengthened any suspicion Marion might have had. But now – now – she caught at her breath. Had Allan become engaged to Meg simply because he believed Claudia to be irrevocably lost to him?

Claudia flashed Allan a challenging glance:

'I had no idea,' she said smoothly, 'that this family regarded such an engagement as a foregone conclusion. Which only shows how wrong it is to jump to conclusions.' She managed to introduce a note of flippancy into her voice. Then: 'All the limelight, you see, belongs to Meg and Allan, as it happens.'

Duncan, uncertain and a trifle bewildered by events he in no way comprehended, said:

'More celebrations.'

'And,' Claudia hastened, deliberately hurting herself, 'since Meg and Allan are being married so soon–' She broke off, the sentence unfinished and, turning to

213

Marion, added: 'You will be very busy–' She met Marion's troubled gaze and lowered her own swiftly.

Allan knew an agony of remorse in those moments; knew the desperate bitterness of reflecting upon what might have been. Had he any right to dare to hope that Meg would release him of her own free will and could he, in all fairness, seek his own escape without the taint of dishonour? How could he hurt Meg at this stage after all her sympathy, devotion, and understanding? It was, he decided, a hopeless and impossible situation.

And Claudia wrestled with her turbulent thoughts. Allan *had* loved her, she would not, could not, ignore that fact. And suppose he had become engaged to Meg only because he believed that she, Claudia, was to marry Raymond... Wouldn't he break his engagement now? And come to her... Could he go through with a marriage that, in such circumstances, would be little better than a farce and which, ultimately, might end in tragedy. She clutched at the thought as a palliative for the torture of the moments through which she was now living. All her hopes, her cherished dreams, could not be smashed just when she had believed most in their fulfilment. If only she had not hesitated when Allan first asked her to be his wife; if only the spectre of her parents' unhappy marriage had not undermined her confidence and instilled the fear lest she might repeat their mistake... She looked at Meg and then at Allan... A knife seemed to turn in her heart as she intercepted a smile that passed between them. After all, might it not be a question of his realizing that the old love was, in truth, the truer and more enduring. Finally, defensively, she told herself that only time would prove such deductions correct and, should she be wrong, even as she had argued before, Allan would come to her, realizing that marriage without love could but cause Meg greater hurt in the end.

Susan, suddenly and acutely sensitive to the atmosphere, the general strain, said gaily:

'And now, how about coming to the Hospital Ball, Claudia? We're all going – Allan's promised me and, if you'd join us–'

Claudia's gaze went straight to Allan and for a second rested in his:

'I'm afraid I've already declined Mr Winters' invitation to the affair,' she said quietly. Then, with a half smile: 'I can hardly appear with all of you, in the circumstances.'

'Then,' beamed Susan, 'why not go with him and we can all have fun. So simple!'

Allan said curtly:

'Don't be facetious, Susan.'

'And don't you be so touchy,' she

countered lightly. 'Meg, you'll have to take him in hand.'

Meg, who had allowed smiles and gestures to suffice thus far, spoke in a slow, self-satisfied voice:

'Fortunately, he doesn't need it, darling.' A subtle pause. 'A man loathes to be "taken in hand", anyway. Am I not right, Allan?'

Allan managed to smile. But his nerves were taut; the conversation futile and trite. He longed to talk to Claudia alone; tortured himself with question after question to which he could find no conclusive answer... Suppose she were really in love with him and had been prepared to marry him, after all. He had to appreciate that she had not really given him her answer to his ultimatum – an ultimatum which had not yet expired... And now it was too late... He met her gaze; for a second it seemed that they stood together in a word isolated from the others; a world entirely their own.

'Do we,' he forced himself to say, 'have to stand talking like this? Surely a drink is called for.'

Claudia exclaimed hastily:

'I must be going. I came only to explain about the newspaper item which was pointed out to me only this morning.' She managed to smile at Meg. 'Perhaps you will come over to "Stoneways" sometime ... although I can imagine just how much you

216

have to do in the next weeks.' The words appeared to burn her tongue and she found herself tensing before Meg's steady, uncompromising stare.

Allan said:

'We'd love it... I'll run you back, now.'

Meg took a step forward but Marion, for a reason she couldn't define, exclaimed:

'Meg, I wonder if you'd give me a hand; I'm so behind with everything today: the excitement of your home-coming.' She smiled at Duncan. 'And if you make yourself scarce darling, it will help, too. One can get *on* so much better once the men are out of the way.'

Meg bit her lip in mortification. The last thing she wanted was for Allan and Claudia to be alone together but, gracefully, she had to acquiesce.

Allan remained silent for the first few seconds of the drive back. Then:

'My – my engagement surprised you, Claudia?' He spoke hoarsely, aware that the question was absolutely inadequate and far short of that which he longed to say.

Claudia replied in a low, tense voice:

'Frankly – yes.' She drew upon her pride and her courage as she added: 'But, then, it never does to try to fathom the emotions of any human being. They are an eternal mystery.'

Allan glanced at her, feeling a pang as he

did so; aware of his need of her, of the love that consumed him.

'You have always been that mystery to me,' he said thickly.

'I?' She betrayed her surprise. 'Aren't you rather confusing mystery with caution, Allan? My only fear was lest I might repeat my parents' mistake.'

The tension mounted; a pulse seemed to beat between them – passionate, inescapable.

Allan whispered in a breath:

'Meaning that, but for your parents, you would have' – he paused imperceptibly before adding huskily – 'cared, Claudia.' And as one who cannot bear the strain a moment longer, he demanded: 'Would you – would you have married me, in the end?' The words were wrenched from him; they fell upon the silence with all the precision of hammer blows; blows that beat into Claudia's brain, weakening her.

She replied and her voice shook with emotion:

'You don't expect me to answer that, Allan – not while you are engaged to marry another woman.'

A dull flush mounted his cheeks.

'I'm sorry,' he murmured. 'I'd no right ... forgive me.' He looked at her and then sharply, eloquently, said: *Claudia.*

She clenched her hands as they lay idly in

her lap; bit on her lower lip in an effort at control. Hadn't she every reason now to believe that he still loved her; that his engagement was a mistake? Would he be talking like this unless the past still haunted him? Didn't the mere utterance of her name tell her more than a multitude of sentimental expressions?

She made no effort to speak; the silence throbbed with the passion of their unspoken thoughts. At last, slightly confused, she said:

'You liked being in Scotland?'

'I love Scotland.' His tone implied: 'But I detested the circumstances.'

'Will you stay at "Cloverdell" after you are – married?'

He answered her almost abruptly:

'I could never tear myself away from the old place for long.' It was agony for him to talk of his marriage, even to think of it. Now that Claudia was free, the very idea became abhorrent and fantastic. If only he'd waited. If only, from the very beginning, he'd curbed his blind, unfounded jealousy. And now it was too late. Claudia was lost to him. Following the trend of his turbulent thoughts he asked abruptly: 'How was it that announcement came to be in the papers. If I were you–'

'I've already seen the editor,' she assured him. 'It was not, however, his fault. I have absolutely no case.'

'Then–'

'I'd rather not talk of it,' she said quickly. 'It doesn't matter now.'

He glanced at her; their eyes met and, swiftly, she turned away, just as 'Stoneways' came into view.

'Will you come in,' she managed to say as the car stopped outside the door.

'No, thank you.' He faced her and looked at her with a great intensity as one who would photograph her image on his brain. Then he said hoarsely: 'Claudia, will you be at the Ball tomorrow night?'

She puckered her brow as she murmured: 'I told you the circumstances.'

'I know.' He gave the words a curious inevitability. 'And I cannot suggest that you change your mind and accept Winters' invitation – much as I want you to be there.' He pulled himself together, mastering the overwhelming desire to reach out and draw her into his arms.

Claudia looked at him; her voice was low, tremulous:

'Then perhaps I shall be ... good-bye, Allan.'

Without a backward glance she ran into the house, hearing his car chunking down the drive and feeling slightly sick as she reflected that he was going back to Meg. No amount of conjecturing, could, after all, wipe out the fact that they were engaged.

The very contemplating was like dying a little.

Her mother called to her from the lounge. She went in.

'Was that Allan's car I saw just now!' Helen asked fearfully.

'Yes.'

'But–' She could do no more than feel her way, terrified lest some cataclysmic happening had brought him home again – sooner than was expected. 'But I thought he was remaining in Scotland until next week.' She looked at Claudia searchingly: 'Is anything wrong, darling: you're terribly pale.'

Claudia flopped in the nearest chair.

'Which is precisely how I feel,' she admitted. Emotion was surging within her; suspicion again reared its head. Suppose her mother had schemed with Raymond to separate her from Allan... The hateful, festering thought persisted and she knew it was one with which she could never make friends; but one that would grow out of all proportion to place their relationship in jeopardy unless she found the courage openly to challenge her and learn the truth. Suddenly, almost abruptly, she asked: 'Mother, did you know anything about Raymond's intentions so far as that newspaper announcement was concerned?'

Helen gripped the arms of her chair and, for a second, experienced absolute panic.

Then, almost defiantly, she tried evasion:

'My dear child, what is all this? You rush out of the house like a mad thing this morning and you return to it looking like a ghost. I haven't the faintest idea what it is all about. What on earth do you mean: "Did I know anything about Raymond's intentions".' It struck her that, since she was supposed not to know that Raymond had inserted the announcement, equally she must be careful not to assume that Claudia had learned the truth in the meantime. She added wearily: 'What *intentions?* Really, darling! I wish you wouldn't be so dramatic.'

Claudia explained the facts, telling of her visit to the newspaper office and, also, to 'Old Place', ending with:

'So you see, Mother, I'm hardly being dramatic. I think I have a right to be inquisitive. I must know where I stand.'

Helen simulated a calm she was by no means feeling as she asked, casually:

'Did Raymond mention me in connection with all this?'

'No,' Claudia said frankly, adding: 'He did ask me if you knew I had been to the newspaper office. Why?' She was tensed, alert.

'No reason; I was just trying to fathom what put such an idea into your head – why you should accuse me of–'

'I didn't accuse you, Mother,' Claudia hastened. 'I *asked* you.'

'The same thing.'

'And you haven't replied to my question,' Claudia persisted.

'I consider it an insult. Do you imagine for one moment that Raymond would confide in me. I'm your mother,' Helen said impressively.

Claudia wanted desperately to believe that her suspicions were unfounded and she cried:

'Raymond knows how anxious you are for me to marry him. He sees an ally in you.'

'He *has* an ally in me,' Helen admitted, knowing that Claudia would be deceived by her apparent frankness. 'But that does not make me your enemy – as you seem to think... Really, darling, I don't know what has come over you lately: you're just not yourself. It worries me dreadfully.'

Claudia rested her head back against the cushions; she was weary, dispirited. It was like being in a strange and unfamiliar world; she had lost all sense of belonging. Perhaps it had been unforgivable to suspect her mother, and yet...

'I've done no more than fight for my happiness,' she said dully. 'And that newspaper announcement has probably killed every hope I ever had,' she finished bitterly.

Helen leaned forward.

'What – what do you mean?' It was a breathless inquiry.

Claudia made no attempt to prevaricate.

'Just that the news reached Allan while he was in Scotland and, as a result' – she spoke very deliberately – 'he is now engaged to Meg.'

Helen experienced a relief that was almost overwhelming. Happiness bubbled within her bringing an excitement she longed to betray. So Raymond's plan had worked, after all. Now, at last, everything would smooth itself out. She managed to keep her emotions in check as she said sympathetically:

'Darling, I'm sorry. I tried to prepare you for this, but you wouldn't listen.' She hastened: 'And for you to imagine that the announcement of your engagement is in any way responsible for Allan having chosen Meg... Claudia, my dear that would be simply tragic. *Everyone* knew that Allan would marry Meg... I just cannot understand your attitude.'

Claudia got up from her chair. It was as though her heart were hurt as from a mortal blow. If only she could *talk* to her mother as a friend; unburden her mind, find solace in the wisdom that should blend with the tolerance of years. But it was as though they stood facing each other across an unbridgeable gulf. Restraint forbade further confidence. She made a last stand, however, as she said:

'And you were in no way aware of Raymond's intentions, Mother?'

Helen argued that it was her duty to tell a white lie in the circumstances. What she had done was in Claudia's interests as time would prove. She said firmly and with just the right touch of annoyance:

'Obviously I was not. I thought I had made that quite clear before. I think you owe me an apology, darling ... you are not very kind, Claudia. You've hurt me more than I can say.'

'I'm sorry,' Claudia said wearily.

Helen could not resist making another appeal:

'If only you'd see *reason* in all this. Allan is engaged to Meg and he's never been in love with you. Oh, he might have been infatuated, but the moment Meg reappeared... It's the old story, Claudia. You're torturing yourself with hopes–' She studied Claudia intently, desirous of probing the depths of her mind, of discovering her future intentions, as she ventured: 'Even now, you are not convinced – are you?' Helen experienced a frustration and impatience that she found almost impossible to curb.

Claudia's voice was low, tremulous:

'Do you mind if we end this discussion, Mother? It has become a painful subject to us both.'

'Only because you are so stubborn.'

'And you just don't understand,' came the swift reply.

Helen sighed.

'Ah, well, it will be a very great blessing when Allan Russell is really married. He's caused you quite enough misery and uncertainty and you cannot expect me to feel any sympathy for him,' Helen exclaimed with a maddening and illogical self-satisfaction. 'My concern,' she went on impressively, 'is for you. I want to see you settled and happy.' She looked at Claudia's white, strained face and all that was true and gentle in her thwarted nature surged in an uprush of emotion as she said softly: 'I really *do* want your happiness, Claudia – you must believe that. I've been so miserable myself that–'

Claudia's smile was wan.

Wasn't that very fact the crux of all this... The present debacle but the miserable past casting its shadow...

'I know, Mother,' Claudia whispered. 'I know.'

Alone, a few minutes later, Helen 'phoned Raymond.

'Have you heard the news,' she said in a voice only just audible at the other end of the wires.

'What news,' Raymond demanded testily.

'Allan and Meg are engaged. Claudia has just come back from "Cloverdell".'

Raymond's voice was soft, sibilant, and oozing self-confidence as he replied:

'I considered that a foregone conclusion. I don't make mistakes... I shall be over this afternoon.'

He arrived soon after three, joining Claudia as she sat in a deck chair under the shade of massive beech trees.

'May I?' He indicated a chair beside hers.

Claudia stared at him, uncompromisingly.

'If you wish,' she murmured coldly.

'Still in your bad books?' He sighed.

'I think I made myself clear this morning.'

'More than clear,' he said with a wry smile. Then: 'Let's call a truce, Claudia. I'll climb down and give you the victory. How's that?'

'It doesn't impress me.'

He frowned.

'I'm sincere,' he insisted. 'I haven't known a moment's peace since I saw you this morning. Out of character, you may think but, well–' He glanced at her. 'There it is.'

Claudia longed for solitude. She was in no mood to argue and words could not change the present situation. She said wearily:

'I'm so tired of discussion, Raymond.'

Raymond lit a cigarette and remained silent for a few seconds. Then:

'Will you change your mind about the Ball tomorrow night?' He held her gaze. 'Just to show that I'm forgiven?'

In that second Claudia heard again Allan's words: 'And I cannot suggest that you change your mind and accept Winters' invitation – much as I want you to be there.' She clung to them almost as a means of salvation. Would he have spoken in such a way unless he still cared?...Wasn't it obvious that his engagement to Meg was a hideous mistake for which Raymond Winters was morally responsible. And, just then, she hated the very name of Winters; hated everything about it and all the upheaval and misery it had caused her. Yet, was this the time wholly to cut adrift from him as she had so firmly intended. She said, almost sharply:

'Very well; I'll go to the Ball with you.'

'Thank you.' Of course, he knew she would, he told himself airily, asking himself for the hundredth time why he bothered with her when there were so many other women who would fall into his arms. That was just it ... the acquiescent type made no appeal to him. He wondered whether his regard for Claudia would prove enduring – once she surrendered... A cynical smile touched his lips. She would always attract him physically and she would grace 'Old Place' but, after marriage there would be fresh pastures... All that, however, did not alter the overwhelming desire he felt for her at the moment, nor the fact that he was – as far as he was capable – deeply in love with her.

Wisely he refrained from mentioning Allan and it was left to Helen, who joined them some minutes later, to broach the subject.

'That engagement is hardly news,' Raymond said airily. 'It was a foregone conclusion before they went to Scotland. In fact I promised that I would give a party for the happy couple.' He laughed. 'Susan was thrilled.'

Claudia said coldly, challengingly:

'Certainly the family didn't expect any such engagement. And Susan was as surprised as the rest.'

Raymond turned a bland smile upon her.

'There are times, Claudia, when the well-worn phrase: "There are none so blind as those who won't see" is very applicable. This, where you are concerned, if I may say so, is one of them.'

Colour stole into Claudia's cheeks. She felt shaken, incapable of retaining a mood or a thought that might bring solace or reassurance. Only that agony of suspense, that need of Allan, was real. She got to her feet.

'If you will excuse me,' she said.

'I must be going.' Raymond stood beside her. 'I'll call for you tomorrow night – about eight.'

Helen glanced up in surprise.

'The ball,' she gasped.

'Yes; your daughter is going to allow me to take her, after all. Will you join us?'

Raymond's glance dared her to accept his invitation and she said swiftly:

'Not tomorrow, Raymond; thank you all the same. I'm going out to dinner, as it happens.'

Claudia was in a state of feverish excitement and anxiety the following evening as she dressed for the Ball. Nothing of which her wardrobe boasted satisfied her fastidious taste and, finally, she selected a gown of crinoline design in ivory chiffon, embroidered with gold thread. It was by no means a new frock, but she recalled Allan's praise of it and that it had always been his favourite. Her heart-beats quickened. Over and over again she repeated to herself the words he had uttered to her ... 'much as I want you to be there'.

The ballroom was already crowded when she and Raymond arrived and, even as they crossed the threshold, Meg saw them and, instantly, drew Allan away so that he might not be aware of their presence. Only one thought dominated her – Claudia! A Claudia still free. She must keep Allan away from the dangers attendant upon such a meeting in that atmosphere of glamour and romance. To visualize his dancing with

230

Claudia was an agony and she was determined that, if it lay within her power, she would prevent it. Meg was becoming hardened; she had neither mercy nor pity for Allan and considered it her duty to save him from the folly of marrying a woman of Claudia's type. She had, in fact, mesmerized herself into believing that the course of action she was now adopting was more than justified and entirely glossed over the fact of having schemed with Helen Lomond to create just this situation.

Allan had never been more depressed. Iron bars appeared to enfold him and he was not blind to Meg's attitude of possessive determination and knew that any hope he might cherish of her setting him free was foredoomed. He said briefly:

'Pretty dud show.'

Meg smiled sweetly, but could not resist the barb:

'Claudia probably anticipated that it would be... Darling, let's slip away?'

Allan had waited, tensed, for Claudia to appear, praying that she might come after all and yet dreading the idea of being condemned to watch her with Raymond. Unlikely she would arrive now.

'Very well,' he said dully. 'Where shall we go?'

'Home.' She slipped her hand through his arm and managed to turn so that his back faced the direction in which Claudia and Raymond might come. She edged him away, almost holding her breath lest he might sense her nervous apprehension. 'The family will understand. And not miss us in this crowd.'

They began to move towards the side exit. And just as Allan reached out and opened the door, a voice said:

'Just seen Claudia.' Susan swirled past them. 'See you later at the buffet. I fixed it with Raymond and said I'd tell you. He wants us to join forces. Has some idea of a party afterwards at "Old Place". 'Bye.'

Meg felt a burning sense of frustration; a mortification she could not combat.

'I fail to see that those arrangements affect us,' she said firmly. 'Oh, for some air, darling. "Cloverdell" will be heaven after this.'

Allan turned and, in that second, found his gaze drawn to Claudia's as she and Raymond approached them; a gaze that, as ever, isolated them and made it seem they were moving only towards each other.

'Allan,' Meg said sharply, authoritatively.

'We obviously can't leave now,' he said.

'But – darling, of course we can. Mr Winters will understand. After all, we're not beholden to him – if Claudia is.' She knew that her tactics were wrong, but it was more than she could do to curb her jealousy.

'Exactly what do you mean by that?'

Allan's expression was grim.

Meg's tone became suddenly purring.

'Nothing, darling … but I just don't want to be drawn into that Raymond Winters's circle and I know you don't, either. Claudia enjoys it – which is fine for her. I just don't happen to care for that kind of life.' She sighed and smiled up into his face. 'You leave it to me: I'll make our excuses – perfectly.'

It was at that moment Claudia and Raymond reached them.

Meg stood there, shaking, fearful, yet with an implacable resolve.

'We are just slipping away,' she said confidentially. 'Fresh air–' She nodded at Claudia and Raymond. 'Forgive the "hello" and "good-bye", won't you?'

Allan managed to free himself from her restraining hand.

'I think we'll change our mind,' he said with determination. He looked at Claudia. 'The evening has only just begun, after all.'

'But–' Colour flamed into Meg's cheeks.

The music started. She glanced swiftly at Allan who said quietly:

'Claudia… May I? It is quite a while since we danced together.'

CHAPTER TEN

It was impossible for Claudia to resist Allan's appeal and she inclined her head, glanced swiftly at Raymond and Meg, then as one impelled by a force over which she had no control, moved forward from the carpeted surround to the shining parquet of the dance floor.

Allan drew her close to him and held her with that possessiveness eloquent of their former association and understanding. His eyes met hers and his voice was husky as he said:

'I had given you up.'

Her heart quickened its beat and seemed to merge with the thudding of his as she murmured:

'Should I be flattered that you were sufficiently interested even to notice my absence?' She tried to overcome the emotion now swirling upon her like a soft, warm tide.

He asked tensely:

'Do I detect a certain cynicism, Claudia?'

It was impossible for her to know what attitude to adopt. Certainly she must not allow him to suspect the nature, or depths, of her feelings; yet, equally, she was loath to say anything calculated to alienate him, or reveal jealousy of Meg. It was a position both delicate and difficult.

'No,' she said quietly, 'I am not cynical, Allan. Curious, perhaps; but that is not the same thing.'

Allan longed to confide in her; to tell her the truth about his relationship with Meg and of his overwhelming love for Claudia. He realized how baffling it must be to her to accept the fact that he was now engaged to another woman when, such a brief while before, he had professed eternal devotion to her. Could she be expected to appreciate just how great had been the impact of that newspaper announcement, or the lengths to which the folly of anger and jealousy might drive a man; a man who erroneously believed himself to have been both fooled and deceived.

Abruptly, he changed the subject, not daring to enlarge upon her remark lest his defences fell before the ever-increasing desire that engulfed him.

'By the way,' he said somewhat startlingly, 'how are things with your father? I understand he has gone to Canada–' He broke off, aware of the futility of trying to make conversation, and of seeking to avoid anything subjective.

'I've not heard since he left,' she said, managing to keep her voice steady. But her heart felt that it had dropped a few inches. Obviously it was not his intention to discuss his own affairs.

'I'm so sorry, Claudia,' he murmured regretfully, 'that things haven't turned out better between your parents.'

She looked up at him; her eyes were darkly mysterious.

'People who are not happy together are far wiser to part,' she said resolutely.

'The hazard of marriage.' It was a remorseful sound.

She caught at her breath.

'Weren't you the one to believe in its permanency and enduring qualities? Now, engaged to Meg—' Her voice died away, throbbing into silence.

'And you were the sceptic; forewarned by your parents' example.' It was a low, hushed sound.

'Which goes to show the tremendous effect of example,' she said half bitterly, 'and its repercussions.'

His lips seemed to touch her hair; she was conscious of his arms drawing her nearer and yet so imperceptible was his caress that she almost wondered if it were not the figment of her imagination and overwhelming desire.

'Do you still hold the same views about – marriage?' he asked hoarsely.

'Perhaps.'

His gaze was penetrating.

'Will you ever marry Winters?'

Claudia managed to control her emotions as she answered him quietly:

'Do we any of us know tomorrow, Allan?' She dared to add: 'Surely we have proved that.'

Was that jealousy that leapt into his eyes; was that tightening of his jaw line evidence of concern. She felt that she was holding her breath as one standing on the very edge of a precipice not knowing whether she was to be hurled to destruction or drawn back to sanctuary; a sanctuary such as only Allan's love could provide.

'I had,' he said stiffly, 'no right to ask the question in any case.'

A pang shot through her. Would he talk in such a strain if he had any intention whatsoever of breaking his engagement to Meg? Wasn't she clinging to a forlorn hope if she imagined that his heart was not in it and that only circumstances had been responsible for his taking the step in the first place?

She allowed her gaze to rest in his as she said swiftly:

'Surely, Allan, our past friendship' – her voice faltered slightly as she uttered that word 'friendship' – 'takes us beyond mere polite, conventional interest in each other's affairs.' She caught at her breath. 'Some things in life can never change.'

He whispered hoarsely:

'If time could stand still.'

Claudia trembled. It was all so unreal; she could not satisfy herself on any given point. One moment it would seem that Allan was irrevocably lost to her: the next, that she had every reason to believe that he still cared. It was a position fraught with an agonizing suspense. She knew only that she must not allow emotion, pride, to sway her towards any defiant retaliation. Her life's happiness was at stake and she refused to jeopardize it by any precipitate action. Involuntarily she said:

'I wonder just what moments we would choose to perpetuate could that be possible.'

Allan did not speak; he knew that had he attempted to do so he would have betrayed himself completely. After a few seconds, he glanced across the ballroom to where Raymond and Meg were dancing and with all his soul wished that it was Raymond Winters to whom Meg was devoted... A sense of responsibility and obligation weighed down upon him crushingly: how could he cut adrift from Meg, now; it was no conceit on his part, he argued, which made him realize just how deep and steadfast was her love for him; that love had been his for almost as long as he could remember...

And, just then, Raymond said:

'You've played your cards very well, Meg.'

Meg resented that. Now that she was engaged to Allan, she tried desperately hard to convince herself that her conquest had been genuine instead of by virtue of mere expediency. Her whole nature had undergone a complete change as a result of all she had patiently borne and she was in no mood to face facts about herself, or to be reminded that subterfuge and circumstances had won Allan to her side and not any true, romantic love.

'I don't quite understand you,' she said innocently.

'You mean that you don't *want* to understand me,' he said smoothly. 'I have cause to be grateful to you,' he went on. 'But for your timely help I've no doubt but that our two cooing doves would be very nearly married by now.'

Colour flamed into her cheeks. She had not expected Helen Lomond to confide in this man and it both angered and annoyed her that, obviously, it was so.

'I'm afraid,' she said severely, 'you must count me out of all this scheming, Mr Winters.' She argued that by adopting an implacable attitude, and refusing to comprehend his subtleties, she might convince him that she was in no way in league with Helen Lomond.

He smiled at her.

'If you are unaware of the situation, my dear Meg, how can you possibly know that there has been any scheming? Come, now; you don't imagine that you can fool me, surely.'

She was not dismayed and said firmly:

'I should be exceedingly dull of comprehension if I was unaware of the fact that Claudia's mother was most anxious to secure you for a son-in-law and–' She paused, then: 'That you were equally eager to become that son-in-law. The sequence of events so far as Allan and I are concerned followed inevitably: we've always been in love – from our kid days,' she added coolly.

He corrected her:

'It is very obvious that you are in love with Allan, my dear.' He spoke deliberately, knowing that the surest way to guarantee that she would cling tenaciously to that which she now held, was to challenge her right to it!

Her eyes narrowed:

'Meaning precisely what?'

'That Allan is madly in love with Claudia,' he replied. 'And that you know it.'

'I know nothing of the sort; are you suggesting that I am holding him against his will?'

'I am suggesting that this whole situation suits both you and me very well. The only difference between us is that I am honest about my desires and intentions. Go ahead… I'm with you every step of the way.'

Meg burst forth angrily:

'Allan is going to marry me because he is in love with me; if he weren't then what is to stop his breaking our engagement?'

Raymond's voice was clipped, insinuating:

'The best way you can convince me of that is to marry him as quickly as you possibly can. I shall believe you, then.'

Meg's eyes flashed; her face was set and tense of expression:

'I'll accept that challenge,' she cried.

Raymond swallowed a smile.

'Splendid … that is a charming frock you're wearing.' His eyes appraised her. 'Blue suits you.'

'So I've been told before,' she remarked, somewhat haughtily, hating him for his brutal frankness and fully cognizant of the truth of his words, which merely added to her annoyance and chagrin.

She was tormented with fear as she danced with him and her gaze was drawn continually to Allan and Claudia who seemed deliberately to keep over the other side of the ballroom. Suppose Allan should ask to be released. Suppose, after all, she were to lose him. The very thought made her feel physically ill. If only the music would stop so that she could get him away

241

from Claudia who, no doubt, was endeavouring to be her most charming and alluring.

To Claudia that dance was a form of exquisite torture and she was thankful when it ended, even though an acute depression assailed her as she reflected that it might well be the last time she and Allan had the opportunity of being alone together before his marriage – should that marriage take place.

As the music died away, he said tensely:

'Have you any plans for the future, Claudia?'

Emotion engulfed her. Plans! Without him the very word became a mockery.

'No.' She looked up at him as his arms dropped to his sides and they began to walk towards Raymond and Meg. 'Why do you ask?'

He might not have heard that as he exclaimed abruptly:

'You will come over to "Cloverdell", won't you? I mean...' He broke off, aware of his invidious position which made everything he said either disloyal or liable to be misconstrued.

Claudia managed to say shakily:

'I shall always love your family.'

'And they you.' It was a heavy whisper.

'Your mother has always been so very kind to me.'

'Not a difficult task.'

For a second he held her gaze masterfully, possessively.

It was strange, Claudia thought suddenly, how the atmosphere had changed between them since the announcement of his engagement to Meg. Before, cynicism, even bitterness, had prevailed and he had been intolerant of her desire for caution and suspicious lest Raymond Winters would, ultimately, be her choice. Now, all that was gone; there was a curious stillness between them – the stillness of silent thunder as their inflamed emotions demanded almost superhuman control. Ostensibly lost to her, he had never seemed more close.

'Will you – will you be married locally?' The words were wrenched from her.

There was a second of throbbing silence. Then:

'I don't know,' he said dully. And, added swiftly as one anxious to avoid further discussion along those lines, 'Thank you for the dance.'

They reached Raymond and Meg and Allan turned all his attentions to her as she moved to his side and slipped her arm through his, smiling up into his face with an adoring and intimate suggestion of their belonging.

Allan knew that he could not endure the torment of another moment in Claudia's company and that he had almost reached breaking point; every nerve in his body appeared to be on edge; depression seeped into his heart and mind and he knew that only Claudia could assuage that agony of suffering. Above all, he longed for the ability that would allow of his being brutal to Meg and, there and then, telling her he could not go on with the engagement. He in no way overlooked the fact that she, herself, was aware of the truth: he had not pretended where his feelings for Claudia were concerned and he had to admit he was surprised at Meg's attitude in the circumstances. One thing was evident: she had no intention of making things easy by releasing him and, loyally, he insisted that he could not blame her; most probably she now believed that his happiness lay entirely with her and that her love and devotion would soon inspire reciprocal affection in him. Almost tersely, he said:

'I think your idea of getting out into the open is a good one, Meg.'

'You would like to leave altogether?' Meg shot Raymond a triumphant glance as she spoke.

Raymond smiled. He had no need, now, to fear – as he had done – that Meg would back out of the engagement and do the magnanimous thing and he argued that his challenge was by no means wasted.

Allan's gaze was drawn to Claudia almost as by a magnet.

'Yes,' he said hoarsely.

Meg beamed. It was more than she had hoped for.

'I'm sure Mr Winters will excuse our not joining him afterwards, won't you,' she said sweetly.

'Most certainly,' came his suave reply. 'No one is more mindful of the cliché than I that "two is company…" I, alas, must stay for a while; otherwise, I should be persuading Claudia to come for a long run with me – probably to Land's End!'

Meg's smile was sugary, but spiteful beneath its sweetness:

'I am sure that Claudia would not require any persuasion. Would you, dear?'

Claudia bristled inwardly. Slowly and deliberately she exclaimed:

'I do not take kindly to persuasion; neither do I appreciate those who seek to indulge it… It becomes forced medicine in the end.'

A hard, steel-like glint flashed instantly to Meg's eyes and because she was aware of her precarious position and of the fact that she, herself, would go to any lengths to persuade Allan to her will, she accepted the barb and it went deep.

Raymond chuckled.

'Claudia always has an answer; even if it is, alas, no!' He looked at Allan. 'But now that

I know the lady does not like persuasion –
simple!' He spoke banteringly. 'So depressing to have to contradict newspaper
announcements,' he added blithely.

Allan, restless, impatient, ended the conversation by saying:

'Perhaps we shall see you at the farm
sometime... Good-bye, Claudia...' His
voice was uneven.

'I hope,' said Raymond smoothly, 'that I
am invited to your wedding.'

'But, of course,' said Meg detesting him
more every moment.

'And when is it to be?'

'Next month,' she answered promptly.

Allan, confused, wretched, added to that:

'We may have to put it back a matter of –
of weeks–'

Raymond adopted a confidential air as he
addressed Meg:

'Keep him up to the original date, Meg...
We men aren't to be trusted. Eh, Allan!'

Allan stared at him, baffled by his attitude.

'I take it,' he said coldly, 'you are speaking
for yourself.'

'Naturally, my dear fellow. Quite frankly,
I've never been worthy of any woman's trust
– until Claudia cast her spell – all a matter
of degree.'

Allan winced.

'Yes,' he murmured, as one half talking to
himself: 'all a matter of degree.'

Meg, infuriated by the remarks, said dictatorially:

'Come along, Allan; I cannot stand this heat another second.'

Out in the air, some moments later, she said crossly as Allan settled himself in the car beside her:

'Loathsome man, Raymond Winters. How Claudia tolerates him I shall never know. And—' She drew in her breath sharply, jealousy goading her on: 'It is perfectly obvious that she is only playing on his feelings and has every intention of marrying him in the end. Some women think that clever and adds to the keenness of a man but—'

'It does,' said Allan laconically. 'Practically all the other women in the town would have snapped him up the moment he so much as breathed a word about marriage – and they'd have taken good care he didn't escape them.' Bitterness seeped into his voice; a bitterness subconscious because of his own position.

'I don't agree.' It was a stormy sound.

Allan glanced at her.

'I really cannot see that you have any cause to be so obviously antagonistic towards Claudia.'

Meg's voice rose.

'Antagonistic! Towards Claudia! Don't be absurd.'

'I'm not being absurd.' His tone was firm.

'You made it painfully obvious and–' He drew in his breath sharply, 'I don't like it, Meg. Claudia is not only my friend, but the friend of the family and the last thing I want, or intend to have, is unpleasantness.'

Meg was out of her depth, incapable of combating the emotions now churning within her; emotions foreign to her normal conception of things. It was as though her love for Allan and her fear of losing him had created a monster of jealousy within her that was fast threatening to devour her. Her hatred of Claudia was purely obsessionist and without the slightest justification. A matter of only weeks ago she would have been horrified at the very idea of it. Now, she was its victim, her whole nature distorted. She panicked as she reflected that she and Allan were already on the edge of a quarrel and she knew that she dare not – in her present position – drive him too far. In fact, at all costs, she must placate him. Once Claudia became an issue between them she could not continue as his fiancée and hold him to their engagement without a complete negation of dignity and pride. She said softly:

'I'm afraid I've behaved in a manner calculated to make me misunderstood, darling. I have nothing but affection and admiration for Claudia. In fact I am intensely sorry for her.'

Allan shot her a swift glance.

'Why?' It was a clipped utterance.

'She's had such a rotten background and, obviously, doesn't understand the meaning of love. How can she, never having seen it in her own home. Naturally, she is cautious and cynical and determined not to be hurt by an unsatisfactory marriage.'

'And you believe she regards marriage to Winters as – satisfactory,' Allan demanded jerkily.

'In a way – yes,' Meg said guardedly, gently. 'He has wealth and position – the solid realities. It isn't a question of being mercenary – Claudia isn't that – but rather a matter of clinging to the stable things. After all, when one isn't in love with anyone it makes so much difference.' She turned a sweet smile upon him. 'I've watched Claudia very carefully,' she said with compelling earnestness, 'and, as a woman, I just know she isn't in love with anyone. All I hope is that she doesn't find the right man after she has married the wrong.'

Meg felt that to be a very clever and subtle innuendo, conveying to Allan that had she believed Claudia to be in love with him then she, Meg, would now be adopting a vastly different attitude. Those words: 'I've watched Claudia very closely', were far reaching in their implication and had not, she knew, been lost on Allan.

Allan's thoughts were turbulent and chaotic as he sat there; the memory of Claudia's gaze upon him; the passionate fervour of her voice... How easy it would have been to convince himself that she was in love with him... And how bitter to reflect that even were it so, he was still not free. Free, he told himself fiercely, and he would so inspire her with the depth of the love he professed, that she could only accept him... No longer would he allow jealousy of Raymond to warp his judgment... Oh, to be able to make her understand all the conflict associated with the past; to be free to tell her that there never had, and never would, be any other woman in his life.

Meg said carefully:

'You want to postpone our wedding date–' Her eyes met his, adoring, pleading. Instantly he was weakened; instantly it was forced home upon him that he could not betray her, now ... and yet, hardly an hour passed, when he was not arguing as to the rights and justification of such a step.

'I think,' he said awkwardly, 'that we shall have so little time in which to plan and there are things to be done to the cottage–' He broke off. How he had pictured Claudia in that cottage; visualized their returning to it together; the ecstasy of working and knowing that she would be awaiting him on his return ... *home.* Something deep within his soul cried out in anguish against the idea of any other woman sharing his life, a woman who could never, he knew, share his dreams or, in any way, be spiritually one with him.

'It would be fun doing it afterwards, darling.' She added hastily: 'But so long as we fix a date... I want the arrangements to be as you wish.' She slipped her hand into his. 'Have I ever told you how I – I adore you, Allan?' Her voice broke.

'I – I don't deserve it,' he said painfully.

'Will it sound conceited if I say that only you could ever deserve all I have to give?'

He groaned inwardly. What could a man do in such a position? Oh, for that ruthless, brutal nature that would have allowed of his breaking that conventional tie...

Meg didn't expect him to answer her and she beat down the dark jealousy that rose within her as she realized that, in his honesty, he could not utter any words to her that were not from the heart; could not tell her that he adored her in return ... but only, she thought bitterly, if he were truthful, that he adored Claudia... She said quietly:

'Suppose we make it six weeks ahead, darling.'

'I'd prefer – two months. I could just about do all I feel to be necessary, by then.' He looked at her. 'You will be going home, I take it, Meg, to arrange things and it will give you more time.'

Home! To leave him here, with Claudia always at hand.

'No,' she said resolutely. 'I shall remain with you here, darling. The family will come to me; shopping in London – all the fun of it.'

Allan's heart sank.

'You've told them about us?'

'But, of course!' She betrayed suitable surprise. 'I wired them … you know I did, darling.'

'Yes, yes, of course.' He spoke apologetically. 'My memory isn't what it might be.'

It was after the rest of the household had gone to bed that Marion approached him that night.

'Meg tells me you are not to be married quite so soon, darling.' She sat down in the chintz-covered armchair in the sitting-room and studied him as he bent over the account books spread out on the circular table.

He answered her without looking up.

'Yes … not for two months.' He tried to change the subject. 'I'm a penny out on this fodder account and–'

'If your mind were on it you might have better results, darling.'

He jerked his head up.

'Meaning just what?'

Marion leaned forward; her heart was thudding as she said:

252

'Allan, I've never interfered in your life – have I?'

'Never,' he said warmly. 'You've been wonderful.'

She forced him to meet her gaze as she said suddenly, bluntly:

'Don't go on with this marriage, Allan.'

He puckered his brows and pleaded ignorance.

'But I don't understand.'

'Do you,' she asked him earnestly, 'seriously imagine that you have deceived me for a moment?'

He got up from the table, thrust his hands in his pockets and took up a stand in front of the fireplace. Then:

'No,' he said hoarsely. 'But there are some things in this life that one just cannot do – to some people, Mother.'

She said urgently:

'Do you think that it is ever justifiable to marry someone you don't love when you are already madly in love with another woman?'

A dull flush mounted his cheeks.

'So you know that, too,' he said jerkily.

'Yes; I've always known in my heart that it was Claudia.' She added bitterly, 'And I sometimes think that by repeating all that Mrs Lomond said to me that night, I influenced you... Oh, Allan, there is so much in all this that doesn't ring true; so much that I cannot understand.'

'I don't follow,' he said in a puzzled tone.

'And I cannot voice suspicion without being able to substantiate my fears,' she said dully.

'Then all this will not get us anywhere,' he said firmly.

'But for that newspaper announcement you would never have asked Meg to marry you – would you?' Her voice was urgent, breathless. 'Would you?' she insisted.

'No.' He met Marion's gaze steadily.

'And Scotland was conveniently far away,' she murmured tensely.

'Oh, darling, let's not talk about it,' he exclaimed. 'It's done and–'

'It can be undone, Allan.'

He said stubbornly:

'You know that isn't possible, Mother. Would you have me treat Meg – Meg of all people – that way?'

Marion felt that a knife was being turned in her heart.

'And what,' she said quietly, 'of Claudia?'

He lowered his gaze.

'The mere fact of Claudia not being engaged to Winters doesn't make her automatically in love with me,' he said steadily.

'True.' Marion got to her feet somewhat unsteadily. 'But your heart tells you, nevertheless, that she is in love with you.'

He said almost violently:

'I've no justification for that belief. Had

she loved me she would have agreed to marry me before.'

Marion shook her head.

'You would not be so much on the defensive, Allan, unless you knew that I was right.'

He spread out his hands in appealing gesture.

'Right or wrong, Mother, I've made a bargain: I believe that the very nature of the circumstances bind me to Meg; that there is, in fact, no honourable way out – no matter what I may think or feel.' He added tensely: 'Whether or not Claudia really is in love with me I shall never know; I haven't the right to ask her, now. Please don't make things harder.'

'But–' It was a desperate cry.

'I'm sorry, Mother; there's nothing on earth I wouldn't do for you, or to please you; but this – no! If you have any sympathy for my feelings, don't let's speak of it again.'

Marion's hand went out and rested on his shoulder; she beat down the sobs that appeared to be lodged somewhere in her throat. Her agony was her very helplessness to combat the forces so powerfully ranged against him.

'Very well,' she said softly. 'But never forget, darling – I'm here, always, and if you should ever need my help–'

'Bless you,' came the husky reply. Then,

without another word he turned swiftly and went from the room.

The weeks passed and each one, for Claudia, was lived in a feverish suspense. Every day that dawned brought the silent question to her lips: perhaps Allan will come to me today... If he loves me... If he loves me...

And gradually the power of those words, inspired by a fragile hope, lost their strength. Could she, after all that time, continue to believe that his engagement was a mistake? And, at last, Helen who had patiently bided her time, said:

'Well, Claudia ... only three more weeks and Allan will be married. I heard yesterday that they have chosen the old Parish Church and that there is to be a big affair at "Long Barn"... Darling, can't you see how futile it is for you to go on hoping? Can't you see that Allan would have married Meg in any case and that the announcement of your engagement had nothing whatsoever to do with it?'

There was a moment of tense, almost electrical silence in which Helen waited in agonized suspense. Then, slowly, deliberately, Claudia said:

'Yes, Mother. I do see. You were right and I was wrong.'

CHAPTER ELEVEN

There was a certain defiance behind the resignation in Claudia's voice. In that second, she saw the situation with what she believed to be a dazzling clarity, sternly taking herself to task for having clung so tenaciously to what she had now proved to be no more than a foolish dream. Allan was lost to her and the sooner she accepted the fact and ceased to dwell upon the past, the better it would be for her, she argued somewhat fiercely. Useless insisting that he had once cared: his recent actions belied the possibility: it was quite obvious that he was now in love with Meg and was going to marry her.

Helen tried to compose herself, but an overwhelming elation surged upon her as she murmured:

'I'm so thankful that you realize the truth at last. I've been so worried.'

There was a certain poignancy in Claudia's solemnity.

'We are all reluctant to turn our backs upon happiness, Mother.'

Helen cried:

'You must not think like that, darling. *Your*

happiness has yet to come. There would have been no happiness for you with Allan, believe me.'

Claudia's smile was wistful:

'That is something I shall never be able to prove.'

There was a second of tense silence which Helen broke by asking:

'You will marry Raymond?'

Claudia studied her mother with a curious reflectiveness; there was something impressive in her calm as she said:

'It would mean a very great deal to you if I were to marry him – wouldn't it?'

Helen didn't prevaricate.

'It would mean everything to me. Raymond can give you all the things I have dreamed of your having, Claudia. And for my own part, it would be idle and hypocritical for me to pretend that my life would not be transformed by such an event. I can only beg you to believe that my own interests, for all that, are by no means my primary concern.'

As Helen spoke she genuinely believed that the sentiments thus expressed were true. It was a case of having mesmerized herself into a state where self-deception became reality.

Claudia held her breath... To marry Raymond...

'It would,' Helen went on, gaining con-

258

fidence, 'be such a *good* marriage for you, darling; good in every sense of the word. What could any woman possibly want that Raymond cannot offer... Oh, you think in terms of loving him, but you will quickly learn to do that; just as you will realize that the emotion you felt for Allan was mere infatuation.'

Claudia sighed and shook her head.

'That is what you would like to believe, Mother.'

'It is what I know,' Helen persisted almost sharply. Then, gently: 'He is devoted to you; there's nothing he would not do for you, Claudia.' She added with a certain practical air: 'In any case, love is merely a state of mind. Tell yourself that you are in love with this man or that and sooner or later you will be.'

Claudia's gaze was steady and unnerving.

'A very convenient formula, Mother. But I hardly think your own case proves the point.'

Helen flashed a warning look; her cheeks grew red.

'That is entirely different,' she said loftily.

'Our own affairs always are.'

'You can,' said Helen wearily, 'be most exasperating, darling – really!' She darted her a rather fearful glance. 'Are you going to 'phone Raymond?'

'Definitely no.'

'But–'

'He will call as he always does,' Claudia said coolly.

'I marvel that he has continued to pay you any attention after the way you've treated him.'

'And you are a little afraid lest the fact that he hasn't been here for two days proves a lessening of his interest?'

Helen looked uncomfortable. It was precisely what was in her mind.

Claudia said cryptically:

'I almost wish that were so: the matter would be taken out of my hands then.'

But at six o'clock that evening Raymond's car drew up outside the house.

'I've come,' he said, by way of greeting, 'to try to persuade you to have dinner with me at "Old Place" tonight, Claudia. I tried to ring you earlier in the day, but you were engaged and I was down in Bournemouth – been there since Tuesday.' He drew her gaze to his: 'Have you noticed my absence?'

Helen who was hovering around, obviously delighted and relieved, murmured:

'We were just commenting upon it when you arrived, Raymond. So strange.' She gave a nervous giggle as she met the somewhat impatient expression in his eyes.

He said:

'Will you come, Claudia?'

Claudia's head appeared to lift slightly:

there was something near to defiance in her tone as she replied:

'Yes; yes, I'd like to do so.'

Surprise at her acquiescence clearly revealed itself in his attitude.

'Wonderful,' he exclaimed. 'I want you to see the sunken garden I've just had made. You'll like it.'

It would have been impossible for Claudia accurately to have described her feelings when, later, she and Raymond reached 'Old Place'. She looked upon it as one seeing it for the first time, aware of its nobility of line, its stately grandeur; its shining white walls set against the turquoise of the evening sky and shimmering in the soft heat haze that still lingered, like a chiffon veil, beautifying the landscape.

And as one who would convince herself, she murmured:

'It really is beautiful here, Raymond.'

He glanced at her swiftly, aware of a subtle change in her attitude that quickened his pulses. Was it possible that his scheme and plans were about to mature?

'It could be,' he answered her deliberately, as he assisted her from the car.

She stood immobile, gazing upon the gardens that stretched illimitably; vivid green of velvet lawns patterned with the shadows of age-old trees that offered peace and sanctuary. And, suddenly, as though a

261

rough hand were pulling at a string tied to her heart, she had a vision of 'Cloverdell'... No meticulous planning, no flawless pattern dictated the splendour of those broad acres flung like a tapestry against the heavens... She felt a sob rise in her throat because the emotional atmosphere of her surroundings at the moment brought a nostalgic longing and as she met Raymond's eyes, she saw only Allan and the longing increased and became more acute.

Raymond guided her inside that now familiar and vast entrance hall; her feet sank into the thickly piled ruby carpet. And she remembered the first occasion of her visit there and thought of the flat that, with but a word from her, awaited her mother...

'We'll wander around the grounds afterwards,' Raymond suggested. 'That is, if you agree?'

'By all means.'

He studied her with great earnestness.

'There is something very different about you tonight,' he said hoarsely.

Claudia forced a smile.

'Women pride themselves upon always being "different",' she said lightly.

'You,' he retorted, 'are not "women". Above all else I appreciate the fact that you are free from the wiles and subterfuges of your sex. There's no pretence about you.'

She gave a little laugh.

'I'm not clever enough for such sophistications.'

'You mean that you are too clever to need them,' he countered. 'Sherry?'

'Please.'

He had reached a magnificent walnut cocktail cabinet which revealed a display of crystal that reflected dazzling light and, as the sun caught it, threw off prisms of crimson and amber and deepest blue.

Claudia's thoughts were racing. This would be her home; all the luxury now surrounding her would, in time, become a part of her life should she marry Raymond... Furs, jewels, dresses transcending anything she had hitherto dreamed about. And she knew, almost with a sense of desolation, that while she appreciated beauty and was not indifferent to luxury, nevertheless without Allan it was as a body without a soul. She took herself to task. Where was her pride that she allowed her every thought to be obsessed by a man who preferred another woman? Tonight she must make that final decision... Marriage to Raymond would bring her mother great happiness: a 'good marriage' she had said! Well, Claudia thought defiantly, why not? There was no question of disloyalty since she would certainly not profess to love she did not feel. She sipped her sherry from the glass Raymond handed to her, fascinated by the thought that this occasion might well mark her last visit to 'Old Place' in the capacity of a friend.

Raymond said abruptly:

'I received an invitation to the wedding – it came this morning.'

Claudia tried to sound casual.

'Allan's?'

'Yes.' He looked at her very levelly: 'I was wondering if you might be disposed to help me choose a gift of some kind. I know so little of their tastes.'

Claudia knew that he was deliberately seeking to inflame her emotions so that he might study her reactions. A faintly sadistic gleam came into his eyes as he added:

'You should be able to enlighten me – at least so far as the bridegroom is concerned.'

Calmly and coolly, even though the effort were superhuman, Claudia managed to retort:

'Anything in the electrical gadget line would appeal to Allan – and to Meg.'

He stared at her, faintly astonished.

'Really! I hardly associate modern devices with farm life.'

'That,' she retorted, 'is where you are wrong.'

He moved until he was within a few inches of her and stood looking down into her challenging eyes:

'Yes,' he said quietly, 'that is where I am wrong and you are very game, my dear.' His hands gripped her shoulders. 'Claudia–' It was a hoarse whisper as, swiftly, he drew her into his arms, his lips finding hers in a long, suffocating kiss.

Tensed, he waited for her angry resistance, but she made no effort to repulse him and while in no way responsive, nevertheless he knew that her entire attitude towards his attentions had changed and with a cry he released her murmuring:

'Is it possible that you–' His voice was clipped, emotional. 'Claudia, marry me–' It was an urgent appeal. 'I can't go on like this,' he finished almost sharply, yet still staring at her in incredulous amazement as he waited for a rebuff.

For a second Claudia felt that every drop of blood had drained from her heart; she was trembling violently as it seemed that her very life was being flung into a vortex. Then, breathing deeply as she spoke, she said slowly:

'Yes, Raymond, I will marry you.'

He cried:

'I daren't believe it.' And although triumph was quickening his pulse and feeding his sense of power, success brought a certain shock. He drew her gaze to his and, fearlessly, she said:

'You may, provided you are ready to accept the fact that I am not in love with you. I cannot marry you under false pretences.' Her voice was firm. 'If that is enough—'

'It is enough – for the time being,' he reassured her and his tone betrayed the confidence he felt about the future. 'I'll soon make you love me once you are my wife, darling.' He finished sharply. 'But I'm not prepared for any long engagement.'

'And I have no desire for one,' Claudia admitted honestly. Having taken the step the prolonging of their engagement could but heighten the suspense. Marriage would, at least, she argued, give her certain responsibilities and, also, in her mother's security, she would find compensation.

It struck her forcibly as she stood there that her father would not easily be reconciled to the situation, but she thrust aside the thought as she reflected that it was unlikely he would be back in England until it was all over and then his views would be modified in the light of her contentment... Contentment! The word was incongruous, but she insisted that having taken the step she would spare no effort to make the future a success.

They dined out and, afterwards, Raymond took her over the house for the second time.

'I knew,' he said with supreme self-confidence, 'on your first visit here that one day you would be mistress of it all, Claudia, and—' He paused and looked at her intently:

'You are at liberty to make whatever changes you think fit – structurally or otherwise.' There was a significant change in the tone of his voice as he added: 'And it is a foregone conclusion that the flat is available for your mother – for her lifetime.'

Claudia murmured:

'You are very kind.'

He laughed rather harshly and suddenly a violent jealousy possessed him as he thought of Allan... Obviously she was still in love with the fellow and now the idea stung. Having won the battle he desired all the spoils of victory. It occurred to him that for his own peace of mind he should get her out of England as quickly as possible. He said tentatively:

'I think we'll make a world tour our honeymoon, darling.' He lit a cigarette. 'Be away about a year.'

Claudia started with obvious anxiety.

'But–' She stopped, aware of his gaze intently upon her.

'The idea doesn't appeal?'

'Yes ... it was just that it seems strange to think of being away so long.'

'Away from your friends, you mean,' he suggested pointedly. Then: 'Ah well, you'll have the supreme satisfaction of knowing that they, also, will be married and that, in any case, nothing would be the same.'

'True,' said Claudia flatly. 'Nothing would

be the same.' She brightened. 'It would be wonderful to see the world,' she exclaimed, realizing that she owed him at least some enthusiasm.

He smiled and tucked her hand through his arm as they wandered across the smooth, green lawns.

'I can't believe that you are here beside me – that I can re-insert that announcement in the newspapers!' He chuckled. 'How indignant you were that morning!'

Claudia was conscious of a complete sense of unreality as she listened to his words. She was going to marry Raymond Winters against whom she had fought so tenaciously... Now, she must concentrate upon his good points instead of enlarging upon the bad.

'I felt indignant,' she said with a smile.

'You were irresistible,' he murmured. Then, suddenly: 'Do you want a "big" wedding–' There was faint mockery in his voice.

Claudia thought of the publicity, the surging crowds, the general fuss and upheaval and shuddered. Swiftly, she exclaimed:

'Oh, no! Not unless you particularly wish it.'

To her surprise, he said:

'I wish only that which makes you the happier.' He put his arms around her possessively, demandingly, and his lips sought hers; she tried to respond, but every instinct resisted his touch and the ache in her heart for Allan increased unbearably.

It was just before eleven that he took her back to 'Stoneways', and acquainted Helen with the news.

'I've won at last,' he said smoothly. 'No opposition, I hope, on your side, Mrs Lomond?'

Helen managed to murmur weakly.

'None... I'm so glad for you both.'

For a brief second reaction set in and she felt both nervous and apprehensive. This was something for which she had deliberately schemed and her moral sense was by no means so blunted that, having achieved her objective, she could wholly ignore the situation as it affected Claudia. The maternal instinct flared, subsided and died in the light of the material advantages now within her grasp. To live in the luxury of 'Old Place'; to see Claudia its mistress... Of course the child would have cause – as the years went by – to thank her.

The following morning, Claudia said:

'I'm going to "Cloverdell", Mother. I want to tell them all of my engagement rather than that they should read it in the papers.'

Helen darted her a reproving, critical glance.

'That is hardly necessary,' she insisted. 'And hardly fair to Raymond. Really, Claudia, you are quite impossible when it comes to your relationship with the Russells. Allan is engaged and–'

'That fact in no way lessens the fact that I count him and his family among my closest friends,' Claudia retorted. 'And if it will set your mind at rest, Raymond is aware of my intentions and is calling for me there after midday. He would have driven me to "Cloverdell", but he had an appointment.'

Helen looked sheepish. Then, abruptly:

'Is it your intention to tell your father about all this?' She paused and resumed in a confidential tone: 'Far be it from me to interfere, Claudia, but I cannot help feeling that it would be wiser if you didn't worry him until after you are married. One sees everything out of perspective when one is thousands of miles away and–'

Claudia said slowly and thoughtfully:

'I shall write to Daddy in the normal way. Unfortunately, he cannot be home for the wedding. I know that he won't approve, but many things have changed since he was here. I see no reason to make a secret of my affairs, Mother.'

'I wasn't,' Helen exclaimed, 'suggesting that you should do so.' She added somewhat viciously: 'Your father is not the most reasonable of men and, with ridiculous prejudice, didn't approve of Raymond.'

'He knew,' said Claudia imperturbably, 'that I was not in love with him.'

Helen lapsed into silence. There was nothing more she could say. She had to be profoundly thankful that Charles was out of England; most probably he would, otherwise, have smashed all her carefully-made plans, for no better reason than that *she* had made them and considered them to be in Claudia's best interests!

When Claudia reached 'Cloverdell' she found Marion and Allan together in the kitchen.

'Stealing the hot cakes,' Marion explained, smiling indulgently at Allan and then kissing Claudia affectionately in greeting.

'Nothing unusual,' said Claudia crisply. 'He always did that.' She glanced at the tempting, golden brown morsels that reposed appetizingly on their wire tray. 'May I, too?' Her smile was spontaneous and, momentarily, happy as she added: 'No one can make them just like you.'

There was something so homely in the atmosphere; something that made the visit natural and intimate and took Claudia back to earlier days when there was all the suspense and wonder of a love as yet undeclared.

Marion studied her with great intensity, noticing the rather pinched expression; noticing, too, that she was thinner and aware of a desperate frustration at her own helplessness. It was so obvious to her that

271

these two were still in love... Allan had admitted it and Claudia's very attitude proclaimed it to her discerning eye.

'I came,' said Claudia, 'to tell you my news and because I wanted you to be the first to know.'

Allan's gaze leapt to hers; there was a moment of almost electrical silence as he echoed:

'News?'

Claudia had the feeling of one suddenly plunged into icy water as she said:

'Raymond and I are to be married.'

Marion spoke in a low, almost hoarse tone:

'I suppose, Claudia dear, we should not exactly be surprised but, somehow...' She broke off, then: 'You know we wish you every happiness.'

Allan managed to add to that:

'Of course.' The sickness in the pit of his stomach made him feel almost faint; jealousy burned within him like a flame. He went on, somewhat cynically, seeking release from his own torment in anger and bitterness: 'So the newspaper announcement was really right, after all.'

Claudia stared at him.

'On the contrary,' she commented forcefully.

'Are you,' asked Marion jerkily, 'being married quickly?'

'Yes; although the actual date has not yet been fixed.' Without her being aware of the fact there was a challenge in the look she flashed at Allan. 'It might well be that it synchronizes with your wedding.'

'You are not,' he said abruptly, 'wasting much time.'

Claudia tried to compose herself, but every nerve appeared to be tingling; emotion engulfed her as she looked at him, knowing only the overwhelming longing for his love; the yearning that it might be him whom she was so soon to marry. She managed to reply:

'Only a fraction less than you, Allan.'

Marion, unable to bear the strained, tense atmosphere, made some excuse and left them alone together.

Allan said jerkily:

'Let's go outside ... too hot in here.'

Claudia moved in step beside him, coming upon the panoramic view of the farm with the same breathless appreciation that marked her first glimpse of it.

'"Cloverdell" never loses its charm,' she said softly. 'It seems to hold all the romance and beauty of the universe.'

'"Old Place" must surely now take precedent,' he exclaimed somewhat cynically.

'"Old Place" is magnificent,' she agreed; 'but it is formal and of man's designing. A farm, somehow, seems to be quite apart – a natural vital expression. A heritage.' She added in a whisper: 'You taught me that – if I needed teaching.'

The words were wrung from him.

'How different it all was then, Claudia.'

Something in the tone of his voice made her turn and her heart-beats quicken.

'Very different,' she murmured shakily.

He gazed out across the far-flung downs.

'I suppose I always knew you would marry Winters – eventually,' he said half-bitterly.

She looked at him and emotion surged between them.

'Then you knew far more than I,' she whispered.

It was one of those moments when both their defences were down; a moment when the soft, sensuous breeze, laden with honeysuckle, the warmth and gold and blue of the day made them sensitive to each other's mood; a moment when passion would not be denied. Hoarsely, demandingly, Allan said:

'Claudia... I must know–'

And just then Meg's voice came smoothly cutting across the echo of those words:

'Hello, there! That was a very earnest conversation. Claudia, I've just heard the news. At least this time I can wish you happiness without it being in vain.' She spoke warmly, and with enthusiasm. 'Marriage seems to be in the air ... only three weeks left for us, now... Where are you going for your honeymoon?'

Allan cut in, irritated and impatient:

'I doubt if Claudia can answer that question at this stage.'

Claudia experienced a sickening jealousy in that moment as she watched Meg take her place by Allan's side... His words still echoed in her ears... What was it he must know?... And could she deny the fervour of his tone, the intensity of his gaze?

'On the contrary,' she said, pride coming to her rescue and enabling her to speak with some semblance of control. 'We think of going on a world tour – being away a year or so,' she added half defiantly.

Allan felt that something within him was slowly dying. A year without Claudia ... without sight of her; without the sound of her voice. It seemed more than he could endure; jealousy tore at him leaving the gaping wound of bitterness.

'But how perfectly wonderful,' Meg purred. 'Allan, don't you envy them, darling? Makes our fortnight at the Lakes seem rather plebeian, doesn't it?' She sighed and then smiled dazzlingly. 'But, the world, the Lakes, or any other spot – what does it matter when two people are in love?'

Faint colour rose in Claudia's cheeks; she was conscious of Allan's presence beside her; of his gaze upon her and of the fierce and ungovernable emotion swelling like a tide within her.

Allan managed to speak after a moment of awkward silence. His voice was sharp:

'Two people *have* the world if they have love.' He added hoarsely: 'But how many can qualify for that state of Elysium?'

Meg darted him an angry, warning glance which he ignored. It was Claudia who broke the tension by saying:

'And how many unintentionally turn their back on that Elysium only to realize their folly when it is too late?' She was trembling as she spoke, her endurance almost at an end. Never again would she visit the farm alone. It was utterly impossible for her to be with Allan and stifle the love she felt for him; impossible, too, for her not to search for some sign from him which might suggest that he still cared. There was a certain thankfulness, therefore, in her greeting of Raymond when, a few moments later, he arrived, and after a matter of ten minutes or so, drove her away.

Marion watched Allan with increasing anxiety as he attempted to eat his lunch. His face was pale and drawn; there was a disconsolate air about him that tore at her heart. And even as she studied him she made a resolve. She could not sit back idly and allow this untenable situation to continue.

'I'm going to see Helen Lomond,' she informed Duncan when they were alone together and the meal over.

Duncan's head shot up above his newspaper.

'What for?' he asked, suspiciously.

'To see if I can't do something about these engagements,' she said briskly. 'I can't sit back and let Allan – to say nothing of Claudia – wreck his life.'

Duncan shook his head.

'Interference–'

'I shan't interfere,' she said with solemn reflectiveness. 'I just want the truth ... and I believe Helen Lomond can supply it. I'm not satisfied that Meg is entirely innocent, darling. I must know.'

Duncan didn't speak.

'You agree with me – don't you?'

His blue eyes surveyed her lovingly:

'Do I ever do anything else?' His voice was gentle. He stretched out a hand and clasped hers. 'I'm with you, darling. Go ahead.'

Marion reached 'Stoneways' just before tea, having made quite certain that Claudia would be out. Helen received her with effusiveness and when, finally, they were seated in the lounge, began:

'It is so nice of you to come along, Mrs Russell; I've always felt that we've not seen nearly enough of each other.' She paused. Then: 'Just what was it that you so specially wanted to discuss with me?'

Marion didn't prevaricate, but answered bluntly:

'The future of my son and your daughter.'

Helen nerved herself to meet that steady gaze. She was ill at ease and a hateful presentiment gripped her.

'Surely,' she said lightly, 'their future is already decided.'

'It would appear so ... but you know, Mrs Lomond, that Claudia and Allan have always been in love with each other and that only tragedy can result if they–'

Helen cut in icily:

'I know nothing – nothing of the kind. And if I may say so, I consider it an impertinence that you should make such a suggestion when you know that Claudia is to marry Raymond Winters. Is your opinion of her so poor that you imagine she would become engaged to him without being in love with him?'

'My opinion of Claudia couldn't be higher,' said Marion calmly. 'As for her being in love with Mr Winters – you know she never has and never will be in love with him.' She leaned forward and said urgently: 'I believe that, with your co-operation, we could put things right. Oh, don't you *see*–'

Helen felt that she was being gradually dragged down into a quagmire. Her position was so delicate that one false move might well prove her undoing. She looked at Marion very sternly:

'On no account, Mrs Russell, would I dream of interfering in my daughter's life. And if you will take my advice you will refrain from interfering in Allan's affairs. They have made their choice and there the matter, so far as I am concerned, ends.'

Marion's voice came with a deadly significance.

'If I could feel that they have made their own choice,' she said slowly, 'I should be the last person in the world to interfere.'

Helen's lips parted in apprehension.

'Just what do you mean by that?' she demanded.

'That circumstances created by others have forced – shall we say – the issue and been responsible for their present actions.'

Colour mounted Helen's cheeks. Anger showed in her eyes – anger born of fear.

'That is fantastic!'

Marion remained impressively calm.

'And you refuse to help me?'

'Most certainly, since there is absolutely nothing wrong. Claudia is ideally happy. If Allan isn't … well, I'm sorry, but really Mrs Russell, he is hardly my responsibility, after all.'

Marion knew that nothing was to be gained by entreaty. She got to her feet and, with implacable calm, said:

'You know in your heart that Claudia is anything but ideally happy, just as you know that it lies within your power to save her – and Allan – from life-long misery.'

'That – that,' Helen protested violently, 'is absurd.'

Depression weighed upon Marion as she left 'Stoneways'. She could not substantiate her suspicions and she knew that one false move would be fatal. Suddenly, like a light piercing impenetrable darkness, she thought of Charles Lomond... He would help and had ever been antagonistic towards Raymond Winters. And it went far deeper than that, for might it not be argued that the repercussions of his unhappy marriage had brought about this present situation?...

She would cable him and urge him to fly home. Only he could deal with Helen Lomond...

CHAPTER TWELVE

The moment Marion Russell left 'Stoneways' Helen 'phoned Meg asking that she should come to see her immediately, and assuring her that there was no danger of her meeting Claudia.

Meg arrived as speedily as was possible;

she was fearful, agitated.

'What is it?' She spoke nervously.

Helen explained the details of Marion's visit.

'So *that* was where Auntie was going – to see you,' Meg gasped. 'I thought it very mysterious.'

'Is it possible that she can know more than we think?' Helen asked anxiously. 'Her suggestion that neither Allan or Claudia had made their choice freely and were in love with each other–'

Angry colour flamed into Meg's cheeks.

'What possible right has she to make such an assertion? Obviously Allan wouldn't be marrying me unless he wished to do so.'

Helen said with some impatience:

'Suppose we stick to the facts, Meg. You know and I know that, but for our scheming, you would not now be engaged to Allan, any more than Claudia would be engaged to Raymond. Don't,' she added testily, 'pretend to me. If you were to offer Allan his freedom at this minute he'd take it with both hands. Only his sense of honour–'

Meg's eyes blazed with jealousy.

'You can't speak for Allan,' she cried.

Helen stared at her coldly.

'We are in this together, Meg,' she said with a quiet but challenging tone. 'And I *can* speak for Allan.'

Meg sat down weakly; she was trembling.

'If you're going to ask me to do the noble thing and give him up—'

'Don't be ridiculous,' Helen snapped. 'It is just as much in my interests to keep you engaged to Allan as it is to keep Claudia engaged to Raymond.' She hastened. 'Of course, I know that all this is for Claudia's ultimate good but—'

'So you,' said Meg with a half sneer, 'want to whitewash yourself, too.'

Helen flushed.

'Nothing of the kind. But if I believed that Claudia's life would be ruined by all this then, naturally, I should not have been a party to it in the first place.'

'She doesn't love Allan,' snapped Meg, 'or she would never have hesitated in the first place when he wanted to marry her.'

Helen smiled.

'I wonder just why when a woman loves a man herself she hates to think of another woman doing so... Come, Meg, I didn't ask you here for all this nonsense.'

'What did you ask me here for?' said Meg stubbornly.

'To suggest that you persuade Allan to slip away somewhere and be married secretly.'

Meg said with some impatience.

'I should have tried that if I'd had a hope of success.'

Helen suggested subtly:

'Don't you realize that, with Claudia out

of Allan's reach, you now have that hope?'

Meg lowered her gaze; her heart was thudding. She hated the very sound of Claudia's name because she knew the injustice she had done her.

'Heaven knows,' she said taciturnly, 'that I'm sick of it all.'

'Then,' persuaded Helen, 'take my advice. Allan would, most probably, be thankful to escape the fuss and bother of an ordinary wedding.'

'There's Auntie to consider: so many plans have already been made but–'

'Better to face the annoyance of the family than to lose Allan,' persisted Helen. 'And I feel that Marion Russell intends to prevent your marriage at all costs.'

'But what can she *do?*' Meg was in a perverse mood; conspiracy was foreign to her true nature and in those seconds, she hated this woman who had inveigled her into such a situation. Nevertheless, she knew she hadn't the courage to withdraw from the fight now; the obsession of her love for Allan, and her determination to marry him, was so great that neither sentiment nor justice would swerve her from her objective.

Helen snapped:

'Obviously, if I were aware of your aunt's intentions I could have dealt with the matter myself. I may be unduly fearful but–'

Meg faced the grim spectre of losing Allan

and cried sharply:

'Nothing shall defeat me now. I've held on pretty stubbornly, and I'll do as you suggest. Allan has to go up to London on Monday – a perfect opportunity.' She looked angrily determined. 'It won't be my fault if I don't succeed.'

'That's better,' said Helen, brightening. 'Days narrow down the possibilities of trouble, but anything can happen with three weeks still to wait and a woman of your aunt's tenacity to deal with.'

Meg nodded and glanced at the clock.

'I'd better be going; I may catch Allan at tea and I don't want any awkward questions to be asked as to where I've been.' She said swiftly: 'By the way, you know we've all been invited to the dance Raymond Winters is giving at "Old Place" on Saturday? He 'phoned this afternoon… I'm going to fight to prevent Allan going. The very thought of his being thrown into Claudia's company–' She clenched her hands, and as one who conceives a brilliant idea, cried: 'I know! I'll try to persuade Allan to go to London on Saturday; that will avoid it all and we can be married. Yes – that's it.' Her eyes gleamed. 'We can wire the news of it to "Old Place" … quite a sensation. And time to get a special licence.'

'Ah,' said Helen approvingly, 'now you are talking.'

Meg said viciously:

'Raymond just wants to flaunt his possession of Claudia over Allan – and–' She stopped abruptly. She would not admit that such a procedure would pain Allan.

Helen maintained a discreet silence for a second, then:

'It is to be quite an informal affair to celebrate the engagement.'

'Dancing,' countered Meg, 'can be dangerous.'

She left a little while later and, on her return to the farm found Allan eating alone – his tea on a tray – in the sitting-room. He glanced up at her casually and she noticed, not without chagrin, that he refrained from asking her where she had been. How obvious it was that he had no interest in her actions.

'All alone?' She sat down beside him on the settee.

'Yes… Mother's in the town shopping. At least I presume that is where she is.' He looked at her. 'Did she tell you she was going out this afternoon?'

'No,' Meg said swiftly. 'I've not the faintest idea where she is.' A faint pause, then: 'Allan?' Her voice was low, suggestive.

'Yes?' He looked at her inquiringly. 'What is it?'

'I've been thinking about – us,' she began. Allan started and immediately showed avid interest. Was it possible that she was going to suggest the breaking of their engagement?

'What about us?' he said in clipped, precise tone as though he were holding his breath as he spoke.

Meg plunged as her hand reached out and clasped his.

'All the fuss of a wedding here, Allan – wouldn't it be a relief to both of us if we slipped away quietly somewhere?... The family wouldn't really mind and it would save a great deal of expense.' She paused. Better not say too much and become involved in any details.

'You mean – get married secretly?'

She hastened:

'Yes, although since everyone knows we are to *be* married, the only secretive thing about it would be the time and place of the actual ceremony. I dread all the publicity here...'

Allan's heart sank. How foolish to imagine that she thought in terms of releasing him.

'Can't say I exactly like it myself.'

She grasped the opening eagerly:

'Then why not let's go up to London this Saturday?' she cried. 'We could be married and make the – the weekend our advance honeymoon... Oh, darling, it would be such fun and mean so much to me. The peace of it... Everyone would understand and you know how sweet your mother is over everything. Probably be a great relief to her, too.'

'I suppose,' he said dubiously, 'we could run to a special licence but ... is it worth it, Meg, when in three weeks?–'

'That's just it,' she insisted. 'In three weeks we'll have all the palaver... I thought I should love it, but, frankly, I don't. My dress can be made into an evening frock and isn't in any case finished. It would be so simple. Let Claudia and Raymond have their fashionable wedding – we don't want it, do we?'

Allan said tersely:

'We are hardly in a position to compete with Winters in any case!' He had tried to keep his thoughts from Claudia, but now they took possession of him to the exclusion of all else. The realization of how completely she was lost to him intensified his agony of mind... If Meg wanted things this way why not allow her to have them? It was little enough he had to give her in exchange for her devotion... And useless harbouring any grievance against her because she had not offered him his freedom. Engagement or no engagement, Claudia would have married Raymond. He said abruptly:

'Very well... Saturday it shall be – if that is how you want it. Mother will understand – she always does, bless her.' He stopped, then: 'There's the affair at "Old Place" – have you overlooked that invitation which has been accepted?'

'I had,' she lied easily, 'but when I come to think of it, what difference will our not being there make? It is merely for Raymond to flaunt his engagement ... we couldn't care less – could we? I don't feel that you wish to be there and I certainly do not!'

Allan's expression hardened:

'No,' he murmured grimly, 'I have no wish to be there.' He got up abruptly. 'Must get back to work.'

'And everything is settled, then?' She looked at him with adoring tenderness.

'Yes,' he murmured. 'I can't say that I like the thought of secrecy, Meg, but–' There was resignation in the shrug of his shoulders.

'It will save so much fuss,' she commented. 'And it isn't as if Auntie won't understand; or is the type to be hurt.'

Allan recalled all that his mother had said to him. No, she had already been hurt by his unhappiness; it struck him that she might well be thankful to be spared the actual ceremony.

'Oh, Allan!' She slid her arms around his neck and pressed against him, seeking his caress.

Allan turned his face so that his lips brushed her cheek. Then, swiftly, he managed to break away.

She stood there watching him, triumph gleaming in her eyes. She had won the battle; in a matter of days he would be out of Claudia's reach for ever: nothing else mattered. And suddenly she remembered that a few wedding invitations had already been sent out. Not many, but sufficient to create a somewhat awkward situation. Defiance possessed her. Did it matter what anyone said? A party could be given on their return and the matter smoothed over. She could only hope that Allan, manlike, would forget that phase of it.

She 'phoned Helen.

'It's all arranged,' she said swiftly. 'I can't say more. Someone coming.'

As Helen replaced the receiver, Claudia, who had just returned, said jerkily:

'Who was that?'

'Wrong number ... always getting them.'

Claudia studied her intently.

'You seem very agitated, Mother, and do you usually say "Splendid" in that tone of voice when you receive a call not intended for you?'

Helen flushed. Then, with a laugh:

'Did I really say that?'

Claudia stared at her with faint concern.

'Is anything wrong?'

'Don't be absurd,' Helen rebuked her gaily. 'Wrong! Why, I've never been so happy in my life, darling. If my behaviour is slightly odd, you must forgive me...' She stopped as she caught sight of the square-cut diamond on Claudia's engagement finger. 'Claudia! Your ring ... why, it's magnificent.' She studied it more closely as Claudia held out her hand. 'What a lucky girl you are ... and why didn't you show it to me before?'

'I forgot,' came the honest reply.

'"Forgot"! Really, darling, you are a strange girl.'

'Perhaps; I'd still prefer a rose diamond from the man I loved, Mother... By the way–' She hurried on anxious to avoid an argument or discussion, 'I wrote to Daddy today and told him all that had happened.'

'I see.' Helen remained calm. There was nothing for her to worry about, now. Meg and Allan would be married before Charles even had time to reply. A gleam of satisfaction came into her eyes. Thank heaven Charles could no longer have any influence; how relieved she was that he was out of England.

Twenty-four hours later Charles Lomond was stepping out of the 'plane at London Airport. Marion's cable, acquainting him with the news of Claudia's engagement and suggesting his immediate return, had been cloaked in terms of such urgency that in a matter of hours he had taken over a cancelled passage and was on his way home.

He 'phoned 'Cloverdell' before leaving and Marion explained the situation as she saw it, apologizing for having the temerity to cable as she had.

'I'm thankful you let me know,' he said stoutly. 'And I agree with you: there's more in all this than there seems to be. I'll get to the bottom if it – never fear ... and, don't be afraid that I shall betray your confidence. I shall know nothing when I arrive at "Stoneways".'

He reached there just before six o'clock. Helen saw the station taxi sweep up the short drive and gasped:

'Who on earth is this? I'm–'

Claudia cried out in astonishment and delight:

'It's – Daddy! It's Daddy!'

Helen paled.

'It can't be.' There was terror in her voice.

Claudia rushed into the hall and flung open the front door.

'Daddy! I can't believe my eyes... You!'

Charles Lomond beamed at her.

'A not unwelcome sight I hope, darling.'

'Unwelcome! Oh, it's wonderful – just wonderful.' She flung herself into his arms and hugged him, feeling a surge of affection and understanding, even of security, as he held her and kissed the top of her head. Then, raising her gaze and looking up into his face, she asked shakenly: 'But you weren't to have come back for weeks?–'

He chuckled.

'Can't a man change his mind? I guess I wanted to see you, darling. I came straight from the airport.'

She became aware of his absence of luggage:

'Left it at the hotel,' he explained. 'Didn't want to butt in.'

'Oh!'

Helen appeared in the hall as the front door shut. Her attitude was frigid, forbidding; her voice uncompromising and harsh as she said:

'I think you might have let me know it was your intention to descend upon us in this fashion, Charles.'

He ignored that.

'How are you, Helen?' he asked politely.

'Never better,' she retorted. 'You've had tea, of course.'

'Yes.'

'Will you be staying to dinner?'

Claudia cried admonishingly:

'Mother, of course he will.' Her glance was critical and accusing.

They went into the lounge and Claudia poured him out a drink, which he accepted, settled himself in his chair and began:

'Now tell me all the news.'

Helen preened herself and looked triumphant.

'*You* have a few surprises coming.'

'Really!' He eyed her with unnerving intensity. 'I'm accustomed to surprises.'

Claudia felt slightly sick; the atmosphere reopened old wounds; the misery of other days washed over her. She said abruptly:

'Mother is referring to my engagement to Raymond Winters, Daddy. I'd just written to tell you about it.'

Charles glanced from face to face.

'That is a shock,' he said harshly. 'An unpleasant one.' He composed himself, realizing that it would be fatal to betray anger or antagonism. 'What has brought about such a thing?'

Helen said swiftly:

'What usually brings about an engagement? I always knew Claudia and Raymond would come together in the end.' She added gloatingly: 'Show your father your ring, Claudia.... Wonderful, isn't it, Charles? She is an exceedingly lucky girl.'

'Suppose,' he cut in, 'you allow Claudia to speak for herself.'

Helen's lips curled.

'You certainly haven't improved,' she snapped.

Charles looked at Claudia.

'Well?' he prompted.

Claudia lowered her gaze.

'What is there to say?' she murmured.

'That you are happy and in love,' he

293

suggested firmly.

Claudia gave him an imploring glance. Helen exclaimed sharply:

'Claudia isn't a child, Charles, and if you cannot realize how happy she is and how fortunate–'

Charles got up from his chair.

'In that we differ,' he said implacably. 'Most certainly I can find no happiness in Claudia's eyes; neither do I consider her other than unfortunate in her choice of a future husband.'

'Please Daddy–'

Charles spoke with great feeling as he said:

'Listen, darling: if you can look at me and tell me that you are marrying Winters because you are in love with him – sincerely in love with him – then you need fear no opposition from me and I'll do my damnedest to see him, in future, through your eyes. Come now, that's fair enough–'

Helen, her heart thudding painfully, fixed Claudia with a gaze so compelling as to come near to mesmerism as she willed her to give her answer. Then, unable to bear the strain and tension a second longer, she burst forth:

'Don't be so ridiculous, Charles. Why on earth should Claudia be marrying Raymond unless she loved him. Really, you–'

Charles stopped her with a look.

'My remarks were addressed to Claudia,'

he said with deadly calm.

Helen made an impatient sound. Then:

'For goodness sake, Claudia, give him your answer and let's have done with this melodramatic nonsense.'

There was a second of almost electrical silence before Claudia, trembling now as she met her father's steady, unflinching gaze said:

'I am marrying Mr Winters for reasons of my own, Daddy. But let me assure you that, as I cannot now attempt to deceive you, neither have I sought to deceive him. Whatever my feelings may be, he is aware of them.'

Charles's expression became grim.

'I see.' A pause. 'And Allan?'

Helen interposed, sneeringly:

'Allan is marrying Meg in less than three weeks. Does that satisfy you?'

Charles said quietly:

'For the time being.'

'Meaning just what?' Helen was conscious of a hateful fear taking shape in her mind. Suppose at this eleventh hour something happened to smash all her plans.

Claudia's nerves were strung to breaking point.

'Don't let's talk about me,' she pleaded. 'Daddy, tell us about you – all you've seen. Do you like it out there?'

'Love it ... when are you being married?'

'A month today.'

Helen said breathlessly:

'You didn't tell me.'

'I hardly had time, Mother; we settled it only this afternoon.' She added. 'Incidentally, Raymond told me to tell you that the flat is there for you to look over and rearrange any time you like.'

'Flat?' Charles looked bewildered. Thus far, nothing had emerged beyond the fact that Claudia was obviously marrying for reasons quite removed from love.

'Yes – flat.' Helen said haughtily. 'You probably have forgotten that "Old Place" boasts one – a beautiful flat with every conceivable luxury and convenience. Raymond has offered it to me – as my permanent home.' She glanced around her. 'And shall I be thankful to get away from here.' A sigh. 'He's the most thoughtful and generous of men.'

Charles bristled... Here, a chink of light pierced the darkness. Marion Russell was, obviously, unaware of this phase of things. Was it possible that Helen had persuaded Claudia, even schemed, to bring about this marriage, simply for her own gain.

'I'm sure you find him so,' he commented subtly. Then, changing his attitude for Claudia's benefit: 'Well, we shall see; meanwhile, I hope you feel that my return calls for a celebration?'

Claudia brightened. Anything, provided

her feelings and emotions were not placed under the microscope.

'Of course we do – don't we Mother?'

Helen's voice was cold.

'I think that your father and I have got beyond that. We are, after all, separated.'

Charles spoke solemnly:

'I hadn't overlooked that, Helen.' He turned to Claudia: 'I'd like a word with your mother alone, darling ... would you mind?'

Claudia smiled and went swiftly from the room.

Helen took up a position near the window; her body was taut, her shoulders squared as one poised for battle.

'Just why have you come here?' she demanded.

Charles lit a cigarette and blew a tiny cloud of smoke into the air.

'To upset your plans, Helen,' he answered smoothly and deliberately. 'You don't imagine that my being here is coincidental, do you?'

The colour faded slightly from her cheeks.

'What do you mean?' It was a gasp.

'Simply that I have no intention of seeing my daughter made a burnt offering. She would never have become engaged to Winters unless–'

Helen interrupted him, her voice was raised in anger:

'She is engaged to him and I have no

intention of listening to your – your vapouring about it. Didn't I hear enough before you went away? Now, you come back and have hardly stopped talking on the subject.' She finished malevolently: 'The truth is that you cannot bear to see my life made secure or happy and you are trying to find a way to wreck it – for the second time.'

He shook his head.

'You do me a grave injustice, Helen,' he said patiently. 'But that isn't important.' His voice grew stern again, and he looked at her very levelly: 'It is my belief that you have engineered this engagement; I'll even go so far as to say that you've schemed with Winters and that the two of you have conspired to separate Claudia and Allan. So far you've succeeded, but Claudia shall never be Winters' wife if I can help it.'

'Very amusing,' she scoffed. 'And just what do you propose to do? Claudia isn't a child to be dictated to, or influenced in any way.'

He stared at her, baffled and pained by her attitude which while being very little different from that which he had expected, nevertheless increased his anxiety.

'There must,' he said pleadingly, 'be some vulnerable spot in your make-up that allows unselfishness to creep in. Claudia is your daughter – how can you sit back and watch her making a loveless marriage – encourage it for your own ends.'

She flashed him a fiercely antagonistic look.

'You make me tired,' she said rudely.

He leaned forward.

'Look here, Helen, you don't fool me, even if you can fool yourself. All you are thinking about is Winters' position and the luxury of the home he is offering you. There's a very ugly word for all that you have done.'

'I've done nothing,' she insisted, unnerved by his calm deliberate manner and the truth of his words.

He looked at her long, searchingly:

'We're both morally responsible for all this,' he said gravely. 'But for our example, Claudia would have married Allan in the very beginning and all the Raymond Winters' on earth wouldn't have swerved her... But what had she seen of marriage to recommend it to her? Nothing; nothing but our bickering and incompatibility–'

'That wasn't my fault,' Helen stormed.

'It was *our* fault,' he answered. 'I'm quite ready to take my share of the blame.'

'Very magnanimous.' She felt ill at ease; the truth of all he was saying stung.

'That won't help – that attitude,' he said sternly. 'Look here, Helen, why not meet me half-way? I'm ready to draw a curtain over the past, begin again ... if you are.'

'Because,' she rapped out, 'you believe that in the event of our reconciliation, Claudia wouldn't go on with her marriage – that's what is at the back of your mind – isn't it?' she added fiercely.

Charles didn't seek evasion.

'Yes; it is … but that is by no means the only reason for my making the suggestion. Don't you think we owe the child the happiness she would experience through our harmony, our reunion? I'm ready to do anything – anything that lies within my power to atone for the past, Helen; to give you as much as my position allows... What do you say?'

For a moment there was a heavy silence. Helen hated the emotion that swept over her … hated the sensation that gripped her as she felt that prickling of conscience, that awareness of truth in all that had been said. But a vision of 'Old Place' insinuated itself before her eyes... And she said sharply:

'I will not even consider it, Charles. Now I have my freedom and, in a month, I shall have the kind of home that most appeals to me... My answer is no – emphatically, no.'

Charles looked at her and there was a warning gleam in his eyes as he exclaimed:

'So be it, Helen, but I warn you … this is war. I'll get to the bottom of all that has been going on and heaven help you if my suspicions prove correct.'

Helen laughed nervously.

'You talk like someone in a second-rate melodrama.' She added fearfully: 'Where are you going?'

'I'm going to "Cloverdell",' he replied quietly.

Helen's heart missed a beat.

'Why "Cloverdell"?' Her voice was thin, apprehensive.

'I rather think that is my business.' He went to the door as he spoke, opened it and called for Claudia who almost immediately appeared. He gave her a loving glance. 'Come up to the farm with me?' he asked lightly.

She felt a sudden surge of excitement at the possibility of seeing Allan.

'I'd love to ... when?'

'At once...' He turned to Helen. 'We've nothing more to say.'

Claudia was too obsessed with her own thoughts to make any inquiries. In a matter of seconds she had slipped into her light coat and was ready by her father's side.

'And if Raymond should ring?' Helen spoke sharply.

'He won't,' came the composed reply. 'A masonic dinner tonight.'

'Oh!' It was a bleak sound; a sound that had in it the semblance of defeat. She bolstered up her flagging spirits with the consolation that she could 'phone Meg and prepare her for this visit. Trust Meg to keep Allan out of Claudia's way.

But, as it happened, Allan met them when they were some few minutes away from the house. Charles watched his expression very carefully, noticing the light that came to his eyes at the sight of Claudia; aware of the tension, the fierce emotion lying between them, and after the usual greetings were over, Charles said:

'I'm going ahead ... want to have a word with your mother. You two follow on... Oh, yes, I'm not so old that I can't hurry. See you later.'

And with that he strode on.

Allan drew Claudia's gaze to his, deliberately, masterfully, and it was as though his lips touched her, so passionate was the look he gave her.

'I hoped I might see you,' he said hoarsely. 'Somehow, I wanted *you* to know–'

Claudia felt that the air had been squeezed out of her lungs; she tried to keep her sense of proportion, to remember that he was engaged to Meg, but all she was really conscious of was her overwhelming love for him and the aching longing for his arms.

'To know – what?' she whispered.

'That Meg and I are to be secretly married in London on Saturday,' he exclaimed and his voice was almost harsh as he added: 'I knew I *had* to tell you, Claudia.'

CHAPTER THIRTEEN

It flashed through Claudia's mind in that split second how amazingly easy it was to see future events in the haze of unreality. And just so long as there was a reasonable time lapse, to imagine that some miracle would happen to prevent the ultimate tragedy... Allan was to be married in a month... Allan would not be married for two months... Allan was to be married in three weeks... But, now, it was narrowed down to three *days* and that truth struck inexorably; there was no further escape, or respite, in the anodyne of hope and faith. She managed to say unevenly:

'Saturday–' And it seemed she was incapable of further utterance.

'Yes ... somehow I hated the idea of your being told about it – afterwards.' He broke off awkwardly. 'Not that it matters to you–' He looked at her and although he in no way realized it, his expression pleaded for a contradiction of those words.

Claudia drew on the remnants of her courage and pride as she murmured:

'I'm glad you told me: we've been friends for so long that it would have hurt to feel that you didn't trust me.'

He said thickly:

'Trust *you* – to the ends of the earth.'

'Oh, Allan!' Her voice broke and she hastened to cover up her emotion: 'I pray you are very happy. I–'

'Will you be?' It was no more than a whisper in which desire echoed like the lullaby of the wind then sweeping across the nearby fields.

'I–' It was a strangled sound; her defences were down no matter how she struggled against the weakness. Allan's nearness; his tall, lithe figure beside her, the deep tan of his skin against his cream, open-necked shirt ... they created emotions she was incapable of fighting, or of ignoring, any more than she could deny the answering passion in his eyes as they met hers.

And into the uncanny stillness came the sound of a voice raised harshly. Meg's voice, calling... Then, around the bend in the lane, the sudden awareness of her presence. It was like the shattering and discordant note in a perfect symphony.

'Oh!' She stopped as one surprised to see Claudia yet, nevertheless, fortified by Helen's 'phone call. Then, pleasantly: 'I didn't know you were here, Claudia.' She moved to Allan's side with that possessiveness which everyone knew so well, then beaming up into his face, said: 'I looked for you everywhere.'

Allan mastered his annoyance, his overwhelming disappointment, his sense of frustration.

'I'm afraid that a farm offers many loopholes for escape,' he suggested.

Meg laughed, but her laughter concealed a jealousy and anger that was flooding over her body like poison.

'I must remember that – eh, Claudia?'

Claudia said subtly:

'Surely that isn't necessary; we seek escape only when we are tied.'

The words fell almost involuntarily from her lips, betraying her mood to some degree. It was so obvious that Meg hated to see Allan out of her sight and, Claudia argued, with a quickening of her pulse, was that not tantamount to confessing herself unsure of his feelings for her.

Meg's temper flared dangerously. Claudia always placed her at a disadvantage because she, herself, was so jealous that she was incapable of adopting a calm and objective attitude towards any discussion or conversation.

Allan said ruefully:

'How true.'

Meg maintained a sullen silence for a few seconds. Then:

'Raymond not with you?' she inquired.

'No; he has a masonic dinner tonight.'

In that second Meg caught sight of Claudia's engagement ring and gasped:

'What a magnificent stone... Allan, isn't that simply glorious?'

Allan glanced down at the offending gem.

'Yes,' he said, almost curtly, and sought Claudia's gaze.

'Who wouldn't marry a wealthy man?' Meg exclaimed pointedly. She flashed her modest ring. 'But I'll still have you, darling,' she said, gazing adoringly at Allan, 'without the wealth, but with the love.'

Claudia refused to be baited. She despised Meg's attitude and was at a loss to fathom it.

They walked to the house in silence. Claudia's emotions were deadened by the numbing effect of an unhappiness that lay upon her like a pall. Allan was to be married on Saturday ... this was the last time she would talk to him before he became Meg's husband. The thought was an agony.

Meanwhile Charles was saying to Marion.

'This whole thing is outrageous,' he insisted. 'It's so obvious that Claudia and Allan are in love with each other.'

'I know,' she said wearily, yet with a touch of desperation. 'I just had to send for you, Mr Lomond. I've tried; I've talked to Allan.' She caught at her breath. 'Youth can be so stubborn, but it isn't only that ... this situation was not brought about merely because of that stubbornness. In my opinion it has all been deliberate; part of a subtle plan.'

'Do you trust Meg?'

Marion hated having to say:

'I'm not sure; the idea of misjudging her is hateful to me; but she's had several rather mysterious 'phone calls and–'

'You are really trying to say that she and my wife–'

Marion looked at him fearlessly.

'Too much is at stake for me to pretend at this stage. Yes; yes, I do feel that there is some conspiracy between them...'

Charles groaned.

'I've spoken to her, already; told her that I was not satisfied with the situation–' He flung out his hands. 'To no avail and it would be useless trying to get at Winters.'

'I realize that.' She looked at him apologetically. 'I'm afraid I acted very impulsively when I sent for you.'

'I'm thankful you did cable me,' he assured her. 'I should have returned, anyway, the moment I received Claudia's letter.' He didn't flinch as he met Marion's steady, honest gaze: 'You see, Mrs Russell, I'm deeply conscious of the fact that the unhappy background of Claudia's home life has been morally responsible for all this. Claudia had seen so much of incompatibility that she was afraid of marriage in the first place, distrustful of everything connected with it; afraid of repeating our mistakes.' He looked strained, anxious. 'Somehow, I've got to put things right or have that knowledge on my conscience for the rest of my life.' He added apologetically: 'You'll forgive the sentiment, I know.'

'I understand everything,' Marion said gently. 'The question is, just what can we do?'

'Vague accusation is futile,' he said thoughtfully. 'As I see it, given the opportunity, Allan and Claudia are our only hope – flung together their defences would be down.' He looked at Marion very steadily: 'And unless I am very much mistaken they've seen very little of each other recently and then always in Meg's presence.'

She said breathlessly:

'That's true, certainly.'

'For instance, where is Meg, now?'

'I don't really know! She ran out of the house a few moments ago–'

'After talking on the 'phone?'

'Yes, why?' Marion puckered her brow. 'But she said it was a wrong number.'

Charles shook his head.

'Far more likely that she was being warned of our visit.'

'"Our"?'

'Yes; I left Claudia with Allan – purposely.' He broke off. 'I've an idea–'

'We've so little time left,' Marion said

urgently. 'And somehow I've a feeling that Meg is planning *something*... I can't explain but, just before you arrived, Allan talked of going up to London this coming Saturday... Meg insisted on accompanying him. Suppose she should have persuaded him to get married secretly. I know she is terribly anxious and–'

Charles said soothingly:

'Don't worry ... I think we can sort this out between us.' He looked at his watch. 'It's now just after eight. I want you, around nine-fifteen, to get Allan alone and tell him that Claudia wants to see him urgently – at "Stoneways". I don't think you need have any compunction about saying that she 'phoned – the motive more than justifies the deception. Do you know his plans for this evening?'

'I believe he will be in...'

'Splendid.'

She looked puzzled.

'You think he'd go to her?'

'I'm certain of that.' He spoke with conviction.

'Don't let Meg know anything about it until after he has left here–'

Marion said anxiously:

'She will follow him.'

'That is precisely what I am gambling on.'

She shook her head in bewilderment.

'There are times in life when allowing for

309

human nature can be more effective than all the complicated schemes.' He got to his feet. 'Trust me to see it through... I'm going to take Claudia back to my hotel for a meal, now, and then return with her to "Stoneways". I shall remain there until Allan has been. This is a case calling for two people to keep vigil... And now, thanks to you, there *are* two of us, Mrs Russell.'

She asked breathlessly:

'And just suppose it is not possible for me to do as you suggest?'

'If Allan hasn't arrived by ten-fifteen, I shall know that the plan didn't work.'

'All the same,' she insisted, 'something very unforeseen will have to happen for it not to do so. I'll keep him here, somehow!'

'I'm sure you will... Ah! Here they come and Meg with them, as I suspected.'

Meg simulated surprise at the presence of Charles, crying as she greeted him:

'Claudia, you didn't tell me your father was home–'

Charles kept his gaze steadily on Meg's face as he said:

'Apparently, I am only just in time. A great deal seems to have been going on in my absence.'

Meg was conscious of a sharp uneasiness as she stood there. Just why had he returned so suddenly? Of course it might well be that his business in Canada was completed, yet there was something in his expression that unnerved her, almost as though he had the power to read her thoughts.

'Hasn't it!' She spoke gaily. 'And now you have to give the bride away – such a lucky bride, too.' She glanced at Allan. 'And we shall, naturally, insist on your dancing at our wedding, too, shan't we, darling?'

Allan hated her cool, easily uttered words; they struck a harsh, and a false note since she well knew that they were to be married secretly. He felt himself resenting that idea, too, in the light of reflection. Yet, what did it matter?... Apathy stole back, born of anguish; an anguish from which he sought escape.

'We shall have to see about that,' Charles said subtly. He added swiftly: 'And, now, Claudia, we must be getting along.'

Marion made no protest and the thought registered in Claudia's brain that it was un-like her not to have offered them hospitality. Normally, at no matter what time of day one called at the farm, there was always the invitation to remain to whatever meal happened to be approaching. There was something in the atmosphere, also, that she could not define. She said slowly:

'And have you had your talk with Mr Russell, Daddy?'

Charles remained calm: he had forgotten the very existence of Duncan during his visit.

'Unfortunately, no! These farmers put me to shame – they are always at work. But there will be other days,' he added blandly.

Claudia knew that she was trying to prolong that agonizing moment when she would have to say good-bye to Allan; for now she knew that it was final, irrevocable – that last farewell before he became Meg's husband, and as they faced each other it was as though the secret he had confided flashed between them like a sword.

'We seem,' she said unevenly, 'always to be saying good-bye, Allan.'

He held her gaze.

'Possibly,' he answered in a hoarse, strangled tone, 'because the time we spend together is always so very brief.' His words throbbed into the silence; a silence that Meg broke with a harsh:

'Allan says the quaintest things!'

Charles couldn't resist the light retort:

'The time one spends with – shall we say one's special friends? – is always all too brief.'

Meg bit her lip to keep back the angry flow of words. Objectionable man, she thought maliciously. How thankful she would be to escape from the Lomond family in general. Helen was getting on her nerves with her dictatorial attitude and hurtful comments about Allan and Claudia.

Claudia was thankful for her father's

presence as they left a moment or two later. She realized just how greatly she had missed him and how regretful she felt that things between him and her mother could not be different. She knew, in her heart, and without self-deception or martyred desire for credit, that had her parents' marriage been happy she would never have considered marrying Raymond. As it was, her mother's delight gave it some semblance of purposefulness and made the sacrifice worth while. She wondered if ever the gnawing longing for Allan would subside... Her heart-beats quickened... How easy it would be to delude herself that he, too, cared. Cynicism came to her rescue. Fool to seek the balm of such a belief when he was going secretly to marry another woman rather than wait three short weeks.

Charles said, as they sat at dinner later that night:

'I don't envy Allan his choice of a wife.'

Claudia became tense.

'Why?' It was a staccato sound.

'Far too jealous,' he exclaimed carelessly, having no intention of discussing seriously the situation. Argument at this stage was, he realized, quite useless. 'Particularly of you.'

Claudia paid an inordinate interest to what she was eating.

'You imagine things. She has no cause to be jealous of me.'

'We'll agree to differ on that, darling.'

Claudia put out her hand impulsively:

'I'm sorry, Daddy, that you aren't happy about – about things; but, believe me, it will probably work out for the best.'

He smiled at her; an inscrutable smile.

'I'm sure it will,' he answered reasonably.

'And you'll be – be nice to Raymond? I couldn't bear any more friction,' she said desperately.

Charles smiled inwardly.

'I'll be charming to him – how's that?'

'A great relief.' She sighed. 'I wish I could see you and Mother–' She broke off: 'But I do understand.'

'Just as you understand why I want your happiness so desperately, Claudia – and the right thing for you?' The words escaped him involuntarily.

'Yes.' It was as though Claudia hadn't the breath to say more. Then: 'You're not going back to Canada, Daddy – are you? At least not – not until after I'm married,' she finished shakily.

Charles looked at her very earnestly.

'No, darling; I'm not going back until after you are married.'

'But, you are going back?'

'That all depends.'

'On what?' She looked at him anxiously.

'Many things.'

'You sound mysterious.'

'And you sound curious, young lady. Eat your dinner and don't ask any more questions!'

Marion, meanwhile, was in a state of acute agitation as she waited for the right moment in which to carry out Charles's instructions. Meg remained at Allan's side, as his shadow – never for a second allowing him out of her sight and it was not until nine-fifteen, when Marion's nerves were taut almost to breaking point, that she got up from her chair and said, realizing that she must make a few discreet preparations for Saturday:

'Allan darling, I'm going upstairs for a few minutes – few things I must do. Will you take me for a stroll when I come down – just before bedtime? I love the farm at night and–' She sighed luxuriously: 'It's such a heavenly night.'

Allan hardly glanced up from the account books over which he had been poring, actually without being able to concentrate in any way; his thoughts wild, turbulent; his emotions inflamed at that earlier contact with Claudia.

'Very well,' he murmured.

Meg bent and kissed the top of his head then, smiling at Marion, went from the room.

Marion, her heart seeming to hang perilously on a thread, cried breathlessly:

'Allan... Claudia wants you to go over to

"Stoneways" to see her immediately. It's urgent.'

Instantly he was alert and incredulous.

'Claudia! Wants *me!*' It was a gasp. 'But she was here only an hour ago–' He broke off abruptly, his pulses racing, emotion engulfing him at the very possibility of seeing her again. 'Something must be wrong... Why should she send for *me,*' he insisted.

'I know nothing more than I've told you,' Marion managed to say smoothly. 'I've given you the message... You'd better hurry, darling.'

He had already got to his feet.

'Yes; yes, of course.' He reached the door in a stride; his expression perplexed, agitated.

'I'll tell Meg,' Marion promised, in an agony of fear lest Meg should reappear before he had time to get away.

Allan nodded. Marion knew he had forgotten everything except Claudia and getting to 'Stoneways'.

'Seems so strange,' he murmured half to himself. 'How did she sound?'

Marion realized that he had taken it for granted she had 'phoned.

'Difficult to judge ... you'll know very soon.'

Allan struggled into his sports jacket, walking towards the hall as he did so. A few seconds later he disappeared into the soft darkness of the night. The car snorted and raced off. Marion put a hand just beneath her heart, her lips moved as in prayer.

Allan was in a state of wild conjecture as he covered the few miles to 'Stoneways'. The idea of Claudia 'phoning... Come to think of it, had the telephone been mentioned? His emotions were far too chaotic to grasp anything beyond the fact that she wanted to see him... No matter what the reason might be, she had turned to him in emergency... What emergency? he asked himself in baffled perplexity. His heart was pounding madly as he turned into the short drive leading to the house and as he got out of the car he was trembling as one gripped by presentiment and nervous fear.

He rang the bell and waited apprehensively for an answer; all manner of possibilities took shape in his mind. Then:

'Ah, Allan,' said Charles Lomond, opening the door. 'Come in.'

Allan stared at him.

'Is – is everything all right?' He spoke hoarsely. 'I was told that Claudia wanted to see me.'

'Of course ... come in, my boy.'

'I was afraid something was wrong.'

'Nothing,' beamed Charles. 'Nothing.' He hustled Allan into the library, gave him a cigarette and said, with what seemed to Allan to be a curious air of mystery: 'Claudia won't keep you a moment and if you'll excuse me—'

Allan's bewilderment increased. He couldn't begin to fathom what this was all about.

'You're sure I've done right in coming?' he asked swiftly.

'Absolutely certain,' said Charles stoutly and, smiling, went swiftly from the room, and so to the lounge where Helen and Claudia were sitting.

'Who was that at this time of night?' Helen demanded.

Charles said calmly:

'Someone to see you, Claudia. I've shown him into the library.'

Claudia gasped.

'To see me?'

'To see Claudia?' Helen was instantly alert. 'At this hour? Really, Charles, you take too much upon yourself. Why you were so insistent upon answering the door is quite beyond me. I thought you said it was most likely a friend of yours.'

Charles interrupted her.

'I just happened to be wrong.' Then, looking at Claudia who had already got to her feet and was walking towards the door. 'Strikes me, the fellow is an old sweetheart,' he said teasingly.

Helen demanded:

'And you didn't even ask his name?'

'No,' said Charles with a maddening confidence. 'I didn't ask his name... Claudia, invite the young man in here for a drink after you've had a talk.'

'Do no such thing,' Helen snapped. 'I think I'd better go and see just who–'

'You'll do nothing of the kind,' said Charles sternly and authoritatively. 'Kindly allow Claudia to attend to her own affairs.'

Claudia shook her head and smiled.

'I can't think of any old sweetheart,' she murmured. 'Far more likely to be someone begging for charity!'

Charles chuckled.

'Then be generous, my dear!'

Claudia made her way from the room and so to the library, opening the door with a weary, inevitable gesture as of one bored by the whole proceedings. Then:

'Allan!' It was a broken sound.

'Claudia!' His voice was low, hoarse. He was aware of the intense surprise with which she greeted him and said hoarsely: 'Did you think I should come?'

His words took her back to the time when she had waited for just such a visit from him; waited in the hope and belief that he would be compelled to come to her because his love was so great that he could not keep away... She managed to say shakenly:

'I used to think you would, but–'

'"Used to think"?' He stared at her. 'You

mean that you didn't send for me tonight?'

Claudia stared at him aghast.

'I don't understand,' she breathed. Then: 'No; I didn't send for you.'

'I see.' Hope dissolved into an agony of disappointment. Emotion churned violently within him.

'And you – you,' Claudia murmured, feeling all the sickness of defeat, 'didn't come of your own accord?'

He looked at her.

'No,' he replied hoarsely. 'I was told you wanted to see me urgently.'

'By whom?' She puckered her brow.

'My mother.'

'Oh!' It was a little cry.

He drew her gaze to his and held it masterfully.

'And if I had come of my own accord … what would you have said?'

She struggled against the overwhelming yearning his presence awakened within her; her resistance seemed to be ebbing like a tide, leaving her weak, vulnerable, but drawing on the last slender thread of pride she managed to say:

'Wouldn't that rather depend on the purpose of your visit?'

Allan was fighting against his love for her as he stood there; struggling to fathom the events of the evening and at the same time wholly incapable of concentrating beyond the fact that he and Claudia were there alone together. He said urgently:

'What did you mean just now when you said that you "used to think I should come"... Claudia; tell me–' His voice grew stronger, more demanding: 'What did you mean?'

Colour stole into her cheeks, but she managed to master her emotions sufficiently to murmur:

'Nothing that counts now.'

'Are you quite sure of that?' His voice grew strong, determined.

'Yes.' It was no more than a whisper.

'But if I had come to you–'

'You didn't,' she answered almost violently. 'Suppose we don't talk of it.'

Allan's eyes looked deeply into hers as he said hoarsely:

'You know that we must talk of it – that we can't escape, you and I.'

In that moment the world of reality faded; they were two people in love; two people whose lives were so shortly to be divided for all time and the impact of that knowledge flooded over them like an indestructible tide. An hour before they had endured the agony of what they believed to be a final parting; now, suddenly, miraculously, they were reprieved and together again.

'Answer me,' he demanded. 'Claudia ... would you have sent me away?'

Claudia struggled for a second and then as one who can fight no more, breathed:

'No ... no.'

For a brief second they stood looking at each other, eyes meeting in question and answer and, then, with a sharp exultant cry, Allan's arms went out and drew her to him and he felt the convulsive response of her yielding body, the warmth of her lips beneath his as they met in a passionate adoration; adoration intensified by the denial and misery of the past months, as they clung together in a frenzy of relief and ecstasy while it seemed that the wild thudding of their hearts became as one beat in a perfect mental and physical surrender.

They didn't hear the sharp ringing of the door bell, but in the lounge, Helen cried out:

'What is all this ... who is that?' She looked at Charles. 'Another of your friends who turns out not to be anything of the kind?'

Charles was outwardly calm; inwardly his nerves were taut, excitement gripped him as he realized that this was the moment on which he had gambled all.

'Suppose we *see* who it is,' he suggested.

Helen had already reached the hallway and was opening the front door. Meg thrust her way in and, looking from Helen's face to Charles demanded suspiciously:

'Just what is all this?... Where's Allan? I–'

'Allan!' Helen's voice was clipped, yet suspicious. 'Allan isn't *here*.'

Enraged, terrified to a point where all control deserted her, Meg shouted:

'If you think you can fool me, Mrs Lomond...' She glanced swiftly into the lounge and, then, rudely pushed past Charles and darted towards the library door, flinging it open and in a voice quivering with jealousy and accusation: 'So Allan is not here!'

Charles moved forward; Helen ran; and at the sight of Claudia drawing back from Allan's encircling arms, she gasped:

'Claudia!'

Meg strode into the room, white with rage as she confronted Claudia and cried:

'How dare you? ... sending for Allan; trying to steal him from me... If you think you can get away with it you're very much mistaken. Isn't Mr Winters enough for you? Why–'

Charles studied Helen's face at that moment; every nerve in his body was taut almost to breaking point. And, suddenly, he saw her expression change; the light of battle leap to her eyes as, like a tigress, she was prepared to defend her cub... Her voice was harsh, strong, in its determination as she cried:

'Stop! If you think I'm going to stand here

and listen to that then you're very much mistaken... I think it is time that Allan and Claudia knew the truth...' She ignored the desperate and imploring glance that Meg gave her and added: 'The truth, no matter what it costs me.'

CHAPTER FOURTEEN

Helen was aware of a curious stillness descending upon her as she stood there, as though the selfishness that had previously dominated her life, took tangible and horrific shape, forcing her to gaze upon the monster she had created; gaze and know the sharp pain of remorse as she realized the depths to which she had sunk in her desire for personal gain. She ignored Meg's inarticulate cries as she said:

'A very great wrong has been done to you both – you and Allan,' she added and there was a catch in her voice as she met Claudia's eyes and was humbled by the gentleness she found there.

Charles took a step forward because it seemed that immobility increased the agony of suspense.

'Yes,' Helen admitted, meeting his gaze. 'Your fears were all justified, Charles; that was why I hated you so when we talked together this evening.'

Meg's tone was aggressive, warning, as she exclaimed:

'I think you must have gone mad; the idea that–'

Charles put in peremptorily:

'No one has been accused as yet.' His eyes narrowed as he subjected her to a merciless scrutiny.

'That,' Meg snapped back, 'is where you are wrong. I have every reason to accuse your daughter. She deliberately set out to get Allan from the first and' – her breath came sharply – 'her own mother knows it.' In her last frantic bid for success she threw discretion to the winds.

Helen turned on her.

'You've made just one vital mistake, Meg,' she said slowly. 'Did you seriously imagine I should stand by while you reviled Claudia when I knew how we had conspired together, you and I, to part her from Allan so that you could marry him and I could enjoy the luxury of all that Raymond Winters had to offer.'

Claudia gave a little whimper.

'Mother!'

Helen sighed.

'It's true, Claudia...' she added tensely: 'And in your heart you knew it; you knew there was something strange when that announcement appeared in the newspapers, but you were too generous, too big, to pursue the matter beyond my denial.'

Allan had stood as one incapable of movement or utterance. He stared at Meg, his expression becoming grim, accusing.

'I begin to see it all, now,' he murmured.

Meg cried desperately:

'Listen, Allan, I can explain; it isn't as you think or – or as *she*' – Meg flashed Helen a dagger-like glance – 'would have you believe. There's something behind all this, there's–'

'Nothing,' said Helen implacably, 'that doesn't make me cringe as I reflect upon it and see it all in perspective.'

Claudia breathed:

'And Raymond?'

Helen nodded.

'Yes; he was in it, too ... the prize he offered to me being the security of his home... I think I must have been mad.' She put out a hand and gripped the arm of a nearby chair, steadying herself because, now, her legs were trembling and her heart-beats seeming to choke her, so great was the emotional strain and the revulsion surging upon her. Slowly, sometimes falteringly, she told the whole story, never sparing herself, or Meg; stating the facts honestly, and with directness, and finishing with:

'I cannot hope that you and Allan will

forgive me but–'

Claudia rushed forward; her eyes were suspiciously bright for, knowing her mother, she was in no way unmindful of all the confession had cost her. Excitement mingled with the pity she felt; the excitement of a happiness taking shape as the implication of all that had been said was borne home to her.

'Don't,' she murmured, putting her arms around her mother's trembling shoulders in a caress foreign to their previous relationship, but which now seemed to spring from a new-born understanding. 'It's all over, Mother...'

Allan took his place by their side.

'Bless you for giving me back, Claudia,' he murmured thickly. 'I knew there was something wrong, but I did not dare to hope that she really cared ... now I know and you have given me my release,' he added, his voice becoming firmer.

Helen tried to speak, but couldn't and, without realizing it, groped towards Charles rather after the manner of a child who seeks a comforting and guiding hand in the darkness.

'I knew,' he whispered, as he supported her, 'that you wouldn't let me down at the finish.' He turned to Allan: 'And you may as well know, my boy, that your mother is more than a little responsible for all this ... she cabled me to come home.'

Allan's smile was infinitely tender.

'She would,' he murmured. 'I was never able to deceive her.'

'I thought,' said Claudia breathlessly, 'that there was something mysterious about your sudden return.'

'You,' he grinned, 'know too much.'

Meg had taken a seat a short distance from them as they stood there. Allan walked to her side.

'I'm sorry, Meg. I hoped, prayed, that knowing how I felt about Claudia, you would release me when we returned from Scotland and found that the announcement of her engagement was false... How well,' he added grimly, 'that served your purpose; and how clearly I can see the whole picture: your anxiety to get me to Scotland... I congratulate you on a very clever act.' He looked down at her remorsefully: 'It seems almost impossible to believe you capable of all this.' There was an abrupt pause. 'And I trusted you as a friend.'

Desolation swept over her as those words died into a tense silence. She found herself quivering beneath the whip of his contempt, realizing that she had not only lost his love, but his respect, and suddenly, the whole sordid story appalled her. A matter of months before she had been at peace with herself, reconciled to the fact that her love for Allan was, and always would be, unrequited; she had enjoyed with him a relationship based on deep and genuine affection... Now all that was gone and she was placed in the invidious position of a scheming, unprincipled woman prepared to go to any lengths to achieve her own happiness. She murmured weakly:

'Oh, Allan, I'm so sorry – forgive me.' She drew a hand across her forehead almost as one coming back from some hideous nightmare. 'I've never, never done anything awful before in my life... But my jealousy got out of hand and when I saw a chance of–' She stopped abruptly. 'It doesn't matter; nothing I say now can possibly carry any weight.' She looked at Claudia. 'I'm sorry for all the misery I've caused you,' she said in a thin, pitiful voice. 'I always knew you loved Allan and–'

'Don't,' put in Claudia generously, 'torture yourself Meg. Let's not have any post-mortems ... it's over and, for my part, forgotten.' She glanced up at Allan. 'For us *both*,' she finished as one pleading with him to be kind for, loving him so deeply herself, she could not fail to feel pity for Meg who had lost him – unworthy though her actions had been.

At that second there was an insistent ringing of the door bell.

Claudia smiled.

'We seem to be busy tonight... I'll go.'

It was Raymond whom she admitted, saying in surprise:

'I didn't expect *you.*'

He frowned at the bluntness of her greeting.

'And I hardly expected such a cool reception, my dear. I rushed away from the dinner believing that you would be glad to see me.'

Claudia looked at him very steadily:

'As a matter of fact I am glad – very glad. I've a great deal to say to you, Raymond.'

He started.

'You sound very mysterious.'

'Do I?' She took in every detail of his elegant presence as he stood there; the immaculate evening clothes and the air of conceit with which he wore them; she took in every line of his attractive, but supercilious face; every shade of expression that betrayed itself, not without cruelty, in his alert, yet wary eyes.

He grew uncomfortable at her scrutiny.

'What *is* this?' he asked testily.

Claudia moved towards the library.

'Come in – we were just talking.' She spoke over her shoulder as he followed her.

'I'm in no mood for "talking" my dear girl... I came to see *you*–'

She ignored that as the next second they crossed the threshold of the room and, looking around from face to face, Raymond exclaimed:

'Quite a gathering of the clans.' His greeting of Charles Lomond was somewhat insolent. 'So the wanderer returns ... how did you enjoy your trip?' he asked patronizingly, determined not to betray the sudden alarm he felt at the strange atmosphere predominating. What on earth was that fellow Allan doing there at such an hour? ... and Meg, too?

Charles became the spokesman in that instant.

'Yes,' he commented firmly, 'the wanderer returns ... just in time to prevent my daughter wrecking her life by marrying you, Mr Winters.'

Raymond's mouth opened in startled surprise; his eyes narrowed to suspicious inquiry.

'Really,' he exclaimed, taking a cigarette case from his pocket with very deliberate movements. 'I rather think that Claudia will have something to say about that – eh, darling?'

Claudia felt a surge of excitement and relief as, boldly, she faced him and with a deliberateness of movement that matched his own, removed the engagement ring from her finger. Then, handing it to him, she said:

'I think this will speak for me.'

He lost a little of his poise.

'I don't understand.' It was a clipped sound.

'I know everything,' she explained with a quiet dignity. 'Mother has told us the whole story ... and since you are aware of all the miserable details no purpose can be served by further comment.' She stepped back to Allan's side and slid her hand into his. 'Allan and I are to be married,' she finished decisively.

Raymond knew he was defeated.

'I see.' He raised his head a little higher and flung a contemptuous glance in Helen's direction. 'I must say that you appeared to be in an inordinate hurry to sell your daughter, Mrs Lomond,' he exclaimed contemptuously.

'I have not spared myself,' said Helen with a quiet dignity, 'and there is nothing you can say that will damage me further.'

'Quite touching ... a family reunion. Well!' He turned to Meg. 'And you, too ... all repentant, no doubt.' His laugh was harsh and cynical. His gaze lighted on Allan. 'Your gain is my loss,' he said, 'to use an old cliché. Claudia is worth ten of all the lot of you put together. I did my damnedest to get her – fair means or foul. I offer no apologies. The only regret I feel is because I failed ... and I hate failure.' He moved towards the door. 'Good-bye, Claudia... Don't follow in your parents' footsteps.'

And with that he strode away... The front door opened and shut...

Claudia closed her eyes for a fraction of a second and felt the pressure of Allan's fingers tighten upon her hand. It was almost more than she could grasp to realize that she was free at last.

Meg stammered:

'I – I'm going back to the farm–'

Claudia said gently:

'Allan will take you.'

Allan turned to Claudia; his look caressed her.

'I'll be back in the morning, my darling – very early,' he added hoarsely.

Their emotion was too great, too over-whelming, to allow of further comment; all save their being alone together, was as an anti-climax.

At last the house was still. Charles, Helen, and Claudia faced each other across what seemed to be a river of revelation and possibility. The atmosphere was tense. Charles said:

'I'd better be getting back to my hotel.'

Helen nodded. She felt as one who had come round from an anæsthetic and was still floating in space; it was impossible accurately to grasp the full significance of these past hours, or assess the effect ultimately upon her life.

Claudia's heart missed a beat. Would her

mother ask him to stay? She waited in a feverish suspense, but no invitation followed. Instead, Helen's voice was subdued as she said:

'I'm afraid this hasn't been a very pleasant way in which to spend your first evening back in England, Charles.'

Charles shook his head and smiled.

'Nothing could have brought me greater happiness than to know that Claudia and Allan are reunited,' he said gratefully. 'Too few people can claim to be affinities and when they can, for them to be separated is sheer tragedy.'

'Oh, Daddy,' Claudia said in a whisper. 'You've been so wonderful.'

'Nonsense,' he retorted almost brusquely, because emotion was beginning to threaten his composure. 'I could have done nothing without your mother's help; her silence would have defeated me.'

'I feel bitterly ashamed,' Helen murmured.

'Few of us who cannot claim to have suffered that sensation in our lives,' he said gently, and raised his gaze to Claudia. 'I'm sure Claudia bears you no grudge.'

'No, Mother – no!' It was an earnest sound.

Charles left them. And a hateful pang went through Claudia as she watched him driving away ... even in the light of her own happiness, the dark shadow of his relationship with her mother cast its gloom. She went slowly back to the library where Helen was now crying – the strain of that through which she had passed snapping the last thread of her control.

'Don't, Mummie – please.' Claudia was beside her, sitting on the edge of her chair, comforting her.

Helen looked up.

'It's – it's a long while since you called me – Mummie,' she said between sobs.

Claudia's voice was low.

'It is a long while since I have thought of you as such,' she murmured.

'"Mother" seems so cold, so–'

'I know ... it's going to be different from now on.'

'You've been so good to me – I don't deserve it.'

Claudia felt a sudden rush of affection, as though the ice that had gathered around her heart, because of her mother's unsympathetic, materialistic attitude, had melted.

'It was wonderful to hear you stand up for me, defend me against Meg's accusations... I felt suddenly that I mattered to you and that you really cared about my happiness after all. The whole world changed for me in that moment.'

Helen drew her into her arms and kissed her.

'Be happy, darling,' she whispered, 'and forgive me.'

The silence became deep, yet pregnant with the peace of understanding. Out of tumult and dissension, selfishness, greed and suffering, came the healing balm of a faith restored and love triumphant.

Claudia said suddenly, urgently:

'And you, Mummie – what of you? I must know that you are going to be all right.'

Helen said swiftly:

'I shall be … probably get a small flat; but that need not be any concern of yours, darling. All you have to do now is to think of yourself and Allan.'

Claudia didn't speak; she could not… It seemed that her heart would burst with the weight of its own love for him and its longing to be at his side.

It was just before nine o'clock the following morning that Allan arrived at 'Stoneways'. Claudia rushed out to greet him, her cheeks flushed, her eyes starry with happiness and, as he drew her into his arms she clung to him as one fearing to release her hold lest he vanish as a dream.

'*Darling!*' He looked down at her, adoring her. 'I just cannot believe that this is true; that you are here and that–' Their lips met again, urgently, passionately and as, at last, she drew back in order to get her breath, he whispered tensely: 'When will you marry me

… let it be soon, my dearest.'

'As soon as you wish it,' came her reply and a soft flush crept up into her cheeks.

'Next week?'

'Yes … next week.'

They were oblivious of their surroundings, or of the fact that they were still standing beside his ancient car in the drive. It was their moment and their world and the song of the birds was their orchestra swelling and merging with the music throbbing in their hearts.

'You won't mind my small cottage?'

Claudia gave a little ecstatic sigh.

'I've never wanted to live anywhere else, darling – never.' She added solemnly: 'That morning I came to the farm before you left for Scotland – I was going to tell you that I loved you and would marry you. So you see, you will merely be taking me to the home of my dreams.'

'As simple as that?'

'As simple as that,' she echoed.

'Will you come back with me, now? Mother is so wanting to see you.'

'Will I!' Her laughter was light. 'Come in while I get my coat.'

Helen welcomed Allan with a genuine warmth; she was subdued, but at peace with herself, and her admiration of him and gratitude towards him increased immeasurably as he said with great earnestness:

'You know I'll look after Claudia, don't you? At the moment I haven't any wealth to offer her, but I'm certain I can give her happiness.'

'I'm certain of that, too,' Helen said honestly. 'She will be in good hands, Allan … and, as time passes, I hope you will come to think more kindly of me and that we may be friends as well as two people related.'

Allan's smile was warm and understanding.

'I'd like to feel we were that – now,' he said firmly.

Claudia came running down the stairs towards them at that juncture, having donned the jacket of her linen suit.

'I shan't be very long, Mummie,' she said gaily. Then, a shadow crossing her face: 'What are you going to do?'

'I'm not sure.'

'Will you be seeing Daddy?'

Helen withdrew behind a mask.

'That is most unlikely.'

Claudia made no comment, but as she and Allan drove away from the house she said solemnly:

'If only I could see Mummie and Daddy happy – that is the only cloud on my horizon. All this' – she indicated the sweep of countryside that was bathed in the golden glow of a summer sun – 'and my own happiness above all, makes it doubly unbearable that they are so far apart.'

Allan was too wise to resort to platitudes or offer false consolation. All he said was:

'There is so much that is unpredictable about human beings, my darling, that hope is always left – even in a case like theirs.'

She slid her hand into his.

'I'm so happy with you that I'm almost afraid,' she breathed.

'Cloverdell' came into view a little while later and Claudia drank in its beauty as one who, for weeks, had been sightless.

'It used to hurt even to gaze upon it all,' she confessed.

'Darling.' His voice was hushed.

'I love it so deeply, Allan.'

'Bless you for that.'

Claudia was like a child as, in a matter of minutes, she entered the large, homely kitchen and said simply to Marion, who was awaiting her with outstretched arms:

'I've come home if you'll have me...'

Marion looked down into her radiant face, hugged her, and cried:

'Oh, Claudia! I was so terrified that this moment might never come, and, now' – her voice was lilting – 'here it is and my family is truly complete.' She looked at Allan above Claudia's shining head. 'I hope you realize what a fortunate man you are,' she said absurdly, because it seemed that there was a very large obstruction in her throat.

'Not in the least!' he retorted with a grin.
Claudia gazed around her.

'Let me just drink it all in,' she pleaded, looking lovingly at the red-bricked floor, the massive, scrubbed-white table; the double-ovened range throwing out its orange glow ... the kettle singing ... and Tibs, the cat, asleep on the hearth. 'Home...' She sighed rapturously. 'Nothing can ever quite compare with a farm kitchen; no other kitchen is the same, somehow.'

Allan said comically:

'When you've finished rhapsodizing about the kitchen perhaps I might claim a little of your attention?'

'That's where you're wrong,' came a voice from the doorway and Duncan joined them, wiping his forehead with his handkerchief and approaching Claudia with the light of welcome and affection in his eyes. 'It's good to see you, my dear,' he said heartily, and kissed her, grinning at Marion and Allan as he did so. 'Now,' he added, 'perhaps I may get a bit of peace.'

'Poor man,' Claudia sympathized. She looked at Marion. 'I can't thank you for making all this possible; for understanding when so few mothers would.'

Duncan moved to Marion's side.

'A very wise woman, my wife,' he said lightly. 'Look how she's kept me in order all these years.' He gave her hand a quick squeeze. 'And now what about some of those newly-baked cakes you're so mean about,' he chuckled.

Claudia smiled.

'Even the smell of the cakes cooking – to complete the picture.' She laughed. 'If a smell can complete the "picture"; but if I mix my metaphors today who can blame me?'

'Who indeed?' said Duncan. 'Don't become engaged to a Russell every day!'

'Duncan!' Marion admonished him with a loving smile.

Claudia said and her voice had a catch in it:

'How right you are…' She slipped her arm through Allan's and pressed against him. Then, abruptly: 'Where's – Meg?'

Marion didn't pause in the task of taking the cakes from the oven and removing them from their tins to a wire tray; she said without looking up:

'She went home this morning – caught the very early train.'

'Oh.'

'It was,' said Marion, 'better that way. She'll come back on a visit one of these days.'

Claudia nodded and did not pursue the subject further. She could feel it in her heart to pity Meg, but was conscious of a certain relief because she was gone.

341

Back at 'Stoneways' Helen wandered aimlessly through the house, restless, unsettled, and when, some half an hour after Claudia left, Charles arrived to see her, she was aware of a certain relief. At least he was someone with whom to talk.

He came in with an air of quiet gravity and, when they were settled in the lounge and he had lit his cigarette and hers, he began:

'We must talk about the future Helen – our future.'

She started, saying defensively:

'I suppose you are condemning me for all this?'

He looked at her very levelly as he answered:

'On the contrary. Yesterday is a closed book so far as I am concerned. I'm quite certain that you have condemned yourself sufficiently during the past months, without my adding to it all.'

She stared at him aghast.

'You – you seem so different,' she said in bewildered surprise.

Charles studied her carefully.

'Isn't that rather because you are able to see me as I am, instead of merely as a stumbling block in the way of your plans for Claudia? You resented my desire that she should marry Allan; resented it so fiercely that no matter what I had said, or done, it would have been wrong in your eyes, Helen.'

She sat down rather weakly. There came the growing realization that every word he uttered and had uttered in the past was true, and she said:

'I cannot deny that. I was wrong – terribly wrong.'

'The fault was by no means entirely yours,' he insisted. 'When two people drift apart they mostly contribute evenly towards the ultimate separation ... what I want to know, now, is this: have you any plans for the future? Anything you want to do? I'd like,' he finished, 'to help you if I can.'

Helen's lip quivered; her voice was shaky as she murmured:

'I don't deserve that you should be so – so kind, Charles. I've behaved so abominably and, but for you, might have smashed Claudia's life – and Allan's.'

'Then it was fortunate Marion Russell sent for me... I knew,' he said stoutly, 'that if I could provoke Meg into challenging Claudia you'd soon prove the real worth of your love for your own child.'

'Quite the psychologist,' she said with a watery smile.

He drew a chair up beside her, leaned forward and began urgently:

'Listen, Helen, we've not given Claudia much of a deal thus far, have we? She's never really had any peace of mind about us; our example was pretty shoddy; so shoddy, in fact, that it was morally responsible for her refusing Allan in the first place... Oh, I know I've said all this before, but it will bear repeating. Don't you think we could begin again – for her sake? Give her that send off, as it were, to her new life, feeling that we were happy, too? I know it is asking a great deal but don't you think that our incentive would be very real?' He paused, then: 'What do you say?'

Helen felt that she was choking; a strange, new happiness was upon her; it wasn't that she deluded herself that she was in love with this man beside her, but that she realized how great was her need of him and, most curious of all, how much she had missed him. She put out a hand rather gropingly:

'If you are willing, I am,' she whispered huskily.

He didn't speak, but took her hand and held it very tightly; it was a moment in which they were closer than they had ever been throughout the whole of their married life; a moment when they dedicated themselves to the future, a future in which the happiness of the other took its place as of paramount importance; a moment when they vowed to wrest success from failure, and to see that, never again, should Claudia have cause to be concerned for them.

Abruptly, Charles got to his feet.

'Amazing how different life can look according to the mirror through which one sees it,' he said gaily.

Helen went to his side.

'You do know how I hate myself for–'

He silenced her.

'I know, my dear, and if I hadn't had a certain faith in you and in my ability to bring out the real Helen, I should not have wasted my time in coming back.'

'I've – I've misjudged you, Charles...' Her expression changed to consternation. 'Are you going to Canada again?'

'I am ... just for another few months.'

'Oh.'

'And I'm taking you with me – that is if you'd like to come.'

'I'd love it.' Her voice was light, enthusiastic.

'And when we return we can look around for a really cosy place – something more suited to our needs than this – eh?'

'It sounds good.'

He drew her gaze to his and smiled.

'And let's keep all this to ourselves until the day Claudia is married. Whatever we decide to give her as a wedding gift, nothing could mean more to her than our reunion.'

Helen agreed.

'And Charles?' Her voice shook.

'Yes.'

'Thank you for being so kind.'

For answer he stooped and, very lightly, kissed her cheek.

Allan and Claudia were married very quietly the following week. Only the two families were present either at the church or, afterwards, at 'Stoneways'. Their honeymoon was, at Claudia's special request, to begin at Allan's cottage and end in Cornwall.

The ceremony over, a simple meal followed at 'Stoneways', which seemed to come to life miraculously for the occasion. Claudia gazed around her, aware of the subtle difference in the atmosphere and attributing it to her own great happiness... Allan's wife. The gaze she surreptitiously gave him, was adoring. Still she could hardly believe that the people she loved best in the world were all gathered at that familiar dining-table ... and that their respective families were in complete harmony. She thrust aside the thought that if only her father and mother could be reunited she would have nothing more left in life to wish for. A pang shot through her as she thought of Helen going on alone at 'Stoneways' as it appeared she was intending to do.

And suddenly, with an awareness of increasing tension, she saw her father rise to his feet ... and heard his voice, low, slightly hoarse with emotion, saying:

'And now, just for a moment, may we older folk have a little of the limelight... It is true that there has been one wedding in the family today but that is by no means all, for there has also been a reunion.' He paused and his eyes met Claudia's eager, misted ones. 'Yes, darling,' he said shakily. 'Your mother and I are going off to Canada next week ... so you see – you've nothing in the world left to worry about.'

Claudia never forgot the moments that followed; the confusion of congratulations, kisses; the exquisite relief and happiness she felt.

'Oh, Mummie,' she whispered later as she was preparing to leave with Allan... 'I'm so glad about it all; I just can't tell you how glad.'

Helen looked ten years younger as she said:

'Companionship can mean so much; and tolerance bridge so many gulfs, darling. I've learned a very great lesson and am very happy.'

Claudia sniffed.

'Don't you dare make me cry,' she said and laughed.

Marion and Duncan, Helen and Charles – with Susan darting around like a minnow – gathered in the drive to watch Allan and Claudia drive away. To Claudia it was a scene epitomizing the very richness and perfection of living and, as the car turned the bend in the drive and they were lost to sight, she whispered:

'I'm almost terrified lest no human being could possibly be allowed to keep such happiness as I now feel.'

He glanced at her adoringly:

'I'll spend the rest of my life making quite sure you do, my darling,' he breathed.

It was some ten minutes later that they reached the farm and passed into the sanctuary of the cottage that was to be their home. Through its open windows the smell of honeysuckle was wafted like incense; honeysuckle that mingled with the fragrance of bean fields and the sweet scent of lavender... The silence was heavy ... a listening silence, aware, so it seemed, of every beat of their hearts.

Allan said hoarsely:

'May a man kiss his wife, my darling?'

She curved into his arms.

'A man may,' she whispered, as their lips met in a passionate and ecstatic surrender, where reality faded into the rapture of belonging and time and place were lost on the soft, warm tide of fulfilment; a fulfilment not merely of the moment, but for eternity...

The publishers hope that this book has given you enjoyable reading. Large Print Books are especially designed to be as easy to see and hold as possible. If you wish a complete list of our books please ask at your local library or write directly to:

Dales Large Print Books
Magna House, Long Preston,
Skipton, North Yorkshire.
BD23 4ND

This Large Print Book, for people
who cannot read normal print,
is published under the auspices of

THE ULVERSCROFT FOUNDATION